Tranquility's Child

By Danyne Quinn

For Chris. My Tristan

ISBN: 978-1-916954-66-3

Acknowledgements

There are a few people who helped make this story a reality.

Clair McFarland- Thank you for working on my manuscript and for encouraging me to continue working to get it published.

Kelly Hostetter- Thank you, Sissy, for painting the image for this book. Anything with your art attached can only be better.

Mom and Jayms- For being my cheerleaders and listening to me read aloud for hours, trying to stay away while my monotone put you to sleep!

To my husband, Chris- Who believed this could happen more than I did. Thank you for your unwavering support and love.

Table Of Contents

Prologue

The woman stood on the pier as the sea rolled and raged on all sides. It was darkest night, as clouds snuffed out the moon and the stars allowed only an occasional glimpse of the moon. Below the congested sky, the small figure appeared a statue facing an angry and roiling sea, unaware of the raging waves reaching for her, threatening to pull her into their depths. Her cloak billowed around her with long wisps of silver hair whipping about the hood like snakes reaching for freedom.

The old man was loath to admit it, but he had no idea how the woman came to be on the pier. It was his job to know, and he would swear he had not been lax in his duty. One minute the pier was empty and the next she was there. The storm brought the oppressive black night along with torrents of rain that fell from the sky in heavy sheets, so it might have brought her as well; a wraith conjured from mist and fog.

Just as he began to question whether she was real or if it was his overactive imagination at play, the figure turned and began walking down the pier toward him. As she drew closer, two things occurred to him. First, it was the blackest night. yet she appeared to be illuminated by something, for he was able to see a pale face peeking slightly from the hooded cloak. Second, she didn't appear to be walking. It was as though she was gliding. There was no gait or stride in her movement. She simply floated toward him.

Another man might have been frightened, but William Reed had seen many things in his lifetime, and in this place, anything was possible. He drew a breath and held up his hand, palm down, pursing his lips slightly to blow on the orb that rested on the top of his hand. It expanded slightly with his breath, becoming brighter.

The woman moved off the pier and down the path toward the open shed where Reed sheltered. He rose from his seated position in the recesses of the shed where he kept diligent watch during the designated hours at his post and stepped out of the shelter onto the path to meet the mysterious figure.

She stopped in front of him, waiting.

"My lady, you may not come further. 'Tis a black night to be out and about, to be sure. I know not from where you have come, but I must tell you this is not the way to shelter. There is nothing out here but black storm and the violent sea." He paused to wait for her answer, but she said nothing. She reached inside her cloak, pulled out an object, and handed it to him. Her skin shone white as bone, as though illuminated from within.

Reed took the object. It was a wooden coin with markings few would recognize. He drew in a breath, saying, "I won't ask you how you came to have this. I know the owner, and it would be near impossible to get it from him without his leave to do so." He glanced up at her, his eyes a question as he gave the coin back and waited, once again, for an answer that did not come.

The woman turned the hand of the arm holding the coin to reveal a mark on the wrist. It was a raised scar of a sea creature and an anchor intertwined. The voice that came from beneath the hooded cloak was soft and melodious. "He said you would know what to do."

Reed stared a moment, taking in what he was seeing, then nodded. "Aye lass. I do." He paused for a moment, still collecting himself then continued, "My name is Reed, and I would ask you to follow me. No matter what happens, follow this orb." He held up his arm with the lighted orb perched on his hand like a bird, then furthered the imagery by putting the orb on his shoulder. He turned away from her and stepped forward, taking them down the beach away from the shed. With each step the air became stiller, and the blackness of the night closed in around them in a fog so thick one could cut it with a knife.

Reed took steady steps forward, slow and even. The journey was familiar to him, but he knew, for a person having never gone through the fog, it would be easy to become lost in it. Indeed, that was the point. Many a soul had tried to penetrate the heart of Marauder's Isle and had become hopelessly lost in its magikal defenses, never finding the way out of it. It was a maze, and not knowing the way was certain death sentence. One could hear the wails of those lost, no longer living but not gone, trapped in the dark fog. Their crying made walking through it all the more terrifying.

"Be sure to stay close to me, lass. There is no need to be afraid while with me, but the voices you hear are the souls lost in this black death, and they would reach out and pull you in if given a chance."

The woman did not respond. She seemed unaffected by the magik of the fog or the horrible wailing of its victims.

Reed had never gauged how long it took to get through the fog maze. Sometimes when he went through it alone it seemed only seconds before he cleared it, but when he was taking someone through it, the journey felt an eternity. He wondered if maybe the magik itself stretched time when someone it did not recognize attempted to gain access to the other side.

Reed spent his life on the island. There was a small village set away from the coastline where he was raised. He came from a long line of keepers, men who were raised to know the island and who were to keep its secrets, guarding it from those who were uninvited. Before Reed's eyes, many a trespasser lost his life to the protections in place on the island. He viewed such experiences as no fault of his own, but the consequential result of poor choices made by the individual.

The village knew the island was enchanted, holding refuge for those fleeing the outside world. Not just anyone could escape to its shores, and those who had a place on the shoreline had special coins purchasing safe passage through the fail safes, with him as their guide. The woman behind him provided not only a coin but proof she was bonded with the man who owned the coin, making the coin her property as well. Coins were passed down through families over generations. One side of the coin had the family or clan emblem stamped on it, and the other side had an image of a large crown with imposing prongs shaped like spikes.

Reed wondered about the figure following quietly behind him. He knew the holder of the coin, and he was curious about the chain of events that brought the two of them together and ended with her on the island alone.

So lost in his reverie was he, he didn't realize the fog was thinning until he stepped into the curtain of rain the magik of the fog maze eliminated. He jerked to attention and mumbled to himself, admonishing his old age and wandering thoughts. They moved along the shoreline towards the rolling sea where massive boulders shot out of the ground.

To view them was to see the outline of prongs upon a great and vast crown, with the circlet submerged and the prongs sticking out of the angry dark sea. This was the image encapsulated on the coin. They proceeded down the shore, drawing closer to the crown of boulders until they were standing near one of them. It was just a gigantic shape in the night, but Reed knew the daylight would show a massive rock covered in moss and algae, forever wet with the crashing of waves around it.

Reed took them knee deep into the ocean then turned to the woman. "Now you must stay exactly behind me. Do not veer to the right or left. There will be a path, but if you step on one side or the other you will fall to fathomless depths and be swept by undercurrents. Understand?"

"I do," came the soft, even voice from within the cloak.

Reed turned and took another step in the water. No path appeared until he lowered his foot, and with each step, a stone appeared suspended above the churning sea. They moved steadily if not quickly. The stone steps were wide enough for a man to stand, both feet planted, but they were wet and slippery with water. He wanted to make certain the woman did not slip. This was an often-tragic test, and if one looked down into the dark depths of the ocean, shapes not natural to the waters moved about. Reed knew they were the spirits of those who failed to cross the magik rock bridge – and they were waiting to receive the next victim.

They moved across the sea some distance from the shoreline, with Reed pausing often to make sure the woman was still behind him. They reached a flat rock section in front of the massive boulder and when he had cleared it, he turned to wait for her. When she reached him, he ascended one step to put his hand on the huge rock.

"Ye must find the crevice in the rock. Then put the coin in it like so." He demonstrated as he found the crevice. The coin slid in, and as it did, he said, "Put your hand flat just here." He pointed to a smooth spot just above the crevice and to the left of it.

The woman did as instructed.

"It will know you now," Reed said. "You will not have to use the coin, as you come and go. However, for a while, wear the coin in your shoe as you go down the path to the shoreline. The path will come to know you as well, and after a few times going back and forth, it will recognize your trod, and you will not have to wear it. I will return on the morrow with food and some essentials 'til you get situated. Is there anything you be needing to get through the night?"

Reed's voice trailed off as an arched doorway opened in the rock; a gaping jaw with chilled breath. The woman stepped into the doorway, pushing her hood back as she turned to look at him.

"Dear God, what happened to ye, lass?" he exclaimed, his eyes wide in horror, as he beheld a beautiful face, much obscured in the darkness except what the orb illuminated.

What he saw left him slack-jawed.

It was her hair, or lack thereof. It was as though someone had ripped it straight from her head on the left side, leaving bald patches and only slightly healed sores. The rest of her hair had been hacked off except on the right side, where there were still strands that looked as silver as the moonlight. They escaped from their hiding place under the hood and fell down her breasts to wisp lightly at her waist.

"What have they done to you, lass?" Reed asserted again, staring without embarrassment at her head and the terrible wounds.

"It is a good thing all my magik does not reside in my hair, is it not?" she responded softly, a small smile gracing her lips. She leaned into the darkness of the room beyond. "Thank you, Mister Reed. I am indebted. I apologize for not introducing myself. I am not myself. My name is Ilia."

She paused for a moment to offer him another small smile then said, "Good night."

She waited a moment for him to release her hand, then turned and moved into the recesses of the cave, as the door scraped heavily on across stone to close behind her.

Reed stood for a moment, all his speculations about the woman wiped away with the reality of what he had just seen. A few moments passed as he stood staring back at the shoreline trying to make sense of it. Then he gathered his thoughts and carried them with him back across the path to the shore.

One

Fate conspired to bring them together in the marketplace. It truly was fate, as she was more a child of the night, and he avoided social gatherings at all costs. Yet, there they were, and there they ran into each other - literally. She was standing in the city square transfixed by all the people and the noise. It was chaos, color, sound, and cacophony. She found herself lost in it all and not paying attention to the immediate.

The immediate came in the form of a rather large man plowing a straight line through the circular center to get to the butchers on the other side. He was indifferent to those around him, his head down, as he read the list of items he needed to order.

Generally, the crowds parted when Tristan was anywhere near, so he rarely bothered with making sure no one was in front of him. His large presence and the fact that most people understood who he was, though they would never speak of it, caused most to retreat. He was the Lord Pirate, a man dangerous and feared everywhere. His exploits were legendary, and there was a quality of the feral about him that caused the most solid of men unease.

Tristan did not like being in crowds, because he knew people were afraid of him. Though it made him uncomfortable, he also relied on their discomfort to allow him to get what he needed quickly and without interference. This day, however, there was an exception- the young woman with silver hair and pale skin so caught up in her surroundings she was oblivious to them. He plowed right into her.

Fortunately for Ilia, he had quick reflexes and broke her fall. Her crystal blue eyes locked with his mossy green, and they did not waver as he righted her. For a moment the world melted away as they stood transfixed. Ilia felt her magik rise within her like a seated figure standing up. Her fingertips tingled, and she felt hot rush of power move through her unlike anything she had conjured up on purpose. This came of its own accord, responding, she realized, to the man still holding her in his arms. He brought her entire being to attention, and she had an absurd desire to pull him closer to her.

It was Tristan who broke the spell. He felt the power surge through her as he still had his arm about her waist. He broke the contact and said, "I'm sorry lass. I was not minding where I was going. Are you all right?"

He would forever remember everything about her that first time they met. She wore a light blue smock. It was not the current fashion, for it had no frills. It was the color of the palest sky, made of a soft material that almost seemed liquid as it moved about her. Her hair, the color of moonlight, was a mass of white curls tied back with a ribbon just below the nape. It was slung over her shoulder, the curls cascading down over one breast to reach her waist.

Her skin was pale but not without warmth. He had encountered night walkers, but she was not one of those. Still, he sensed she was a woman from the night world. Her eyes were the same light blue as her dress and had a translucent quality did not waver from his. He had a sense she could see right into the heart of him. No doubt, this was a very powerful woman.

Ilia did a mental collection of herself, bidding the power coursing in her veins to subside, as she took stock of the man in front of her. He was large, formidably framed, and marked by hard labor. He had slim hips and well-muscled legs to match the rest of him. His dark hair was pulled tightly back in a plait, tied with a stock, that hung well past his shoulders. He had a full dark beard that for all its thickness was well groomed and trimmed closely to his jawline.

He wore the clothing of an upper-class merchant. Dark breeches fitted his slim hips and legs and met with high leather boots of good quality. He wore a dark green coat that extended almost to his calves, a black wool vest, and a white linen shirt that was open at the neck, the one component that suggested he was not quite the upper-class gentleman the rest of his attire promised, for true gentlemen wore cravats at the neck. At his waist, he'd tucked a knife into his belt. She could see, through the Y-neck of his tunic, the edge of a tattoo of some sort. He was definitely of the sea-faring folk, for tattoos were a part of their particular distinction. Her magik perked, sensing the ocean about him. His piercing green eyes studied her as she surveyed him for what seemed forever but was in fact only seconds.

"My apologies, sir," her smooth voice flowed over him like cool waters. "I was wool gathering. I don't often come to market, and I fear I am slightly overwhelmed in my senses with it all." She smiled, a faint rosy tint shading her cheeks in embarrassment.

"Indeed, I think we can both take the blame here, but how else would I have met the most interesting woman in the square without such a collision?"

He grinned, eliciting another smile from Ilia. "I am Tristan," he said, reaching out a hand for hers.

She gave her hand, and as he kissed the top of it she said, "You are more than that, sir. You are, I am quite sure, a pirate." She did not stop at the surprised look that crossed his face before he schooled his expressions.

She shrugged, a mischievous glint in her eyes. "I, on the other hand, am just Ilia."

He released her hand, laughing. "Aye, but you are more than that, madam. I wager you are a moon child, and an extremely powerful one at that."

It was her turn to struggle to school her features to mask her surprise. She started to step back from him, and he quickly responded to her action, his face suddenly serious, "Do not be alarmed. I do not fear power in any creature. Power is a thing to celebrate, not shun out of fear."

He glanced around them before continuing, "But I do believe we are drawing a crowd. May I suggest we walk on?"

Ilia looked around and noticed they were indeed drawing a crowd. She knew she should take leave of the stranger and go about her business, but she could not seem to leave him. She suddenly felt a connection to the man was important to explore. She knew, as one knows when a decision is the right one, from that day forward she would be tied in some way to him. "I only need to find the woolsy. I need a new cloak."

He nodded, reaching for her hand to tuck it in the crook of his arm as he steered them through the crowded street to a table heaped with wool goods.

With some haste, she picked out a wool cloak that had been dyed to a deep, dark Indigo blue. It was of excellent quality, and heavy. She seemed to know exactly the one she wanted, and as she paid the woolsy Tristan said, "Shopping with you must be a quick venture. It took you but two minutes to make your purchase."

Ilia glanced up at him, grinning. "I'm not really much of a shopper. I tend to buy what I want and have it in mind before I ever set out." She shrugged, saying, "And I have never had much opportunity to take my leisure either. I draw attention, and that does not lend a comfortable atmosphere for wandering and looking." She fell silent, wondering if she was sharing too much.

But he nodded. "I can identify. I tend to draw attention as well, though in a different way, I'd wager." He sent her a wry smile.

They fell silent for a time until Tristan broke the hush. "So where are we walking to? I don't mind strolling around the town with you at all. 'Tis a very pleasant way to spend the day, but I am guessing at some point you would like to get back to your place of residence."

She smiled and gave a small chuckle. "Yes. That might be good information to have. We are staying at the King's Inn. It's just down this same street."

"I know it well," he said, shifting his stance. "You said, 'we.' Are you here with family? A husband perhaps?"

"No husband. I am here with my sisters." She paused. "Well, they aren't really my sisters. We grew up in the same place and, well…" She trailed off, not sure how to explain. She drew a breath and tried again. Since he did not press her for a more precise answer, she was willing to give him one. "I grew up in a special place, you see. I never knew my parents. So, I was raised in a home with other children like me."

Tristan nodded. "I have heard the stories." He paused, glancing at her. "Shall I tell you what I have heard, and you can tell me what is truth and what is fable?"

Ilia sighed in relief, happy to let him do the talking, as she bobbed her head in agreement.

"Moon children, you are called. Changelings at birth. You were born to mortal parents who saw you were different, and because of the brainwashing and fearmongering of the current society" – he scoffed - "you were left to die in the woods somewhere."

He waited for her correction, and when she said nothing, he continued. "I'm guessing someone found you or was even looking for you, picked you up, and took you to a place where you could live in safety."

"Yes. You have it correct," said she. "There are people who look for changelings for good and for ill. Most changelings are moon children, but there are other kinds. I was fortunate to be found by someone who cared and who was able to give me a good home. Moon children are generally female. We are pale, as you see I am, pale blue eyes, and silver hair. We look as though we have been touched by the moon, and so we have. Some of us are quite powerful. Magik flows from us like breath. Others have only the looks and very little magik." She grew silent.

"Which have you?" he asked.

She gave him a pointed look. "Well sir, you might say I have it all."

Tristan smiled, "I'm sure you do. I knew it when I touched you, but I wondered if you knew."

Ilia chuckled lightly, then sobered, "It is dangerous, and that was a fool thing I did today.

Impetuous. I may as well have announced my presence over a horn at the tallest building." She gave an exasperated sigh, "But I get so tired of living life in the shadows. I sometimes want to live in the sun." She gave a slight bow of her head. "I fear my lack of judgment may cause repercussions. I hope I am wrong."

They walked in silence for a time then Tristan said, "How many of you are there here in town?"

"My two chaperons who are really more like mothers to us, and three of my adopted siblings. There are more of us than that, but as we grow up, we are often placed in different areas throughout the world, especially those of us who have special abilities. We have a benefactor; someone I do not know, who keeps us well funded and has since long before I was born," she paused, not knowing how much further to go with her story.

"So, your sisters do not have special skills, and that is why they are still with your mothers?" It was a question, but he uttered it like a statement.

Ilia nodded, "They are not moon children gifted in the magikal realm. At least two of them are not. One is still too young to tell."

"Then what of you?" he asked. "Where do you fit in?"

Ilia shrugged, "I am something altogether different, and they keep me close not only for my safety; but because my training has been much more extensive than others like me." She brushed a few stray silver strands from her cheek. "And there are people who would like to get ahold of someone with my abilities who has not quite learned the extent of them or how to use them." She trailed off, realizing she had exposed herself to a man she did not know.

Tristan sensed her alarm. "Do not fear. I assure you; I am not one of those people." His smile did assure her, and she returned it.

They were at the King's Inn front door. Ilia was turning to thank Tristan for the walk when the door flew open, and a small dark-haired lady rushed through it.

"Ilia! Oh, thank God! Ilia, the proprietor says we must vacate at once. He said he does not want 'our kind' in his establishment! Can you believe it? Where will we go? There is no place in town for us to stay that is safe. We always stay here. He says we will ruin his business! Oh Ilia, you must do something!" The small woman flailed her arms in the air, her hair in disarray, panic evident in the redness of her face.

Ilia said, in her soft even voice, "Calm yourself Madra. I will deal with this. But we must leave tomorrow morning. I can only make it last through the night; otherwise, there will be damage."

The woman named Madra nodded and became silent. Ilia pulled her new wool cloak about her, and turned to Tristan, "I apologize for the disruption. I must take care of this situation immediately. Thank you for the walk and the conversation." She looked at him with regret then, with an air of dismissal, turned to go into the Inn.

Tristan had no plans to leave her in peril, even though he was not generally the chivalrous type.

He had long held the philosophy that women in peril usually got themselves that way and needed to acquire skills at getting out of peril on their own. Practice made perfect. But this was different. This woman was different, and since she did not wait to see what he was going to do but turned to address her troubles on her own, he felt obliged to follow in her wake.

Ilia moved from the sunny outside into the darkened foyer that opened to a sitting area, where there was a desk for check-in. The lamps were lit all around, but the shutters were closed, and the light creeping in from the sunlit day did little to brighten the room.

Ilia looked about the room, noticing there was only the owner at the desk, and he was coming around it to confront them. Ilia could sense Tristan standing behind her. "Stay behind me," she said in a low voice.

Madra nodded her head in acquiescence.

"Now see here…" the short pudgy owner of the Inn was red-faced and clearly ready for battle of some sort. Ilia found the situation slightly amusing, as the man looked agitated enough to spontaneously combust before she even spoke.

No matter. If that were the case, she would be doing him a favor. She stepped in front of him and waved a hand. The man stilled, as though rooted to the spot. His face lost its angry redness, and his eyes glazed.

Ilia spoke softly and the man nodded at everything she said. Tristan could not make out what she said, but once she finished speaking, she stepped back and lowered her hand.

The man looked confused, gathered himself, and went back behind the desk. "What can I get for you, madam?" he warbled.

Ilia glided to the counter and said, "We shall be leaving in the morning. Thank you for your services. We will receive dinner in our rooms this evening."

“Very good,” he stated.

Ilia turned and walked back toward Madra and Tristan. She cast a glance at them both and said,

“Not here. To our sitting room.”

*

Tristan followed them down a long hall to their rooms. At the end of the hall there was a large room designated for gathering, and off that room were four bedrooms. They entered the sitting room wordlessly. Ilia crossed directly to the decanter sitting on the sideboard and poured a brandy. She tossed it back, something Tristan found rather sexy. He had never seen a woman do such a thing, and he found it appealing. He watched her gather herself for a moment with her back to everyone, then turn to face six pairs of eyes.

“It will only last until morning. As I said, any longer and I would have done him damage. Not that he doesn’t deserve it, bigoted old goat, but I don’t want that on my hands,” Ilia said, as though they had been having a conversation and she was just responding.

The other ladies sat demurely; their eyes fastened on Ilia. It was clear to Tristan, they looked to her for guidance for resolving conflict situations. It was clear they had forgotten he was in the room until he cleared his throat and strode over to the sideboard where Ilia focused her attention on pouring another brandy. He grinned as she handed it to him.

They all started at the action, as though someone had snapped their fingers and brought them back to life, but before anyone could say anything, Ilia said, “Ladies, this is Tristan. I apologize for the familiar first name, but we were short on time. If you need a more formal name, call him…” She paused, grasping for information. “Well. He is a pirate, and anything more you want to know, I guess you can just ask him yourselves.”

Tristan smiled into his brandy glass as he drained it. No need for subtlety with this woman. Then he said mildly, "How do you do, ladies? My reputation for pillaging does not apply in this context, I assure you. I'm at your service." The shock at the discovery of what he was made his admission seem inconsequential.

Ilia introduced Tristan to Madra, to Mena her other mother, and then to Anna, Senza, and Trissa, her sisters. Tristan realized Madra and Mena were twins. Same small round frames. Same dark hair streaked with gray. Same shining brown eyes hinting at a great sense of humor. Identical. He chided himself for not registering the fact sooner.

"But Ilia, we still have several days' worth of business to finish. We can't leave in the morning," said Senza. She had slightly more coloring to her skin than had Ilia, and her hair had a hint of strawberry to it. She was plump and a bit giggly, Tristan noticed. She looked to be the youngest of the group, though truth be told, the sisters all looked about the same age. The mothers, he guessed, were not moon children. They were facing their dotage, but he could not determine the ages of the sisters, nor Ilia, for that matter.

They all sat in silence, each lost in their thoughts. Tristan finished his second brandy and set his glass on the sideboard. "Well ladies, I have an idea that may help you."

They all looked at him in unison. He tried to soften his voice to put them at ease. "I have a friend who has a rather large rambling house just outside of town. She lets rooms, and I have known her for many years. I have no doubt she would be happy to have you stay. It is the off-season, so she is not so busy just now. That is why I find the innkeeper's wanting to get rid of you so nonsensical."

"It is because of what we are," Ilia said.

"That and the fact that Ilia was walking about town today as if she is just like everyone else," this from Trissa who, Tristan could see, was more forceful in personality than her sisters, and maybe just a bit jealous of Ilia.

"Trissa. You have no say in what Ilia does. She is the reason we are as safe as we are, and you are being spiteful!" exclaimed Senza.

"She is most likely why we are as hunted as we are." Trissa retorted, her chin up at the accusation, as she leveled her blue gaze on Ilia. She was a striking woman in her way. The same light skin, but her hair was straight and cut in a very sleek bob. Her clothing was immaculate and of the latest style. Tristan could see she was a woman who wanted to be first in any situation and might resort to unorthodox tactics to make that happen. Her distaste for Ilia fringed her every syllable.

Ilia steadied her gaze on Trissa and said nothing, but a few seconds of her focused attention and

Trissa flinched as though burned, subsiding back into her chair, her tirade quieted.

"There will be plenty of time for you to express your distaste for me and my actions, Triss. I am more than happy to remove myself from your company at any time. I think we both know who would fare best if that happened." Ilia paused, turning her gaze back to the others, "But for now, we must solve our problem. Trissa is right in that my actions today were reckless, and for that, I apologize to you all. I have nothing to say for my defense except that I needed to get out."

Anna, who sat quietly in the corner spoke for the first time. "Ilia, we have put ourselves in your capable hands before, and this time should be no different. What do you suggest?" Her voice was like a gliding stream, calming and full of harmony. Tristan felt immediately languid listening to her, and he noticed she had the same effect on the others.

Ilia looked at Mena and Madra. They had remained silent throughout the exchange, but both nodded at Ilia to continue. If Tristan had not known better, he would have thought the entire discussion had been orchestrated. It was as if each woman had a role and played only her part.

Ilia turned her focus back to Tristan. "Sir, I think that even though we were to spend the night here, perhaps we should depart later this evening after dark. My mind-altering abilities are generally effective, but I would prefer to not have to rely totally on this one. I would not want to disrupt your schedule, though. It would suit us to leave in cover of dark, but I defer to your final word, as you will need to show us the way."

Tristan pondered her words for a moment then pushed himself away from the sideboard he had been leaning against, "That is fine with me. I have a few things to do, but I will come back for you just after dusk. Do you have conveyance?"

"Oh yes," replied Mena. We have a carriage."

"Very good," Tristan replied. "I will leave you, then, and be back later."

He strode across the room to the door. "Ladies," he said, catching Ilia's eye for a moment before closing the door behind him.

"Well!" exclaimed Madra, "We are fortunate that young man made your acquaintance, Ilia, though it is difficult to determine if the man is demon or angel!" Her eyes twinkled.

"A little of both, I expect" came Ilia's response, her eyes still on the door that had just closed a few moments before.

Two

True to his word, Tristan arrived just after sunset. He had been busy in the little time left before the appointment. He finished picking up supplies he needed to take to the ship, and once he dropped them off, he made sure things were running smoothly with the repairs. He then stopped off to see his accountant, Devlin, to make sure everything was in order on the financial end of his endeavors.

Tristan, being in the line of work he was in, had many "accountants" in various ports. These men were trusted and capable of covering tracks when need be. Tristan never put all his eggs in one basket, for he had all his crew to provide for as well. His crew was his family, and he made sure they and their families were well taken care of. He had never had a crew member defect. They all knew the grass was greenest with him, and their loyalty to him was unimpeachable.

By the time he was ready to meet up with Ilia and her family, Tristan had tied up everything in Portsmith except the completion of the ship repairs. He expected another week or so would see that task completed as well, and he would be ready to get back to the world he loved, the open sea and all the adventures therein.

*

They set out just as the light faded from the skyline. Tristan's right-hand man, Edmond, rode along with him. Ilia had chosen to ride horseback rather than ride in the carriage. Doing so gave the other ladies more room and gave Ilia space from Trissa who continued to snipe. Ilia found

Edmond congenial and eager to chat as they made the trek out of Portsmith into the countryside. He regaled her with stories of their adventures, and Tristan grew an indulgent smile at the embellishments. They were riding behind the carriage, he on one side of Ilia, and Edmond on the other. He noticed Ilia sat her mount as a woman who had always ridden and commented as much.

"We had comprehensive training as young women of upbringing," she responded.

"Horses are not overly fond of moon children, but they make an exception with me, and Anna also does quite well with them."

Tristan smiled. "I expect most all creatures make an exception for you."

"Not all," she said lightly, but her brows had drawn together, and her face held an apprehensive expression he couldn't understand. But he let it go and said nothing.

The three travelled on in companionable silence as the carriage wound its way down the narrow road. The night was still and calm, a chill lingering in the air. They were just entering spring, and winter struggled to give way to warmer nights. The sky was clear, and the moon shone down like a light from the heavens.

Ilia, dressed in her wool cloak, sat astride her mount, her head uncovered, her long hair curling around her like silver bubbles. She shone, with the moon's own light. She tipped her head back slightly, basking in the moonlight as one would normally bask in the sunlight for warmth after being in the chill of shade.

"I know you are watching me," she said, laughter tinging her voice. "You are not very covert."

Edmond had ridden up a bit ahead to steer the coach down the correct lane to their destination, so they were alone. "You caught me," Tristan chuckled. "I didn't want to disturb you, but you must admit, you approach the night and the moonlight a bit differently than would most."

She looked at him, her eyes glowing, as was her skin and even her hair. Tristan started a bit, and Ilia giggled. "Yes, I have an interesting biological reaction to the moonlight. I am not a moon child for nothing, after all. I draw a tremendous amount of energy from moonlight. My sisters do not like to be around me when I am thus, they do not have the same reaction to the moonlight as I do. They do not need to 'refuel' from it as much as I do, but then I am not really like them." She paused for a moment, tilting her head. "Anna is different than the others. She has always understood me, but then Anna is quite a bit older than any of us."

Tristan registered a shocked look. "Anna? How old is she?"

"That would be telling, and a lady never gives away another's age," laughed Ilia. "Suffice to say she has lived many lifetimes."

Tristan was silent for a moment, pondering the new information. At length he asked, "I beg your pardon, but I can't help myself, are you quite old then?"

"Much older than you," she said, smiling sweetly.

Tristan didn't want to badger her, but he had questions, and he didn't know when he would have her alone again, so he plunged on. "You say Anna knows you better. What about your other two sisters? "

"What about them?" she responded, then continued on a slightly different vein. "Senza is a frivolous little girl, sweet-natured, and will always be naïve, I think. Trissa, well Trissa does not like me. She never has. I am never sure just how deep her dislike for me goes, but I would guess her jealousy is just the tip of the iceberg. I try to stay away from her."

"Why do you think she dislikes you so?" he asked.

"Well, I expect it is because I am, um, unique? I naturally possess what she has always wanted.

Yes, I think that is it." She finished by pursing her lips as though she'd solved a big conundrum.

"What do you have that she does not have," he asked, though he wagered he already knew the answer.

"Power" she replied. "A tremendous amount of power." She sighed and continued without waiting for an answer. "But she cannot help how she feels, just as I cannot help what I am. And she is, for all accounts and purposes, my sister. At least for my part, anyway. So, I am very indulgent toward her."

The bridge between her silver eyebrows knitted. "I suspect she is the one who stirred up trouble with the innkeeper. It is just the kind of thing she would do. It is not the first, nor I wager, the last time" she finished matter-of-factly.

Tristan sat silent, digesting what Ilia had shared. "How did you know I was a pirate?"

Ilia chuckled. "Well I guessed, but I knew you spend a great deal of time on the sea."

"How could you know that?"

"I could sense it on you. It is deeply embedded in your, shall we say, nature," she said warmly. "I sense other things in you, as well. I sense magik in you, but that is a conversation for another time. You are much more than you appear, and I expect that is your intention, Lord Pirate." She grinned at his shocked expression and then looked away.

They finished the journey in silence, each to their own thoughts, and soon they were in front of a three-story house. It was the tallest building for miles, and Ilia suspected it had been a major talking point among residents of the area for some time. The house had white columns on either side of a flight of the stairs leading up to the front door. They gleamed in the moonlight.

The inhabitants descended the carriage, and as Tristan helped Ilia dismount, she pulled her hood up over her head. "Wouldn't want to frighten our new hostess, now would we?" she said breezily.

"It's the glowing eyes that might cause alarm more than the glowing hair and skin," he chuckled. "Though Ella is made of some pretty stern stuff, and having known Edmond and me since childhood, I can promise you she has seen some things, though nothing like you, I'm certain."

"Well, once I'm inside the light will deflect, and I will no longer look so…otherworldly," she said, moving to join her mothers and sisters.

Tristan led the group up the stairs to greet Ella, who was standing in the doorway, with a hug. He then made introductions. Ella was much younger than Ilia had supposed, though with Tristan mentioning they were children together, she should not have been surprised. She didn't know

Tristan's age either, but then they all seemed young to her. Age to Ilia had stopped mattering when she learned she would age very slowly over many human lifetimes.

She stood watching Edmond join the group and the easy communication they shared. She concluded it must be one of the rewards for maintaining long-term relationships. She had known Madra and Mena a very long time, but there was a reserve that existed between them that kept them from a more intimate connection. Ilia wondered if that reserve was more self-preservation.

She wondered if she scared them on some level, and that prevented the nurturing relationship she saw between the two mothers and her other sisters. They needed her mothers, and maybe Ilia never had.

Ilia suddenly felt very alone, as she stood back, detached from the two groups that were beginning to mingle together with introductions. She realized the closest relationship in her life was with Anna, and that was a very formal one. She could not tell Anna her heart. She turned and moved away from the group. She could hear them laughing and talking, and something in her heart twisted.

For the first time in her life, Ilia wanted someone to know her. She was tired of being set apart from others, even those of her own kind. Was there no one who cared enough to know her? Was there no one brave enough to get close to her? She drifted silently around the back of the house and down the back lawns toward a pond set some distance from the house. The sounds of voices faded to be replaced with night noises. Crickets, frogs, an owl hooting, the movement of grass in the breeze along with the nearby trees, and the gentle sound of water.

This was comfortable to Ilia. She drew in a breath and let the night calm her; heal her heart. She extended her long fingers from her cape, the chill of the night enunciating her breath in wisps. Reaching her fingers up toward the moon, she tipped her head slightly until she could see the big orb in the sky. It was a full moon. Her whole body hummed with energy from it. She felt as though she could pull it down out of the sky and step into it. She could wrap herself in it and become part of it.

Instead, she simply spidered her fingers toward herself in a beckoning gesture. Threads released from the moon itself and extended to her. As they touched her fingertips, they stretched away from the heavens in wisps, clinging to her. She dropped her hood and let the cloak fall to pool about her feet. The moonspun gathered around her, enveloping her, coming to her as fast as she could pull it in. She spun around and around, the moonspun like silk, covering her, glowing and directing her in a dance perfect for the enchantment of a full moon.

*

Tristan stood on the bank at the back of the house watching something he would never be able to describe to anyone else. He saw Ilia glide off quietly in the wake of their arrival at Ella's. He had been about to introduce her to Ella when he noticed her disappearing around the back of the house. He did not want to draw attention to her departure, so he made his excuse to leave the group, saying he needed to check his saddlebag in the stable. He crept off in the direction of the stables then circled back around to find Ilia.

Having found her, he stood transfixed, watching her pull something out of the sky. It was silky and shining. It seemed to be almost alive. He wanted to shake his head to make sure he wasn't hallucinating, but he knew he was seeing what he was seeing. He watched her shed her cloak and then move as though in a dance with a partner he couldn't see. The strands moved around her as she stepped and circled. When she raised her hands, fingertips in the air, more strands dropped down from the heavens, down her arms and into her hair as she dropped her head back, her long silver hair a wild mass of glowing curls that hung well past her waist. Her eyes were closed as she twirled around the pond, not needing to see to maneuver it. Her simple white linen dress hung loose around her small body, and though it gave nothing away, showed no curve or any skin, Tristan thought it was the most erotic thing he had ever seen.

"She is moonspinning," came a soft voice from behind him.

Even though it was little more than a whisper, Anna's voice might as well have been blasted in his ear. He jolted to attention, turning to look at her, his eyes wide in surprise.

She came up next to him. "Sorry. It's quite a beautiful thing to watch. I am the only one who has ever seen her do it. I will never forget the first time she took me with her. I danced with her, and the moonspun covered me like cobwebs. Keep watching. It's almost over."

They stood there watching the glowing figure wrapped completely in the bright tendrils, dancing and moving. Finally, the internal music must have stopped, for Ilia stilled and stood, covered in the moon spun. She raised her hands one final time, fingers pointing into the air. As she slowly moved her hands down, palms up, to her waist, the wisps pulsed over her and around her then slowly absorbed into her body, and she floated off the ground. She moved a hand out toward her cloak that lay on the ground nearby, and it floated up to gather around her shoulders, the hood lifting to settle ever so gently on her head. She raised her head. Even from a fair distance Tristan could see her eyes shining from the hood, and they were looking right at him.

"I think this is my cue to head to bed" Anna said. Then, "She is very powerful. No matter how genteel she seems, she has tremendous power. But she is not a weapon. She is a woman; a unique kind of woman, but woman nonetheless. Please do not forget that. The man who can match her will have a life truly worth living." With that, she left as quietly as she had come.

*

Ilia sensed he was there as she drifted to the ground. She wasn't sure how much he had seen, but she had sensed Anna with him as well and knew Anna would likely have done some explaining. No matter. There was little she could do. She was a moon child of the first order, and a full moon dictated certain things. She honored that, as was not only her heritage but her biological need. The ritual was more of a healing experience than anything. Moon children must have the ability to refuel, and city living did not afford enough privacy or even access to the moon to do what was natural.

She walked toward the back of the house where Tristan was waiting. She hoped for little commentary. Her mind was on a different plane and didn't want to have a discussion. She wanted this precious little time to savor.

Tristan seemed to understand her mood and said only, "I will show you to your room. Let us go up this side entrance to the house, and we can avoid seeing anyone."

Ilia guessed she was still glowing and knew her eyes were shining like honeyed orbs in her head. Whenever a moon child had a moon encounter, the traditionally blue, almost translucent eye color changed to glowing orbs with irises the color of rich honey. No one had ever been able to explain to Ilia the reason for the change, and she was grateful when Tristan saw her to the door of her room, his tall frame towering over her as he put the key in the door and opened it for her.

"I am guessing you have questions," she said, turning in the doorway to face him. Her shining face and glowing eyes beamed directly at him.

"I think that was sacred, and the sacred is hard to explain. I am not a man who is easy to scare away. I am at your service as long as we are in one another's company." He backed away from the door. "And," he added, leaning back on his heel, "I'm looking forward to it. Good night moon beam." He grinned and left her to stand in the shadow of the doorway smiling to herself. Moon beam, indeed.

*

The time at "The Bird in Hand," Ella's home, consisted of Tristan, Edmond, Madra and Mena going back and forth to Portsmith. Tristan and Edmond were continuing their preparations for leaving port, and Mena and Madra took turns going back and forth to further the stockpile they needed to last for many months. The place Ilia called home was a secluded spot, hours from Portsmith near a little village called Luna – the name, no doubt, a nod to the generations of moon children brought up nearby.

The people of Luna were both wary and accepting of Ilia and her family. To outsiders, the village closed ranks around the members of the village, which included the moon children. But to Ilia and her family, the village remained aloof and did not interact with them when they were in town.

Ilia could understand their fear. They had grown up with many stories, some true and some not, that instilled fear in the generations. It was natural there would be a wariness towards what they did not know or understand. That, however, was not the reason Ilia and her family went to Portsmith a couple times a year to shop. The village had day-to-day items but not in volume, and Madra and Mena had always made it a practice to buy in bulk and limit interaction with those who did not know them or their ways.

After the first two days, Edmond stayed in Portsmith and Tristan remained at Ella's. Ilia wondered if the reason for that was to put Ella at ease while the woman extended her hospitality to the strange family she had taken in. Ella was friendly and solicitous, but Ilia caught her watching them at different times, as they sat in the large parlor talking over a book or debating a theme that had been introduced, as they had so often throughout their lives.

Ilia enjoyed being outside and spent time walking the large grounds or riding with Tristan. Often, she slept late, as she spent time outside in the night hours where she felt most comfortable. Senza spent her time following Ella around helping her with whatever chores she was doing. Senza loved to cook, and Ella was happy to share her kitchen, even turning the baking over to Senza.

When not making runs into town for various items they had either forgotten or just realized were needed, Madra and Mena sat in the parlor room devouring books Ella had on her shelves.

They were voracious readers, and whenever they could read someone else's books and save their own for a time when options were limited, they did so with zeal.

Trissa's habits were less obvious. She only grudgingly participated in family situations. The things that set her apart from humans, her pale skin, her light blue eyes, and her silver hair seemed to anger her. She was always looking at fashion and spent more than the rest of the group combined on her wardrobe. When they were in Portsmith, she went down to the docks to scan the wares just coming in from other ports. She could bargain with the best of them. She took what she bought and had it made up in the latest styles. She wore her pale hair in revolving trends and found ways to cover most of it in hats and fashionable scarves to disguise its unusual color.

It wasn't Trissa's fashion obsession that concerned Ilia. It was her disdain not only for who she was but for those in her family. She often amused herself by causing problems for the rest of her siblings. There was a streak of maliciousness in her that Ilia found disturbing. Ilia hoped that as she aged, Trissa would lose some of her bent toward mischief. So far, though, quite the opposite had happened.

Since they had been at Ella's, Trissa had often gone off on long horseback rides by herself. When she returned, if questioned, she would simply say she had been riding and then took a siesta under a tree or had been staring out at the beauty of the countryside. Ilia didn't believe her. Trissa didn't like horses, and they didn't like her. Ilia felt a sense of urgency to get back home even though that would mean the end of her time with Tristan.

Tristan. Ilia was experiencing a sensation foreign to her. She was becoming very attached to him. They rode every day together, talked and laughed, shared stories of their lives, and he often shared stories of adventures he had.

Ilia once asked Tristan if he had always wanted to be a pirate.

"Aye." He gave her a sideways glance. "Two of my favorite things, the sea and causing trouble." They were sitting under the shade of a lovely Ona tree. Ona trees were hundreds of years old by the time they became substantial enough to sit under. This tree was large, and its blood-red branches arced into a perfect umbrella all the way around the tree. Silver leaves with pale pink blossoms draped all around them, nearly touching the ground.

Ilia raised her brows in question and grinned at him, and they both laughed.

He became more serious and said, "My life is a bit like yours in the sense that I really didn't have parents. My brother, Roger, raised me, but he was sickly. My parents were quite old. My mother had me late in life. I wasn't but 4 years old when they both died of an illness that spread through our village. It took most of those past their prime. So, my brother took the job of raising me, but I spent most of my time at Edmond's house. He is more of a brother to me than mine ever was. And when we were both grown, we kissed his mum goodbye and set out to serve on the seas for our country."

He stared out at the landscape, chewing on a blade of grass, as he let his mind drift to the past.

"We saw many creatures both in the sea and on land," he continued. "I think those on land might have been scarier, though. You'd think it would be the opposite, but on land, monsters and the magikal meld together, and you can't always see where they are coming from.

Edmond and I always enjoyed our adventures together, but the pirating came later. I would never ask him to take part in something we could be shot for later, but he wanted to serve with me. I earned the reputation for being able to outmaneuver a ship through any waters. We got a few bounties and had success with them and earned a reputation for achieving what we set out to.

Edmond doesn't look the part of a pirate, though. He looks a better fit in a fine-cut outfit and is comfortable in a crowd, exchanging pleasantries. That is often where I send him when we make port. He finds out information, and all the ladies love him."

He stopped, and Ilia said, "But not you? Do the ladies not love you? I can imagine you being quite charming when you've a mind to."

"That's the thing. I'm rarely of a mind." His green eyes took on an intensity, and Ilia felt herself responding to something igniting between them.

She didn't break the link between them as she said, "You have been quite charming with me."

"Aye, but with you I am just myself. I feel like I've known you my whole life. How is that possible?"

Ilia shook her head, their eyes still locked, "I have no idea. It's not a kind of magik I'm familiar with."

Tristan leaned forward slowly and touched his lips to hers, their eyes still gazing. It was a soft, questioning kiss. He leaned in again, and this time it was more demanding.

Ilia closed her eyes, opened her mouth slightly and sighed as his lips explored hers, his tongue tentatively touching hers. She wrapped her arms around his neck, and he pulled her up against his chest, as he continued to explore her mouth.

At length, he broke the kiss and looked down into her azure eyes.

She sighed. "My. That was good."

He chuckled releasing her then stood, pulling her up and into his arms. She was quite small, and he was well over six feet tall. When he held her and kissed her, he simply lifted her off the ground and hugged her to him as his mouth covered hers once again.

He released her a few minutes later and set her on the ground. She said nothing but walked over and grabbed the reins of her horse and mounted it. He did the same, and they rode in silence back to the house, both lost in thoughts that traversed the same theme. This was the person. They could both feel it to their core. And they were both about to go their separate ways.

Ilia knew having a man in her life would complicate the fragile hold she had on everything. This man would never be at home in her life. Even she wasn't most of the time. What was going to happen over the next couple of days that would change that? And how, knowing what she knew, could she possibly, ever let him go?

Three

"I need to go into Portsmith today," Trissa announced at the lunch table. "I plan to take the carriage. I was wondering if anyone would like to go. I need to pick up some dresses that are ready. I can pick up anything else we still need if you give me a list," she announced.

"Why so late in the day, Trissa?" Madra asked. "You should have planned this outing this morning."

Trissa sat back, a sullen expression on her face. "Well, I just got a note saying they were ready, and I thought maybe it would be fun to go in and have a nice dinner and stay overnight."

Mena looked at Ella and sputtered, "Of course, we have lovely meals here with you, Ella. It's just so seldom the girls get to go to the city."

"I completely understand," said Ella, smiling gently.

Anna spoke up. "I'm fine staying here. I have no need for an outing. Maybe Senza or Ilia would go with you."

"I don't want you going alone," said Mena. "It's not safe. Ilia, would you go with Trissa? I would feel better if you were with her."

Ilia swallowed her discomfort at being pressured into an outing that involved time alone with

Trissa. "Yes of course," she agreed, avoiding Tristan's scowling gaze across the table from her.

"How soon are you leaving?" he asked. "I can ride along with you, but I have a couple of things to take care of first."

"We must leave right after lunch if we are to get there before the dressmaker closes," Trissa responded, a bit too quickly. She clearly did not want Tristan joining, whether he was in the carriage or riding alongside.

He sat for a moment contemplating then said, "I can join you in town for dinner. That will allow me to spend a little time with Edmond later this evening." Trissa scowled, clearly not happy with the arrangement.

But Ilia smiled, and Mena gave a grateful sigh. "Oh, I would feel a lot better about them being in such a big city if you were there, Tristan. Thank you!"

After lunch, Ilia grabbed a few items and headed downstairs where Trissa was already waiting for her. "You packed quickly," Ilia said, amused. Trissa was usually the last one to get ready for anything. She must really be excited to get her dresses, Ilia thought. "Where are your things?" she asked aloud.

"Oh, they are already on the carriage. Here give me yours, and I will put them with mine." She grabbed Ilia's bag and headed out the door. Ilia shrugged at Trissa's proactive behavior, a departure from her current mode of handling anything, and went into the drawing-room to take her leave.

"Well, we are off. We will not tarry in the morning. I know tomorrow is our last day here and there is lots of packing to make us ready for our journey home." She gave an encompassing smile to the members of her family and said, "Tell Tristan we shall see him this evening." With that, she headed out the door and climbed into the waiting carriage with Trissa.

It was sometime later when Anna dropped the book she had been staring at and not reading. "Oh my God!" She exclaimed. "Where is Tristan?"

Ella looked up from a cookbook she was perusing and said, "I believe he is down at the stables.

He was helping Nathan shoe that colt." Anna did not answer any questions. She stood up, the book falling to the floor, and fled the room.

Anna ran all the way to the stables. It took her several moments to find Tristan, and when she did, she was so out of breath she had to wait a few moments before she could speak. "Tristan!" she shouted.

Tristan turned and came towards her. His pace quickened when he saw the look of alarm on her face. "What is it?"

Anna gave him a stricken look, her eyes filled with fear. "Ilia's in trouble."

"What do you mean? What has happened?" he asked.

"It's hard to say, but it is not good. Trissa is up to something. I have been doing some thinking about her behavior of late, and it occurred to me that she may be meeting with a man. That in itself is not something I would worry too much about, but she said at lunch she had received a note saying her dresses were done.

From whom? The mail was just delivered a few minutes ago, and we received no messages from another source today. I'm certain." Anna was positively vibrating in alarm. "This has something to do with Ilia, Tristan, I know it. And it is not good."

Tristan stared at Anna for a moment then nodded, "I have noticed her sneaking off at different times. I didn't pay much attention, as she is no kin of mine, but I was wondering who she might know around here. You haven't been here long enough to meet anyone local. So, this must be someone she met in the city. Did you have contacts with people in the city before you came?"

"We do not, but I know that Trissa has been corresponding with someone for months, and when we were planning this trip, we had considered going to Leemond, as it is a place with which we are very familiar. Trissa lobbied heavily to come to Portsmith. She said they are more fashionable here and more affordable. She was adamant. I confess, we all gave in, because she so seldom seems to engage in any activity we try to do as a family…" Anna trailed off, her breath quickening.

"This is not good. There are hunters in Portsmith. They take those with magik and do terrible things to them in hopes of procuring their essence. Some they sell off to slavers," Tristan said. As he was speaking, it all started making sense. Trissa had thrown her lot in with one of those nefarious people.

"That is why she tried to get you thrown out of King's Inn," he said, almost to himself. "She wanted you all at a disadvantage so she could control where you stayed and get Ilia in a place where she could be taken." Anger hot and searing tore through him.

Anna must have seen it, for she stepped back. They had only known Tristan as a kind, handsome man who was willing to assist them and befriend them. It had been difficult to correlate the Tristan they knew with what she had heard about him. His reputation was that he was a violent man willing to kill without a second thought. He was not a man to be crossed and one to be feared. Anna could see, in this moment, just how true the stories might be.

"I am going with you", she stated. She moved to grab a horse. Tristan looked to stop her then thought better of it. Maybe it would be good to have her there. His gut told him he might need her and her knowledge before the day was over.

He saddled his horse and joined Anna. "Keep up," he said, and then tore out of the drive, leaving the rest of the family standing in the driveway in consternation.

*

Trissa had done everything right. She couldn't figure out what had gone wrong; what she had missed? A year ago, she met a young man, Chance, in the village where she'd been mailing some items. She dropped a package on her way across the muddy street, and he swooped in valiantly to assist her to the post office. They started chatting, and things went from there. She saw him steadily over the next month. He was staying with some friends and would not be in the area long.

Trissa figured there was no point worrying about her virtue. She would never be married looking like something from the night. She figured if he showed an interest and was leaving, they would have fun until he was gone.

She had lain with him many times during the weeks he was there, enjoying the feeling of control she had over him as she drove him wild with wanting her. She always gave in, because, let's face it, sex could be a lot of fun. Trissa was not a person who fantasized about love. She wasn't even sure she was capable of such an emotion. What she fantasized about was status, the ability to provide her own security without depending on others. She wanted a place of her own where she was the center of attention, and she would do just about anything to get it.

When Chance left, Trissa figured that would be the end of it, but he began to write her. They corresponded for nearly a year, and over that time, a plan unfolded; a plan that involved her sister, Ilia.

Trissa had never considered Ilia her sister. In fact, she hated Ilia. Hated the way everyone gravitated toward her, hated that she was so nice to Trissa, and most of all she hated Ilia for having so much power. Why had Trissa been the changeling born with no powers? Why had Ilia been the only moon child born to two other moon children in a millennium? Ilia didn't even know that. Trissa had discovered that fact when she was snooping through some correspondence of Anna's.

Anna was the historian for moon children, and she kept fastidious records for everyone. When

Trissa uncovered Ilia's genetic heritage, she was so enraged she wanted to burn up all the documentation, but she couldn't let Anna know she knew. The reason Ilia was so unusual was because it was rare a moon child could conceive. Occasionally it happened, but never with two moon children. Ilia was a unicorn in the world.

So, when Chance revealed to her what he did for a living, she knew it was her ticket to bring Ilia down a peg or two and to get herself away from the house and the family where she always felt she did not belong. They came up with a plan, and Trissa followed it to the letter. There was the hiccup with the King's Inn, with Ilia demonstrating the power of persuasion Trissa had never seen – the witch. And then, moving out of town had caused some quick thinking, but here they were, right where they were supposed to be.

Except Trissa had not planned on being bounced along a dirt road draped over a horse after the carriage was hijacked. She had not planned on leaving the carriage at all until they arrived at their destination. She lost her hat somewhere along the way. She loved that hat, but she determined it a casualty of war with the stakes so high.

Then they arrived at a building somewhere on the outskirts of town. Chance handled all the details on his end, so she had no idea where they were. She had been dragged off the horse and caught a glimpse of Ilia being hauled in through a different door than the one Trissa entered.

She thought it strange at the time that Ilia had not made a sound. She had not called for Trissa, and her hands were tied so she could not use her magik. That was something Trissa had insisted they make sure to do, but it was strange Ilia was so silent. For all Ilia knew, Trissa was being kidnapped as well, and yet she had not said a word or called for Trissa. The knowledge of that rankled and made her uneasy.

She shook herself mentally and headed into the building. She sat in a small room, waiting. She wasn't sure how long it would take for them to extract the magik. She wasn't really squeamish, but she really didn't feel the need to watch. She figured it was just extracting with a needle, but she really did not like needles.

She sat a few minutes more. Then the screaming started. It was a high-pitched piercing scream that made the hair on Trissa's neck stand up. What in the world was going on? She waited a few more minutes, but the screams grew louder and louder. Then silence.

Trissa stood and opened the door to the next room. There she saw Ilia on a table with a light shining down on her. Her linen shift had been split from top to bottom, leaving her naked on the table. Her hands were tied to either side of the table. There was blood on the floor by her head, and Trissa sucked in a breath when she saw that Ilia's hair had been cut along with her scalp and removed on the left side of her head. The rest of her hair had been hacked off near the scalp save one section on the right side where it had not been touched. Bruises were appearing on Ilia's porcelain white skin, all over her body, and there was blood between her legs.

Chance was tucking in his shirt as he walked over to Trissa, "Hello darling!" he said grabbing her round the waist and pulling her up against him as he gave her a savage kiss. "Your sister and

I were just getting to know one another a bit better."

Trissa, still in his embrace, whispered, "You had sex with my sister?"

"Well, I wouldn't really call that sex, luv. I was just distracting her while Adam over there scalped her." He kissed her again. "Don't worry she's got nothing on you in the sack." He laughed and released her.

Trissa moved across the room to sit on a chair. Her thoughts numbed, her blood pumping in her ears, as she processed what she had just seen. She hadn't thought this through very well. She had not realized what was entailed in removing magik from someone. She didn't consider herself to have much of a conscience, but as she looked at the figure lying so still on the table as the three men poked and prodded, threatened Ilia, and discussed what course of action to take next without killing her, Trissa's stomach turned.

She wanted Ilia to suffer, but more because she could no longer use her magik, not because she had been tortured to the point of death. When Adam mounted Ilia, Trissa closed her eyes, willing herself to unsee, unhear what was going on. She heard the grunting and heard Ilia cry out. Trissa opened her eyes and saw them running a line up her arm and heard Ilia say between screams, "You. Can't. Take. My. Magik. It. Is. Part. Of. Me."

Trissa heard the other man, James, say "Well we will just have to slave you out if we can't get it."

Trissa was just standing to intervene when the door flew open, and a huge man in a rage like no other came barreling through the door. Behind him a small woman stood silhouetted in the doorway. It was Anna. Trissa realized she had better think fast if she were to survive the event unscathed.

"Anna!" she cried rushing over to her, "They took us..." she started toward the woman, but Anna put up a hand to stop her, her eyes taking in the scene.

She looked at Trissa. "You will answer to him," she said, pointing at Tristan, only a small quiver in her voice giving away the level of her emotion.

Trissa turned to see Tristan throw Adam at the wall like a rag doll, where he slid down it and was still. Tristan grabbed James, who was still in flagrante. He struggled to pull his pants up, but Tristan punched him, and he slithered to the ground. Tristan moved on to Chance who had pulled a knife and was waving it, stabbing at Tristan as a man fighting for his life. And so he was, as Tristan moved forward, quickly grabbing the wrist wielding the knife and turning it around to stab Chance through the torso. He then pulled the knife out and stabbed him in the heart.

It was over in seconds. Tristan strode to the table, murmuring softly to Ilia as he carefully pulled the line from her arm. He gathered her up slowly in his arms as she moaned in protest of the movement. Anna came forward and used Ilia's cloak to cover her.

They progressed toward the door, leaving Trissa standing in the room alone, staring after them. She flicked a glance at James, Chance, and Adam. Chance was dead; no doubt about that, but James and Adam were beginning to come around.

When they reached the door, Tristan paused, as Ilia spoke. He adjusted her slightly so she could see Trissa. Ilia slowly pulled her hands together creating a clear sphere between her two palms.

She spoke in a language foreign to Tristan. As she spoke, she blew into the sphere, and it clouded. She gently tossed it into the air and watched silently as it moved across the room and hovered over Trissa.

Trissa flinched, as if awaiting a heavy weight to fall on her. Ilia looked at her for the first time, her eyes glowing that strange honey-gold color Tristan had seen the night of the full moon. She looked over at Adam and James to make sure they were paying attention. "Is this the power you wanted to see? The power you all wanted to take from me?" Ilia said, her voice a whisper but somehow echoing in the room. "This is my parting gift to you. I am going to give you some of my power, and you may take it with you wherever you go for the remainder of your lives." Ilia snapped her fingers and the globe popped over Trissa's head.

Ilia continued. "You will never speak again. You will never deceive anyone with your lies and your cunning. Your forked tongue is forever silenced." Trissa clutched at her throat gasping, trying to make a sound, but nothing would come.

Ilia looked over at James and Adam, pulled her hands together, creating another sphere, going through the same process as with the first. Tristan noticed the language was different. Ilia sent the sphere into the air, but as it began to move toward Adam and James, Ilia made a slicing motion in the air and the sphere dividing in half, each half moving to hover over the men. Then she said, "You will never be able to hurt another woman again. You will never again have a cock that stands." With that she snapped her fingers.

Ilia turned her head to look back at Trissa, who was still grasping at her throat. "Enjoy it, sister," said Ilia, weakly. "You have earned it." She finished in a gasp and leaned back into Tristan's arms.

He looked at Trissa and the two men. "If I ever see you again, I will end your miserable lives on sight." He trained his eyes on Trissa. "I care not whether you are a woman, for you are none by my definition. You are a vile creature, and she is far more gracious to you than I will be."

He turned and carried Ilia to his horse, putting her on first, then stepped up to sit behind her, cradling her in his arms. Anna did not speak to Trissa. She left her without a backward glance, mounted her horse, and followed Tristan.

Four

There was much emotion and confusion when they got back to The Bird in Hand, but Ilia heard none of it. She used up the last of her resources to dole out punishment. She was unconscious as her mothers, sister, and Ella cried, horror etched on their faces over what had been done to her. She did not hear the wails that came from her mothers when they were told Trissa had been the author of such devastation. She did not know when Tristan broke away from the group and carried her upstairs to Ilia's room to lay her on the big bed, as Anna fetched a basin of warm water and salve to tend to her wounds. Ilia was in the dark for all of it. She was lost to the present, as she shrank away from the violation perpetrated on her body and mind, welcoming oblivion.

*

"I'm worried about the scalp wound," Anna said, her head bent, brows furrowed as she gently examined and cleaned the large wound. "They took all the scalp down to the skull. I do not have healing powers to make it as it was, but I can try to mend it some, and hopefully in time she will have hair there again. The rest of her wounds are superficial."

"It's the psychological wounds I'm more concerned about. She was violated Lord knows how many times before we got there. I know she will heal," Tristan said, "but I'm concerned about her mental state." He ran a hand through his long hair, which had long ago come loose from its stock and was hanging about his shoulders, framing him like a dark lion.

"Let us concentrate on what to do next," Anna suggested. "That may help you work through this for yourself." At his nod of acquiescence, she continued. "She is in more danger now than ever before. You know she will be hunted by the Syndicate now that there are three survivors who have seen her skill. She will most certainly be on their radar, and though this was foiled, they will keep trying, as I have no doubt Trissa will be bent on revenge." She paused, taking a deep breath to steady herself. "She needs time to recover. She needs a safe place to heal. Once she does, she will be able to fight for herself. Do you know of such a place?"

Tristan sat for a moment, lost in thought. "I do," he said at last. He ran his hands through his hair, emitting a heavy exhale fused with anguish and anger. "Bloody hell! Why did she not defend herself?"

Anna paused and looked up from her ministrations. "Well, she will have to give the account, but I wager it was because at first, she thought she and Trissa were being kidnapped together. She was likely waiting for a time and opportunity to get them free. By the time she realized she had been trapped and Trissa was involved, it was too late. Trissa had made sure Ilia's hands were tied in such a way that they could not move.

Tristan took in what she was saying, brows furrowed. "Her hands have to be free to do magik?"

"Yes," Anna responded. She finished by applying a thick ointment to Ilia's head that smelled of earth and green things. Tristan could not place the smells exactly.

"A rudimentary lesson on our magik is in order, I think. I will be quick," continued Anna. "Most moon children have certain areas where their magik is concentrated. Some have power over the mind. Some have power over water; some have power over earth such as what grows from the actual ground itself. Moon children are to make the world better for those inhabiting it. They are to use their abilities to improve the quality of the world." She paused for a moment to gather her thoughts. "Those who have these abilities go out into the world after they have been trained, and they follow through with their missions."

"Who trains them?" Tristan asked.

"We have masters from all over the world who come to where each student lives and trains them. Sometimes the student must go to the master, but most of the time the master goes to them. They train and are commissioned to spend their lives doing what they were made to do."

"Who monitors whether or not the missions are being carried out?" Tristan asked.

"There are moon children who are commissioned as historians. Their powers lie in being able to notate events exactly, have extremely long memories, long lives, and can observe events and remember them to exact detail. The historians are assigned to groups and follow those inhabitants. Historians become a part of the group and are unobtrusive."

"You are a historian, aren't you?" Tristan asked, looking at Anna with new eyes. She was not the dowdy person he had seen originally. She was quite lovely. Her eyes shone with great intelligence, and he noticed for the first time a wave of power emanating from her.

"I am," she said, her face relaxing slightly. "I have been with this group of children for some time. My job is simply to watch. I do not intervene," here she paused for effect, "UNLESS harm is planned against one of the children by his or her own kind. Then I may intervene as needed." Tristan nodded. "There are men as well?" he asked.

"Yes," Anna responded. "But they are never in groups, and they are very rare. They have a different journey than the women, and to be honest, I'm not really sure what that journey entails.

I have never asked." She shrugged.

"Those are the basics. There are of course, many moon children who do not manifest enough ability to warrant missions. Trissa is one, and we are still waiting to see about Senza. She is still very young."

"So, you are really with this group because of Ilia," he replied, more as a statement than a question.

"Yes." She tilted her head, measuring her words carefully. "As I said, I'm still waiting to see about Senza, but I'm mostly here because of Ilia." She looked down at the still form in the bed, a look of concern etching her face. "We have been together for a long time, though she has never really known me as other than her quiet sister." She glanced again at the woman in the bed, so still, and Anna's face softened with affection. "Ilia is very special."

"I have my own reasons for believing that, but what are yours?" asked Tristan.

"She doesn't even know this, but I expect either you or I will need to tell her. If I am not with her when she wakes, it will need to be you. She will understand, probably better than you what you are telling her." Anna paused for a moment to glance at Ilia once again. "Ilia was born of two moon children, a very unique circumstance. I have a letter for her to read when she is more recovered that will explain the story of her lineage, but for now, let me just say that such an occurrence is rare for many reasons, but the main reason is that moon children are not generally able to have children. That is why moon children are considered changelings. They are born to non-magikal folk.

Ilia's parents were both magikal, and they made Ilia. Such an occurrence happens maybe once in a millennium; and Ilia is extremely powerful. Not only is she mighty, but we just don't know of what she is capable. No one I have talked to about her has ever had an encounter with anyone else like her. I have only ever found one record of someone similar in our archives, and it was vague." She screwed up her eyes in recollection. "What was written simply stated, 'a female born to male and female moon children - named Nalia - magikal abilities beyond anything known prior.' The child was taken away to an undisclosed location for her protection and the protection of others until she was able to master her abilities."

"That's it?" Tristan asked, and at Anna's nod, he shook his head. "That's really nothing to go on."

"No, except it does tell us Ilia is not the first, and if at some point she were to try to research her heritage, she would have something to start with. I think that most likely, whoever this Nalia was, Ilia must be directly related to her somehow.

In the meantime, we need to get her to safety and figure out just how much of a threat is out there. She has all the training she needs. Now she just needs time to discover the full extent of her abilities."

Anna paused, glancing at Ilia again and then back at Tristan. "What she did in the building to Trissa and those men, I have never seen, no, never heard of before. I'm not even sure she knew she could do it until she did it. Such power needs time to blossom in the person, and Ilia needs time to understand the full landscape of her power."

Tristan nodded in agreement. "Which brings us back to finding a place for Ilia. A safe place." He contemplated for a moment before responding. "I know of a place, but it has strings she will need to agree to, and you cannot come."

Anna started to protest, but he put up a hand. "No. There is no way around it. I'm sorry. You will have to let her go for a time."

Anna sat back against the bedframe next to where Ilia lay, pondering what he had said. At length, she said, "Is there no other way?"

"You were the one who told me she is going to be hunted now by the Syndicate, no doubt by that nightmare sister of hers. Is it as bad as you say?"

Anna nodded. He continued, "Then I have only one place to take her where I know she will be one hundred percent safe. The only place in the world," he finished.

"Can you at least tell me where?" she asked.

He eyed Anna for a moment, considering her question, and then answered, "Marauder's Isle."

Five

She dreamt she was being rocked. She was in a large wooden cradle, swaying back and forth.

She tried to speak. She tried to sit up, but she couldn't move. The rocking was so intense she began to feel queasy, and panic rose along with the bile in her stomach. She felt she was pushing against something. No. Someone. They were going to hurt her again. Her hands were tied. But wait. They weren't. If she could just get out from under to get movement of her hands…

"Ilia. Stop."

That voice. She knew that voice. Even before she pinpointed it, something deep inside her recognized it as someone she cared for. Her body overrode her chaotic thoughts and began to relax.

"…And try to breathe. Just one thing at a time. It's going to be okay. Just try to relax and open your eyes."

Ilia did as the voice commanded and drew in a deep breath. Slowly, as though laden with an invisible weight, her eyes opened.

Tristan.

She knew it was him before her eyes focused on him. His long hair was loose, his well-groomed beard looking bushy and unkempt. It had been hard to imagine him as a dangerous and feared pirate when she first met him, but now, he looked every inch the villain, his green eyes were piercing as they peered from his tanned face.

She registered the concern in his eyes, as he sat on the edge of the bed trying to comfort her. She struggled to sit up, and he leaned in to help her, stacking pillows behind her so that she could affect a more upright position.

"Tristan," she croaked. "What? – Where…" She looked around and felt a ratcheting pain shoot through the left side of her head. She moaned, and Tristan helped her lay back against the pillows.

"It's okay lass," he said, smoothing her hair away from her face. "You are safe here. I know you will likely have a lot of questions, but I don't think you are in any shape to be asking them, so how about you lie back, and I will fill you in on what you have missed? Then you can ask what

I haven't answered. Will that work?"

Ilia nodded slowly and relaxed back into the pillows, while Tristan filled her in on everything that had happened while she was unconscious. When he finished, she said, "Where is

Anna?"

"I could not bring her on my ship, lass. I'm sorry. I know it would have been a comfort for you to have her, but this is not a ship for women. I can make it relatively comfortable for you, but I can't have two females on my ship. There just isn't accommodation, and having even you here is a violation of our bylaws. Where we are going, she would not be able to go with you." He saw a new question forming on her face, and he intercepted it. "I will tell you soon, but let's dispense with the past before we talk about the future, eh?"

"Where is Trissa?" asked Ilia with a meager half-smile given as her agreement.

"I've no idea. Far from here, I can guarantee. I had my sources check before we left Portsmith, but we had to leave too soon. There wasn't time to get information. I would have liked to have given you a few days on land to recover a bit, but it was too dangerous, and I had to leave on schedule. I have some business I must attend to and am in a bit of a crunch."

Ilia winced at the pain in her left cheek. "Ow." Her eyes watered and Tristan reached over, gently probing the side of her face. "I will have Connor come and give you something for the swelling." Ilia displayed a questioning look to which he responded, "For all intents and purposes, Connor is our doctor. He has some skill with the healing arts, and if you are coming out of a fight and need to be put back together you are in the right place, as Connor is the best. He gets a lot of practice on this ship," Tristan said, grinning.

"But there are some of your injuries he can't help with. Anna looked you over and fixed what she could while she was with you…" he trailed off, suddenly at a loss for words, his eyes locking on hers. Then he got up and walked across the cabin, bringing a mirror back with him as he sat back down, next to Ilia, on the side of the large bed.

"Okay lass, best to just get it over with." Ilia was touching the side of her head tenderly, where a white bandage covered her hairline, above her temple to the curve of her head, and extended equidistant to the back of her ear and down behind it. She drew in a breath and took the mirror with purpose, holding it up to her face.

As her image came into view, Ilia sucked in a quick breath. The left side of her face was swollen and bruised. She could tell the cheekbone was broken. Tristan helped her gently remove the bandages on the side of her head, and she said nothing as she beheld the section where her captors had removed her scalp.

"I know he took my scalp, Tristan. There should be no skin here." Ilia motioned to the wounds. "Aye, but Conner is very good. In truth, I don't want to know how he did it, but he managed to correct some of the damage. I don't know if you will get your hair back, lass, but he's given as much opportunity as possible for that to happen."

Ilia handed the mirror back to Tristan. "I need to thank him. It is more than I hoped for. I know there was only skull there. They wanted to extract my magik, and," her breath caught as she loosened her grip on the mirror, and Tristan gently took it from her, "they did. A bit anyway.

When they took my scalp, I felt the magik syphon out. There is a legend that says if you take a moon child's scalp, you will have their magik for as long as you carry the pelt, and there is truth in that, as with all legends, but it is not truth on the whole."

Tristan found himself struggling to control his anger as he looked at the beautiful, gentle woman who had done nothing to warrant such cruelty. He felt an intense desire to protect her, something he had been feeling since the day he met her, iridescent, standing in the market square full of dull people. He had known then; it was a privilege just to know such a creature. Maybe even a miracle.

His crew had said nothing, as he had spent more time than he ever had away from his ship, the Anemone. They didn't protest when he entrusted Edmond and Rudy with all that was entailed in getting her ready for another run. But he could see it in their eyes. This sudden change in habit and nature in their commander, who was generally so methodical and focused, both concerned and intrigued them. He took them into danger constantly, and they trusted him with their lives. To see such a change in him was unsettling. But Edmond was the only one who said anything, and even then, very little.

It was the night Ilia was taken. Tristan left Ilia in Anna's capable hands, as he raced back to the ship to let Edmond know what had transpired. The crew were out on the town, their last night of doing whatever a man cannot do on a ship for months at a time.

Standing starboard, looking out to the sea was the only consolation in the aftermath of what had occurred. The ship moved slightly on the incoming waves, but it was something Tristan was so accustomed to it he no longer noticed.

He was playing back what had happened. He had seen many horrors in his life and chosen vocation, but none affected him as had seeing those men bent on destroying Ilia. So lost in his thoughts was he, that when Edmond spoke, he started.

"My apologies, Commander. I wondered if I might have a word?" Edmond's manner was formal, as it always was when they were onboard.

Tristan turned to his Captain and boyhood friend. "No worries, Ed. I was wool-gathering, as they say. What is it?"

Edmond cleared his throat. "Are you sure this is the way to go, sir? I mean, she is a woman. Is there even accommodation for her onboard?" He swallowed. "And what of the crew?"

Tristan gave Edmond a long look. "I don't know what else to do. She is in mortal peril if I leave her here. She won't be with us all the way. I will have her in my cabin, and I can bunk with you."

Edmond's eyebrows rose. "Where are we going to leave her, sir?"

Tristan gave Edmond another long look and said, "I am going to take her to the only safe place I know."

"You are going to take her to Marauder's Isle?" Edmond's eyes widened as he said it. "You can't be serious! How will she survive there? And are you willing to pay that price, for a woman you have known little longer than a fortnight?" He paused, scanning Tristan's features. "Ah, I see.

Does she feel the same?"

Tristan gave a frustrated sigh, running a hand through his hair. He had removed the stock that contained it, moving away from the niceties required in polite society, and had gone back to his natural state. It rained down in dark waves past his shoulders. "I hadn't planned on having to make this kind of decision so soon, but I would have either way. I would have liked to have her consent and know she holds me in the same regard, but I made the only decision I could, in good conscience, make. I only pray she feels the same."

Edmond snorted, losing his earlier formality. "Tris, this is Marauder's Isle, man! She won't have a choice. You know that only those who have the coin or give the coin to someone *bound* to the coin owner may access the Island."

"Don't lecture me, Ed," Tristan said in a steely voice, a tone that would put fear into the hearts of most men but didn't faze Edmond. "I will do what I can. That's all I can do. I hope she will be willing. I have some, and I will tell her everything, but I can't give you answers I don't have."

He paused for a moment, gathering his thoughts. "For now, tonight, I need to address the crew." He looked at Edmond, and knowing what he was about to say, intercepted him. "No. Not you. I need to do this. This crew has followed me into the mouth of hell and back. I owe them all the details. I want them to agree on this."

Edmond pondered the statement then said, "I don't think you will have issues with the crew.

They will just want to know they still have you as their leader, first."

Tristan nodded, reassured. "Well, they have their captain regardless, so I would imagine this will not have too much impact on them or the journey."

Six

Just as Edmond surmised, the crew expressed little concern about the new addition to the ship. Edmond attributed their loyalty to Tristan's openness toward them. Tristan had a unique relationship with his crew. He viewed himself as the commander of a band of brothers, and that was an apt description, as they grew up together, navigating through many sticky situations together over the years.

Tristan rarely took in new members, and there was no need, so long as everyone stayed alive. He left daily dealings to Edmond, but when they were in battle, or when they were heading into a dangerous situation, it was Tristan, who dictated how they were going to get out. They trusted him, and he had never steered them wrong.

Edmond leaned against the railing of the ship, watching Tristan interact with the crew. Edmond served in a dual capacity as captain and sailing master. Most pirate ships had a man for each position, but Tristan and Edmond had learned early on that the crew functioned very well in their day-to-day roles, which allowed Edmond to take on the sailing master role. He was also well educated, and that education helped tremendously in navigating the seas and mapping out locations.

The master gunner for the ship was another childhood friend of both Tristan and Edmond, named Rudolph, or Red Rudy, as he was called. Red Rudy was in charge of the cannons and the crew who maneuvered them. He had a tricky job, as the goal was, generally, to disable a ship, not sink it. He was a fun-loving Celt with hair to match his name. If Tristan was ever unable to give commands in a battle situation, Red Rudy would be the one to make whatever tough calls were necessary.

There were two boatswains on the Anemone, Jan and Michael, who supervised supplies, inspected the ship every day, oversaw deck activities, which included the weighing and dropping of the anchor and the sails on the ship. There was the physician, Connor, whom Edmond suspected was closer to a miracle worker than a traditional physician, as what he could do with healing was nothing short of magikal. Then there was a carpenter named Benjamin, the newest member of the crew. He was shaping up to be a superior craftsman. Other crew members included sailors who rigged sails and steered the ship, as well as keeping watch and working cannons. Other positions included the rigger, Kale, who monitored and worked with the sails and the rigging, as well as two cabin boys, Emmitt and Dicken, both of whom were sons of crew members. The pirate life often ran in families.

Tristan carefully selected the crew, with Edmond's help. Tristan considered Edmond his equal, but as in their childhood days, Edmond preferred a secondary position. It wasn't that Edmond lacked confidence. He simply preferred the capacity of confidant and adviser. Tristan valued Edmond's counsel and knew better than anyone that the success of the Anemone the result of Edmond's ability to analyze and work with his leader in solving problems. Edmond was not overly ambitious. He was not interested in commanding his own ship, and he trusted Tristan with his very life, just as Tristan trusted Edmond with his.

Edmond watched as Tristan conversed with the crew, listening intently to their escapades from the night before. He knew Tristan did this to connect with the crew, but he also had an uncanny ability to extrapolate information and glean insights from the crew members that would assist them in their endeavors. Many times, Tristan had picked up on a thread of information relayed by a crew member from something they heard in passing, which led, alternately, to unclaimed treasure or warnings the Anemone needed to heed in sailing towards bounty.

Edmond smiled to himself. Tristan had a way of winning people over. It wasn't that he was a showman. Quite the contrary. He was a man who said what he meant and left it at that, but there was a genuineness about him that belied his intimidating exterior and his occupation. He simply cared about people, and it showed, most recently in Tristan's decision to bring Ilia on board the ship. In doing so, he broke one of the articles of agreement under which the ship sailed. They made their decisions as a democracy, for the most part, and they had the option of voicing their opinions. They were not to steal, and they were not to get in drunken brawls or become so intoxicated they could no longer answer for their actions, and they were not to bring women on board the ship.

By bringing Ilia onboard, Tristan violated one of the articles, and even though the crew pproved the violation based on the circumstances, the punishment would still stand. Edmond could see Tristan already acting on the punishment. He had selected Red Rudy to mete it out. Tristan was in the process of removing his vest and his shirt, as Red Rudy pulled a long thin whip from his waistband.

Their leader, stone-faced, put both hands on the railing of the ship, his bare back exposed, waiting for the first blow.

And it came, along with nine others. Tristan did not move or make a sound the entire time, and Red Rudy did not go easy. Edmond could see red welts with thin streams of blood leaking from their angry centers. The crew stood by in solemn observation until the last crack of the whip was done.

Tristan, who had not moved an inch the entire time, lifted his head, staring out at the sea for a few moments. He then turned to face the crew. No one said a word, but Red Rudy reached in his shirt pocket and pulled out a flask, handing it to Tristan.

Tristan accepted it, unscrewed the cap and took a deep pull on the flask. Then another. He eyed his crew and said, with a grin, "We may be down on our luck at times, but we never run low on good rum!" He lifted the flask in the air in salute.

The crew cheered and laughed, as Tristan handed the flask back to Red Rudy. The Celt took a couple deep pulls of his own.

Tristan turned to look up at Edmond, who was standing on the main deck looking down on the lower deck. Edmond nodded at Tristan and watched as his commander followed Connor with stilted movements below deck to treat the wounds on his back.

Now everything was settled.

Ilia was accepted on board, and they had never seen her. Edmond suspected the crew was in for a real experience once Ilia was restored. He knew none of them had ever seen a moon child. Moon children like Ilia were myths in their world. Magik was a part of their existence, but over the years, magik had become watered down, and instead of living legend and mythology that promised the possibility of true magikal experiences, the idea of a real encounter with the magikal realm had become staid and tepid. Clans who were once mighty in power now exhibited only moderate skills at best. But from what Tristan had told him about Ilia – and what she had done to her sister and the men who had attacked her – she held the magik of olden days.

He was interested to see what would unfold.

Edmond's thoughts shifted back to Tristan. He wondered if Tristan had said anything to Ilia about who he was; what he was. Edmond doubted it. Even the crew only knew a moderate amount of information. They knew what Tristan was but had never seen what he was. Only Edmond, Connor, and Red Rudy really knew. Oh yes, the journey could get very interesting.

Edmond pushed back from the railing and turned toward his cabin. He had some modifying to do to their map. He had to make arrangements for a stop at Marauder's Isle.

Seven

Ilia was sitting up in bed when Tristan knocked and entered at her permission. She looked much better than she had the day before. Her head was covered in a type of turban, the material a downy dove gray. On the side where her hair was intact, soft white curls escaped from the turban and tumbled over her shoulder to lie across her breasts. She was wearing a light blue shift that was what Tristan could only describe as shimmery.

He provided some trunks for her to use that had material and women's apparel. They had been sitting below deck for some time, booty gathered from the last ship they'd commandeered. Tristan had Dicken, the youngest cabin boy haul them to the cabin, and as soon as Dicken met Ilia, the lad became her servant, never wanting to leave her side.

Tristan indulged this, as Ilia needed someone to wait on her. Dicken lived with five women, four sisters and his mum, before his dad rescued him and whisked him away to become a pirate like his pirate father. Tristan was glad Dicken had so much experience being around women, for he was right at home with Ilia and not only waited on her hand and foot, but entertained her with stories and card tricks he learned.

Ilia always clapped with enthusiasm, never alluding to the fact the boy was attempting to deceive a wizardess with card tricks; and though the irony was not lost on her, she never let it get in the way of her enjoyment in watching Dicken attempt to work his own brand of magik on her.

Ilia smiled at Tristan as he moved closer to the bed and pulled a chair up next to it. At closer inspection he could see the bruises on her face were changing in color, and while the swelling on her cheek and eye socket was still extensive, the bruises had gone from red and blue to purple and a tinge of yellow. The healing process had begun.

"Do I pass inspection?" she said, her eyes twinkling, a smile playing on her lips.

"My apologies, lass," chuckled Tristan, realizing he had been scrutinizing her for some minutes.

"I didn't mean to make you feel uncomfortable. I was just looking to see how you are healing."

"I am as good as can expected, considering what the past few days have rendered," she said, her smile fading. "I am not used to not being able to do for myself, and poor Dicken has been conscripted into taking care of me."

Tristan snorted, "Poor Dicken, indeed. The boy is smitten. This may ruin him as a pirate. I suspect you may never get rid of him."

Ilia giggled. "He is certainly committed to his task. I finally sent him away to be out in the sun and wind. It is not good for a boy to be cooped up with an invalid."

Tristan frowned, "I do not want you up and about any more than necessary, Ilia. Connor says you have experienced a great deal of bodily trauma." He cleared his throat, giving away his discomfort in speaking further on a topic he felt he should address. "He says you were damaged a good bit from what those men did to you both physically and psychologically…" he trailed off, hoping she understood what he was saying.

Two pink spots appeared on Ilia's cheeks, and she raised her chin slightly to look directly at him. "Connor did a thorough inspection while I was unconscious. Thankfully, I was not awake for that." She paused, letting her thoughts line up for organized distribution. "I am bruised and cut, but nothing permanent on the physical front. I'm just tender, and it is painful to sit up for too long. Psychologically, I don't know how damaged I am. Time will tell, I guess. It's not something I plan to dwell on." She closed her eyes to shut out unwelcomed images, as she actively implemented her statement. "But I'm concerned about how the combined damage will impact my magik. Magik is my lifeblood. I feel it is still coursing within me, but the power has waned. Again, time will tell, but I am very concerned about this impacting the potency of my magik."

They sat for a moment in silence, then Ilia spoke again. "You said Anna had a letter for me. I think I am ready to read it if you have it."

Tristan nodded, grateful to be given a task. He got up and strode across the cabin to the large desk that sat against the cabin's only window. He pulled open the middle drawer of the desk and took out a small parcel. As he walked over and handed it to Ilia he said, "I will leave you to your reading then."

She looked up from the parcel and smiled. "Thank you. I know I have put you out of your cabin and disrupted everyone by being on board. Please relay my appreciation to your crew for being so understanding and allowing me to stay on their ship."

Tristan looked at her in surprise. "Why would you say that? "

Ilia smiled again and said, "You forget young Dicken. He keeps me up to speed on the goings-on outside this door." She motioned toward the heavy wooden door.

Tristan wondered if Ilia's admirer had told her about the punishment, but she didn't volunteer the information and he wasn't keen on asking. He would have to have a conversation with young Dicken.

*

After Tristan left, Ilia sat for a moment. The stillness of the room combined with the rocking motion of the ship made her sleepy. She reached tentatively for her magik and felt a slight pushback at her tugging. It was there, but she suspected it was waiting for her to heal in body and soul before surging through her like it usually did when she tugged on it. It seemed almost shy, wary, and possibly wounded, right along with the rest of her. It was almost as though it was concerned about burdening her further with more to carry.

Ilia calmed her senses, closed her eyes, and folded back into herself, breathing expansive, deep breaths that filled and revived her body, calmed her spirit, and allowed her to hear her magik. It was humming deep inside her. It had not been weakened, not at its core. Just like her, it had been wounded but not debilitated for long, and as she healed, so it would as well. Ilia felt a deep sense of peace as hope surged within her. It would take the full moon, as she'd suspected. She breathed deeply once more, pulling herself up and back into the world around her. She reached out for Anna's parcel and opened it.

Inside was a beautiful scarf. It had every color woven into the fabric. Anna was an accomplished seamstress, often working with many different resources to make gorgeous and exotic creations, but the most exotic resource Anna used was moonspun, and the scarf Ilia held in her hands was made entirely of it. It shone and was almost fluid, moving like mercury in Ilia's hands.

Ilia gave a small cry as she held it, tears tumbling down her cheeks. She pressed it to her face and sat for some time that way. Moonspun was very special and rare. Few people could pull the gossamer threads from moonlight and turn it into articles of clothing. She had no idea

Anna was so accomplished in the art. Ilia, herself, had been taught by one of the teachers she had as a child, but they had spent little time on it. The teacher showed her, and they practiced a few times, but that had been the extent of her training in that area.

"This is something you can develop on your own, child," the teacher said. "You were meant for far more significant acts than this, and those are what we must focus on."

Ilia cultivated her ability to pull the moonspun every time she was in contact with moonlight. It wasn't about making clothing, at least not for her. It was about a tangible connection with the moon and the regeneration she found in it. Sitting in a room on a ship bound for, where, she did not know, holding something made with real tenderness and care, Ilia could not have disagreed with her teacher more. There was no magik more important than this.

She wrapped the scarf around her neck and reached inside the brown paper package for the next item. She felt the benefit of the moonspun on her head the moment it touched her. Maybe this was Anna's way of continuing to treat her wounds. Maybe the moonspun would help her heal. Time would tell. Whether or not it helped her heal physically, Ilia knew the psychological and emotional benefit was already in play.

Ilia looked at a piece of parchment that appeared to have been torn from a ledger of sorts. On it, written in a strong hand, was a list of dates and names. She stared at it, confused. What was it for?

Ilia dropped the parchment and went to the last item in the wrapping. It was a letter from Anna, bearing her wax seal in charcoal gray. The seal depicted a dragon moth, Anna's favorite creature. Ilia smiled as she ran a finger over it. She spent many a night out with Anna searching for the elusive insects. It was about the size of a hummingbird but had an elongated neck and wings that looked more like dragon wings than those of a moth or butterfly. They only came out at the full moon, and their wings were translucent but glowed in the moonlight. In the daylight, the creature was quite ugly, but at night in the moonlight, it looked other-worldly and utterly beautiful.

Ilia tore open the seal and started to read:

Ilia,

So much I wanted to say to you, but now I am out of time. I will try to make this as short as possible. First, the scarf is a gift. It will help you as you heal. I hope you like it. I put all my best colors in it.

Second, the parchment. That will take longer to explain. But let me just kill the suspense by saying it is a list of names I took from a ledger. It has the names of your parents and a place for you to start.

Ilia, I do believe your parents are dead. I'm sorry. No other way to say it but straight out.

I know what you are going to say next, and the answer is, I know because I'm a historian. You know the role of the historian, and that has been my role in your household since you were brought to your mothers' house. Historians are tasked with documenting the lives of powerful moon children. Trissa has no power to speak of, and Senza, well, I shall watch and see about her. She is too young to tell. But generally, any moon child who shows particular promise in an area is documented. You, my dear, are the most powerful moon child in a millennium. The last moon child to exhibit your abilities to a degree was named Nalia, but there is little known about her except she was born to two moon children. I think that she may be an ancestor of yours, but I have nothing on which to base that hunch.

You were born to two moon children. Yes, it does happen. Very rarely, but it does happen, and I think that one day you might want to try to find out what happened to your parents. You were brought to your mothers' home as a changeling, but there is a piece missing there, and I think it might be worth your time and effort to find that missing piece.

You are pursued and will continue to be pursued, not only by Trissa, but the entire Syndicate once they discover your origins. It would be beneficial for you to understand as much of the details of those origins as possible and if you have other family.

You are in full possession of your powers, but you do not know of what you are capable, and you are too distrusting of others. Setting yourself apart does not make you safe. It makes you vulnerable, and you need people you can trust.

I am sure I don't have to tell you this, but Tristan is one of those people. I know you have feelings for him. I have watched you with him, because, well, that is what I do. I know he cares for you, and it is important you take this in before you read on in this letter.

Ilia stopped and looked up out the window of the ship across the room from the bed. Part of her did not want to read further. She had a sinking feeling that whatever she was about to read would force her to make a decision that would change her life, one way or another, forever.

Ilia, we had nowhere to send you.; no place you would be safe. You were unconscious, and we, Tristan and I, had to make a decision. He is taking you to

Marauder's Isle. You have heard of this place. It is the stuff of legends, but it really does exist, and it is the only place for you to go to heal and to re-engage with your magik and truly discover the extent of your capabilities without being hindered in any way. I asked Tristan to let me tell you this, as I am the one who made this decision for your life.

In order to be allowed on Marauder's Isle, you must be a member, and the island actually recognizes members. It will kill anyone who is not. However, if you are tied to a member in some way, you are allowed to take refuge on the Isle.

Maybe you have guessed what I'm about to say but say it I must. Ilia, you will have to marry Tristan in order to be on the Isle. He cannot keep you on the ship. It's too dangerous for him, his crew, and for you. The work that he does puts him in constant contact with slavers and traders who would love to get their hands on someone like you. And with you being so severely ill, you would not be strong enough to combat such an assault.

So, I am asking that you forgive me for taking liberty with your life no one should take, and I hope you will accept Tristan and forgive me at the same time.

As a historian, I am not allowed to be close to those I am documenting, but I want you to know you are very precious to me, and I hope in some way I have given you a chance at a better life than the one you were living. Go to the Isle. Heal and learn from the people there. Then go find out about your heritage.

All my best to you-

Anna

Ilia folded the letter and placed it back in the wrapping. She picked up the parchment and looked at the list of names. About halfway down the page, she saw her name, and off to the side was a notation that read, "Born of MC- Micha, Antiera.

Ilia folded the parchment and placed it back in the wrapping on top of Anna's letter. She stared again out at the ocean waves through the window. She didn't know what to feel. She couldn't wrap her head around what had taken place while she was unconscious. And her parents? They were moon children? How could that even happen? When? Where? Anna knew that Ilia would not be able to resist those questions. She would demand answers.

Then there was Tristan. She conjured him up in her mind's eye and realized she literally had two images to choose from, the gentleman she had known him to be, and this new version of him, the commander of a ship of pirates. She had feelings for him, and who knows where the natural progression would have taken them had she not been kidnapped and nearly killed. Most likely they would have ended up in the same place, but she would have had an active decision in the matter. What was upon her was no decision. For self-preservation she would be forced to be impetuous to survive.

A spurt of anger coursed through her, and she felt her magik quicken. She looked down at her fingertips. They were tingling and glowing. She held up an index finger and on impulse, blew lightly on it. Sparks flew from it.

Shocked, Ilia quickly quit blowing, patting the coverlet to smother the embers. Now, that was new. She gazed in wonder. She had felt abandoned by her magik, as though it had gone into hiding at the first sign of trouble, but she was realizing it wasn't hiding. It was waiting for her to call on it, and she needed to refuel by moonlight.

She fell back heavily against the pillows, lightly rubbing her fingers together. The glow was gone, but they still tingled. Ilia sat for some time, thinking of the conspiracy to save her life, the betrothal made while she slept.

By the time Tristan knocked on her door, the sun's rays were creeping over the edge of the horizon like a creature crawling back into its hole, and Ilia had made some decisions.

"Come in," Ilia said, in answer to his knock.

Tristan opened the door, his six-foot-four-inch frame filling the doorway. He lingered there, then came in, shutting the door. He walked across the room and pulled out the heavy desk chair, turning it to face Ilia on the bed. He sat down and leaned back, his expression unreadable.

Ilia studied him. He was dressed as any crewman on the ship, dark gray woolen breeches that were tied at the knees, woolen stockings inside leather shoes, a white linen shirt with no collar, open at the neck showing his tattoo. She could finally tell what it was; an anchor that was partially comprised of some sort of sea creature. His long sleeves were currently rolled up to the elbows, and he had on a dark red vest that was buttoned up to just below the opening in the shirt. His long hair lay about his shoulders in a disarray of dark waves, covered by a gray knitted Monmouth cap.

In the short time they had been on the ship, his skin had darkened significantly. His dark beard covered much of his face, but his full lips showed through where he kept his mustache at bay. He looked dangerous and hard, but intelligent green eyes watched her with wariness and – what was it? - Tenderness? Yes. He was looking at her with tenderness, and in that moment, she knew she was making the right decision, would always make the right decision casting her lot with him.

"Tristan, I have read my letter from Anna." She stopped. Only his eyes stirred.

"Aye," was his only response, but she felt the air tense between them.

"I need to thank you for all you have done for me, Tristan. I have not done that. You saved my life. I am grateful and forever in your debt." Ilia sat back against the pillows, her hands clasped primly in her lap.

Tristan snorted and shifted in his chair, "Is that what you have to say to me, lass?" He pondered her for a moment then said, "And here was me thinking Anna had done the job for me. I guess it's up to me. There is something you need to know, Ilia." He cleared his throat. "There are, uh, stipulations to your rescue, and I need to have an answer soon. I'm sorry to have to tell you this, lass, but…"

Ilia cut him off, "I know what they are. Anna explained everything, and I would be a fool not to accept for many reasons, but before I get into them, I need to know a few things." He relaxed visibly. "As this affects us both, I need to know what your thoughts are on the matter."

"What do you mean?"

Ilia sighed in exasperation, flicking her fingers across the coverlet, only to leave a trail of sparks.

"Oh!" she exclaimed, quickly snuffing them out. Tristan laughed as she gave him a sheepish look saying, "That's new."

Two rosy spots flared on her cheeks. "Yes. Well. It seems I'm a student of my magik once again."

Tristan shifted in his seat and was now leaning forward, elbows on his knees, a smile on his face as Ilia continued. "I need to know how you feel about this, Tristan. Do you want to be tied to me forever? I mean, you may feel you don't have a say in all of this since you were forced into making such a decision, but you do. I don't want us to be tied to each other if you are going to be miserable." Ilia had been looking down as she spoke, but as she finished, she looked up from her fingers that moments before had been sparkling and met his eyes.

Tristan sat unmoving. "Ilia," he murmured, "I would have hoped to ask for your hand at some point. I just needed time to figure out logistics, to plan. I don't exactly lead a conventional life." He sat back, pulling his hat off, running a hand through his hair in consternation. "I have no idea where this will lead us now, but my consolation in this is that you are not a conventional woman, and even if I were a conventional man, who you are, and your abilities, would likely impact any ideas of conventionality."

He smiled at her, "And, so, the way I see it, we are perfectly suited in terms of logistics. As to how I feel, well, I'm not really a man who dwells all that much on how I feel. I live on adrenaline most of the time with little time for reflection, but my feelings for you are not fleeting. And," the intensity of his gaze deepened, "they go beyond just caring for you."

Ilia sat listening, unmoving for fear of shattering a moment she had only dreamed of, her heart thrilling at the words the magnificent man in front of her was saying with such vulnerability.

"But I would know your feelings before we take any more steps in this direction," he finished.

Ilia inhaled, gathering her emotions around her in an effort to fully express what was in her heart.

"You are the only man I can ever imagine myself with. Whatever feelings I have for you can only deepen the more we know each other. You live a dual life, but then so do I. Yours is about vocation, which I know is very much wrapped up in who you are as a man. Mine is about what I am now and what I am certain to become. You and I, I think, are comfortable with life being fluid. We may find that the only stable thing in this world is what we have between us, and I'm fine with that." She stopped, looking to him for a response.

"As am I," he answered. He smiled almost shyly at her. "So, you are willing lass? You would be my partner in this life?"

Ilia nodded, her blush deepening in happiness. "I will." Then her smile faded as she looked at him, tears filling her eyes. "But Tristan, look at me. How could you ever want me? I'm pale as a ghost and I may always be ugly like this." She pointed to her hairless scalp.

Tristan stood and walked over to the bed, kneeling beside it, taking her hands in his. "Lass, you are beautiful as the first new-fallen snow in winter, and the damage you take in this life is less about what was taken from you, and more a testament to your ability to survive and thrive. You are beautiful and other-worldly. I will always feel fortunate to be your partner when I look at you, and grateful I am the man who gets to hold you at the end of every day."

Ilia was overrun with emotion, her tears falling like rain. They looked at one another a moment, and then Tristan stood, leaning over the bed, placing a hand on each side of her as he looked into her eyes. He slowly lowered his head, his lips touching hers in a soft kiss. He pulled away then kissed her again, this time firmer and longer. As he lifted his head, he looked deep into her eyes and said, "I think passion will not be a problem for us. Do you agree?"

Ilia could do nothing but nod, her senses too discombobulated to do anything else.

Tristan moved away, sitting on the bed next to her. "I do have one thing I must tell you. I guess it's best to just say it." He paused to gauge her reaction, but she only sat staring at him, so he continued. "As my partner," he cleared his throat, "my wife, you will have to have a brand. See, like this one." He turned his arm, palm facing upward, to show his wrist where a white brand was raised on his skin.

Ilia leaned forward to see it better. It was the image of his tattoo, an anchor made from the form of a starlet sea anemone. The anemone made up the shank, one arm of the crown. The other arm was clearly metal, and the stock was comprised of anemone tentacles. Ilia ran a finger over the brand and asked, "Why not a tattoo like you have on your chest rather than a brand?"

Tristan shrugged. "You know some religions like the Sakerist faith do not allow for tattoos. We have crew members who are Sakerist and their wives or other members we have brought into our fold. There are other religions out there who do not hold with ink on the body, so we found a way around it. This also saves anyone in a port knowing our mark, as we would have to have someone do the tattooing. None of us are good enough to do a decent tattoo. But we do have a blacksmith on board who is quite gifted. Many years ago, when I first took command of this ship, I had the tattoo done, but I decided the brand was a better idea. It is required of all of us, and those close to us, to have this brand. So, I also got the brand. There are many things tied to it."

Ilia laid back against the pillows. She was stiff and needed some privacy but didn't want Tristan to leave. "Like what things?" she asked.

"Well getting onto Marauder's Isle for one thing. There are also services in different places such as sleeping accommodation, places to trade and get information, and ways to get help if needed, that will only allow this brand. See, we have a network all over. That is how we are successful in what we do.

It takes many people to make what we do work, and that is why this brand is so important. Having a brand rather than a tattoo makes it less obvious and, in many ways, more permanent."

Tristan shifted off the bed and stood, holding out his hands to her. "Come. I think you may need to move around a bit. Maybe a trip to the water closet?" He motioned his head back across the cabin to a small closet that contained the toilet.

"How did you know?" she asked, her eyes sparkling warmly as she reached for his hands.

"Just a hunch," he said, grinning as he helped her slowly maneuver her legs around to gain her feet.

Ilia grimaced when she put weight on her feet. When she allowed gravity a role, she felt every bit of the damage that had been inflicted upon her. It was as though her body was infused with steel rods through her limbs. Slowly she stood, and Tristan all but carried her across the room.

"Can you manage?" he asked, his look skeptical.

"Yes. I'm just stiff," she countered.

He released her and stood back, saying, "I will leave for a bit. Is there anything you need? Dicken has not been in with your food, no doubt because I am here. Anything else you might want?"

Ilia turned to face him. "Well, I don't know if this is possible, but I would dearly love a bath, and maybe one of your shirts. The clothes in the trunk are lovely but not practical for wiling the time away in bed."

Tristan raised an eyebrow. "Dicken and I will put our heads together and make it so. Can you find your way back to the bed?"

Ilia nodded. "I will be okay, now that I am moving," and at Tristan's nod along with his departure, she turned to open the door to the water closet.

*

The trip back to the bed seemed like miles, and Ilia was glad no one was present to see her labored efforts. It felt as though her top half was disconnected from the bottom half. Her legs were like jelly. Her muscles throbbed, and the area between her legs was raw. She felt as though she had been ripped in half. Pain shot clear up inside her, congealing in her stomach. She fought the urge to double over as she clutched her lower abdomen. She stopped at the bed, grabbing the bedframe to steady herself. She squeezed her eyes shut, willing herself to not allow the images that came unbidden across her mind's eye. But they came anyway, looming before her, as if they were happening in real time.

Ilia cried out, still clinging to the bed.

Tristan rushed through the door with Dicken in tow. He quickly made his way over to her, putting his arms around her to hold her up. "Ilia? Ilia!"

From the waking nightmare she heard him calling her name. Was it now or then that he called her? She didn't care. She swam toward the sound, reaching for it as a person drowning grasps for an extended hand.

Ilia felt his arms around her and knew she was safe. She allowed him to pick her up and sit in the big desk chair with her on his lap, cradled like a child. She lay in his arms shaking, soaked in sweat. She heard him say something to someone about a blanket. Then the warmth and heaviness of it covered her. She was safe. This was real. The other was past. Why couldn't she keep the two straight? Her mind refused to give her answers, and her magik crawled to a place deep inside of her, refusing to come out.

In her foggy distress, Ilia could hear Tristan humming a tune of some sort, and it soothed her.

She relaxed against him, the shaking of her body slowing to a stop, and she drifted off to sleep.

Tristan sat holding Ilia, feeling her body melt into his. She was light as a feather, and he wondered if she was eating anything. The shaking subsided, along with the moans and sobs, and when she surrendered to sleep, he sensed it.

Edmond arrived in the open door, his brow furrowed in worry. Dicken was out of his depth and called in more seasoned reinforcements. At Tristan's questioning look, Edmond said, "All is well on deck. It's just a light rain. What can I do?"

"I need a bathtub, Ed, and hot water. Do you think we have something this wee lass can fit in?"

Edmond stared for a moment then said, "I will find out. Give me a bit."

Tristan glanced at the woman in his arms. "I'm not going anywhere," one corner of his mouth lifting slightly, as he pulled Ilia closer to him.

"Did you tell her?" Edmond asked, and at Tristan's nod, "What did she say?"

"She is in agreement."

Edmond nodded and left to find a bathtub.

Sometime later, Edmond returned with Wil, the ship's cook, and Dicken. They carried in a tub and set it in the back of the room near the water closet. Dicken carried a large bucket of hot water and turned to retrieve more. Behind him the other cabin boy, Emmett, carried more water, which he poured into the tub.

"Ed, would you mind going over to that wardrobe and pulling out one of my shirts? Also, we need to put some sort of screen up. See if you can come up with something, would you?" Ed bobbed his head, pulling one of Tristan's crisp linen shirts from the closet. He reached into one of the drawers and pulled out a pair of wool socks and motioned to Tristan, who nodded in agreement.

Edmond put them on the bed and left in search of a screen.

Dicken and Emmitt returned two more times to fill the tub, and on the last round, Edmond returned with a screen.

"Found it below in the pile of loot we never had a use for," he said. "There are a lot of things down there a woman might find handy. It's as though it has all been waiting for her." He smiled and situated the screen around the tub. Then he reached into his pocket and pulled out some items, saying, "Things like this." He walked over and showed them to Tristan. There was bubble bath, a cake of soap, and a bottle of lotion.

Tristan smiled. "Perfect. Thank you." He shook Ilia gently. She woke with a start, and he interjected quickly, "It's just me, lass. Your bath is ready, and I think you will feel better. I will carry you over and help you stand in it, then I will leave you to undress."

Just then, Dicken came in with what appeared to be a big fuzzy blanket and a large strip of linen.

Tristan raised an eyebrow.

"Well Commander, she'll be needing something for her wet hair and to wrap in, won't she?"

"Boy you are handy to have around," Tristan said with a grin. "Never would have thought of that."

Dicken took the bubble bath and went around the screen to pour in a generous amount, then stuck his hand in to stir the water, saying through the screen, "Seen my mam do this. Guess it makes the bubbles bigger." He came back around the screen and left the cabin.

Edmond had also taken leave, and Tristan was left to carry Ilia, who was gaining possession of her faculties, to the tub. He handed her the soap and said, "Not much to that night dress, and it's slippery enough it should come off easily for you. I can see now why you want one of my shirts."

He deposited her into the tub, made sure she was sturdy on her feet, then said, "I will check back in half an hour." He didn't wait for her response but turned and left the cabin.

Ilia pulled the chemise over her head and slowly lowered herself into the tub, to be engulfed in the heat of the water and the heady lavender scent of the bubbles. It was the most luxurious feeling she had ever experienced. She let the heat sink deep into her muscles and reveled in the feeling. She slowly worked her way over her body with the cake of soap, and when it came time to wash her hair, she carefully avoided Connor's work on the left side of her head but managed to wash the rest of her hair. When she was finished, she simply laid back in the tub and relaxed. The lights were low in the cabin, offering enough to see but were low enough to enhance the relaxing experience.

Sometime later there was a knock on the door, and Tristan called out to her. Ilia responded that she was ready to get out. He picked up the fuzzy robe from the chair along with the linen strip.

"Can you stand up, lass?"

"Yes, I think so," she responded, and he heard the sound of the water as she slowly made her way to her feet.

"I will not look at you. I have the robe and will hold it up in front of me. You can put it on, and then tend to your hair. Then I will help you out. That ok?"

"Yes. That will work," she said, reaching for the robe he offered. Once she was wrapped, both hair and robe, Tristan scooped her up out of the tub and set her on the nearby desk chair, where he kneeled down and put the wool socks on her feet, looking up at her as he did so. "Did you have a flashback of that night?"

Ilia nodded; her iridescent blue eyes fixed on him. "It was so real, as it was the first time, but what was different this time was that my magik knew what it was and shrank deep inside me. The first time, it was with me the whole time, and that is how it got damaged. If I can pay attention to how my magik acts, I will be able to tell myself it's a memory and not the real thing.

Tristan finished with his ministrations and was sitting on the floor leaning back on one hand, one knee bent in the air and the other bent in cross-legged position. He pondered her idea for a moment then said, "You might try that, but what I have seen really help in the past is for the person to tell the story of the event to someone."

Ilia shook her head before the final words were out of his mouth. "I don't think I can do that,

Tristan. Besides, who would I tell? You? You were there."

"Not for all of it, and it's not about the person you are telling. It's about putting it into words so the mind cannot continue to inflate it, and it's about getting the mind to understand it's a memory; not real time." He paused to think a moment then said, "I know. Try writing it out first.

Maybe that would help. Do you think you could do that?"

Ilia nodded, "I can try. It's not like I have much else to do while I'm healing up."

Tristan grinned. "Good lass. I will get you some paper and something to write with." He got up and moved to the desk. He pulled out a key from his pants pocket and unlocked the desk, removing several sheets of parchment paper and a pen, then set it all on top of the desk. "It's here when you want it. Shall we get you back to bed?"

Ilia nodded, then noticed his shirt lying on the bed. "I think I would like to put that on first. I think I can get myself over to the bed. I need to start moving around at some point, right?" She asked, giving him a questioning look.

He nodded, "Aye. Now's as good a time as any. I'm guessing you will have a hard time getting in bed, so when you are ready, let me know. Send one of the boys out to get me. I will have them up here taking the tub out." He turned to leave her but stopped and turned back when he got to the door. "Ilia, I don't want anyone putting you in that bed but me." With that, he turned and left the room.

Ilia smiled to herself. Dicken had been helping her in and out of that bed to the water closet since she was brought on ship. Something had shifted for Tristan, and she had to admit, she liked it. She looked over at the pen and paper sitting on the desk. Not tonight. Tonight, she was clean and sitting upright in a chair. She felt relatively human and wanted to just enjoy it.

Eight

The days that followed saw Ilia finding her way out on deck to sit in the sun and watch the goings on with the crew. The sun did wonders for her both physically and mentally. She felt the damage done to her begin to seep from her bones like an infectious disease being driven away with strong medicine. She spent time writing out her experience on paper. It was slow going, as the trauma of the events often captured her and threw her into the moment, causing her to relive everything over again, but she began to find some distance when the flashbacks happened. It was a small sliver of ground she reclaimed, but it was enough to stand on, and as she broadened it, her magik came to assist, giving her strength to pull out of the episodes quicker and easier.

Tristan began to introduce his crew to Ilia. He wanted them to know her and be prepared for when her role changed from his guest to his wife. He didn't expect the crew to have any issues with Ilia, her gentle nature and the fascination with her uniqueness would pave the way, and he was right. The crew took to her like bees to the queen bee. When they saw her above deck sitting out in the sun, watching, they would wave until they caught her attention and she waved back.

Edmond didn't admonish them. Ilia wasn't enough of a distraction to keep them from their work, and he had to admit, he also enjoyed having her on board despite his initial misgivings.

Ilia spent every fair-weather day outside, and it helped her healing process. Connor felt her progress was good. Aside from the physical wounds and the psychological ones, there was the immense trauma to the overall body that she had suffered, but Ilia was healthy otherwise, and once she was able to get out of bed and move around her recovery accelerated.

Evenings she spent playing chess with Tristan or just talking. Sometimes they strolled about the deck. Ilia was able to get around on her own, but she tired easily still, so having Tristan with her to lean on enabled her to see more of the ship from all sides. They would watch the sun set over the horizon as Tristan held her in his arms, kissing her neck until she giggled. They would invariably end up in each other's embrace, Tristan's lips exploring hers.

One evening as they were sitting in Tristan's cabin, chatting about the events of the day, Ilia looked at Tristan and said, "I trust you Tristan. I know it hasn't been long, and the fact that you saved my life certainly plays a role, but I am finding I'm completely confident in what you say and who you say you are. I have never had that kind of feeling about anyone."

Tristan gazed at her, his eyes relaying more than he could ever say. "Thank you, Ilia. I feel the same about you. You know, I never really planned to be bonded to someone. It wasn't that I was opposed to it. I just have a lot of things about me that complicate matters. And I haven't shared them with you, because time has been so short and you have been so ill, but I want to honor your trust in me by full disclosure."

Ilia's eyes widened, awaiting whatever shock he was about to send her way. Tristan softened at the look on her face. "Relax lass, I'm not a night walker, as you well know. I'm not a werewolf either." He paused, studying the azure depths of her blue eyes, trying to see what her response might be. "But I *am* a shapeshifter."

He waited for a reaction, and when she met his scrutiny with a contented stare, he said "See?

Nothing too tragic to endure, at least not for you. For me, well, it has not been so easy."

The direction change forestalled Ilia's words at first, but she finally said "Oh yes, of course! That must have been, must be, very hard on you."

"I have found my life, and it suits me. I have a crew that knows what I am and will only speak of it upon penalty of death."

"Even the boys?" she asked.

He nodded. "Even the boys. You cannot be on this ship without the contract. I cannot compromise my livelihood by bringing attention to myself or by putting a target on my back for those hunting us."

Ilia bobbed her head in understanding then said, "But I have not signed a contract. What about me?"

He inched closer to her. "We will be signing a different kind of contract," he said. "Together."

Ilia pondered that statement for a moment then said, "So you know all about me. What of your life? How did you end up the Lord Pirate? The young man I knew first in Portsmith does not even resemble the one sitting across from me, and I'm not talking physical changes. I know you have explained some about your past life, but I am certain there is more. What is it?"

"Fair enough," Tristan responded. "There are three people in this world, four now with you, who know my story: Edmond, Red Rudy, and Ella. It's not because it's so mysterious, really. It's just that I am a very private person, and with what I do, the lifestyle I lead, I cannot have a lot of people knowing a much about me."

"I grew up on Marauder's Isle. It's a very mysterious island, covered in natural fog a good portion of the time. But then there is also magikal fog and the low-hanging clouds that make it near impossible to find. There is a small village on the island. The village was originally settled by a group of magikal beings who were fleeing persecution. One of those people was a woman with great powers. She cast magik spells all over the island to protect it from just anyone finding it. If you were able to find it, then you could stay. That eliminated many an adventurer from landing on the island, so the village left it that way."

"Over time a lot of pirates seeking safe haven found their way to the Island's shores; men who were escaping the law, those who were seeking refuge from many things. They built rooms in the huge boulders surrounding the island, and many stayed there. The problem with the system was that it did not keep out dangerous people bent on causing harm to others on the island."

"One day a shapeshifter came onto the island. He raped one of the young girls in the village and she became pregnant. The young woman gave birth to a shape shifter. She died while doing so. The babe was raised by the brother of the young girl." He had been looking out over the ocean as he spoke, but he finished and looked at Ilia.

"That babe was you?" she asked.

He nodded. "I was raised by my uncle. I know I said before I was raised by my brother, but it is just something I say to throw people off of the truth. I know I told you a different story about my parents, but I did not know you so well back then." He gave her a look of chagrin before continuing. "He did the best he could. I had a healthy upbringing. I had friends like Red Rudy, Edmond, and Ella. But I was always different from them. They were non-magikal folk living on a magikal island. My very genetic makeup is coated in magik. And I had things I had to learn they did not. Like how to shift and how to shift back. How to do so while attracting the least bit of attention possible. It is easy now as an adult but imagine a small boy doing so. How about a teenage boy?" He shrugged, one massive shoulder following the other. "Lots of things."

"So where did you learn all that?" Ilia asked.

"The sorceress I told you about? Well, she was very old by the time I came along, but she took me under her wing. She taught me a lot of things. She was so angry about what happened to my mother that she went through the entire island and threw everyone but the villagers off the island.

I am told they drowned. There are very deep areas along the isle. You can step off and just fall into fathomless depths, and there are tremendous undertows that will hold you down and drag you to the bottom. Some say it is an invisible sea monster. It's possible," he said, flicking his eyes dismissively.

"The isle has a series of boulders that shoot out of the water. They are in a circle, and some say they are the prongs of a great crown, and the only visible part of an invisible sea monster who has been cursed to stay underwater, but whose crown floated to the surface and lodged along our shoreline." He shrugged again. "It's as plausible as any other story I've heard."

He continued. "There is a wooden coin the members of the village have, and once I had the Anemone, I created a brand for those whom I would shelter on the island. Many of the villagers have brands they have created that speak to their people being able to seek refuge. Mostly, though, the brands are for those of us who travel the seas. This way the villagers know who to let in and who to allow to be swallowed by the dangers on the island. If you come to the island without one or both of these things, you will never get more than a few feet on the shore. It's a dangerous place for those who are not welcome there."

"So how did you become a pirate? You have your own ship, and you are clearly comfortable on the seas. How did you get from that island to this?" Ilia gestured with her hand in a wide, sweeping arc.

Tristan smiled. "Well, that's another story then. When I was of an age, my people sent me to Portsmith for my education. I lied a bit about this part of my story when I told you. Mind, I had plenty of education from the lady. I always called her 'The Lady.' Kind of in the way people call me 'Lord Pirate.' But her real name was Andora. I learned many languages and much history as well as how to read from Andora, but my people wanted me connected with the rest of the world, so I went with Rudy, Edmond, and Ella. Now, Ella went to school for a time and then met her husband Allen. They were married, and then he died from an aneurism in the brain. So,

Ella stayed in Portsmith, and as you know, she runs a room and board business in her home."

The rest of us continued in school then went into the Water Armament. It made sense to go into the branch of military that has to do with protecting the ocean, growing up where we did. Plus, for me, on a ship out on the ocean was better for my, uh, particular genetic makeup. I have never been one who likes to be confined indoors.

In the military we learned more than we could ever want to know about ships. It was hard work, and that wasn't so bad, but the conditions were terrible. We were often not allowed sleep, were given very little food, and were punished brutally for small infractions. You get used to it after a while, but the human spirit will eventually break, or it will rebel.

One day I looked around at Edmond and Rudy, and I knew neither of them were going to last. I had been listening to news from people when we docked at different ports, and I knew pirate ships were thriving. The amount of cargo going back and forth between destinations and the military ships being taken provided a boon for the pirating industry. I didn't know how exactly to get on a pirate ship, but I knew that was where we needed to be. We were all very skilled, and Edmond is even an engineer. I knew that the right ship would use our skills and have a need for them."

Tristan leaned back, stretching his arms, one arms stopping on the way down to massage his neck.

"Here I was trying to figure out how to get us in contact with a pirate ship when, one night, we were overtaken by one. The Commander was a woman called Bonny Anne, and let me tell you, she was bonny." He threw a quick glance at Ilia, who responded with an indulgent smile.

He continued. "They killed most of the crew. Anne wasn't much for leftovers from the ships she commandeered, in terms of humans. She had a crew, see. But luckily for us, they were looking for a few positions. They needed a gunner. Now, Rudy wasn't a master at the time, but in the midst of the fight he must have caught her eye, because in the lineup, she chose him. There we all were lined up before a firing squad, and she went down the line, this very buxom woman with flaming red hair, dressed in men's clothes, making them look like something a man would pay to see then go repent for." He paused again to look at her, hoping he had not offended her, but she only nodded her head to prompt him to continue.

"She sort of swayed down the row and every man was falling at her feet. I realized after some time that she was something akin to a silkie, or a siren, able to draw men in and do whatever she wanted with them. She moves on and picks Edmond saying he will be useful to her. Somehow, she knows his skill sets, or at least knows he is more than an average sailor, and he is just drooling over her like a puppy dog. They all are."

"Then she comes to me, and though I can appreciate a woman like that, I am not affected like the rest. They are all looking like they are in some kind of trance, and I am just standing there awaiting my fate. She stops in front of me, runs a finger down my face and across my chin and says, 'Hmmm. There is more to you than meets the eye young sailor. You will be my final choice, and I look forward to uncovering what it is about you that makes you immune to my charms.'"

"Rudy, Edmond, and I, and our ship's doctor whom you will know as Connor, are hauled off the ship and onto hers. The rest of the crew, well the stories differ, but after seeing her in action many times, it's fairly certain she had her way with as many as she wanted then killed them all. They took from the ship what they wanted, and then they sank it along with the bodies of the crew that were left. I confess, I wasn't despondent over the outcome. We were poorly treated, and for us to be put on her ship while they met their fate seemed to me pure karma and good fortune all rolled into one."

"Were you her lover?" Ilia asked, jumping ahead in Tristan's story.

"Well not in the way others were. I mean, she controlled them. But with me, well, I guess I was a novelty, and that appealed to her. We were all with her for many years, and she taught me everything she knew about pirating. She knew about my shapeshifting after a time, and we often used my abilities in our endeavors, just as she used hers to advantage."

"I bet you learned about more than pirating from her," Ilia said, offering a teasing smile.

Tristan gave a wry chuckle. "Well, there was that. For many years there was that, but she was a creature whose basic makeup was to feed off men and their sexual desires. She couldn't get that from me or with me, so there were always lots of men, and eventually we just got tired of one another, I think. I was her captain; Edmond became the navigator, ship structural engineer, Rudy learned quickly and became gunner, and Connor became the physician. He was not susceptible to her charms either, but she never showed an interest in him. There is something about Connor that discourages foul play in his presence, and I have never seen anyone violate that."

Ilia nodded, knowing just what he was talking about. There was an earthiness about Connor, like he had somehow sprung from the ground, bringing fresh rain and all that is wholesome in nature with him.

"She did have a go at Edmond," Tristan continued. "He is a good-looking guy after all, but I discouraged her from going after my mates if she were entertaining me with her favors. As a result, she left Rudy alone. He didn't want her to leave him alone. Poor Rudy." He paused with a chuckle, shaking his head. "If you ask him about her to this day, he will tell you she was a vile witch from the bowels of hell. He hated her. Get on a Scot's bad side and there you will stay. I'm not sure what all went down, but it's not hard to guess how she managed to elicit such a reaction from him."

He turned to find Ilia's eyes fill with amusement. "And then one day she got very sick. She lived a long time, as do most magikal folk, and her time was up. Our relationship was long past amorous. Much of the time my involvement with her was one part survival, and two parts the idiocy of youth. For a long time though, it was professional. I was her confidant and right-hand man. She taught me everything she knew about pirating, and she was the best.

When she died, she left me the ship. This ship, the Anemone. I didn't much care for the crew, as most of them were conscripted and held by her particular, charms? I nearly had a mutiny when she died. It wasn't so much that the crew was against me, but with her death, whatever held them captive was released, and they were angry. Connor, Edmond, Rudy, and I along with a few others banded together and held the ship. I had to shift right in front of them to frighten them into acquiescence."

"What did you shift into?" Ilia asked.

He laughed at the memory. "A massive wolf." He sobered as he said, "I understand their fears. Sailors are a superstitious lot. Having the commander die while at sea is bad luck, but we made it to shore with the crew, whom we hadn't had to kill or throw overboard. I paid everyone, which was a new experience for us all, and released those who wanted to go." He sighed, leaning back on the bench, his back against the railing with his arms stretched out on either side as he looked out over the ship deck. "I suppose the shifting is what set off the rumors and earned me my title.

Not very original, but if you spell it as proper, it takes on a whole different meaning." He turned again to look at her, smiling.

"The rest of it is a lot of lore, though I have been merciless many times, and much of my reputation was built when I was with Anne. I did whatever had to be done to survive and protect my mates. Once the ship was mine, I was no longer hunting prey as before. I began hunting bounty, and I got people on my crew who were looking for brotherhood and to collect bounty as well. I had to prove myself to the network of pirates, but it helped to have Marauder's Isle, and to be able to offer sanctuary to pirates in need."

"So, you are a philanthropist?" Ilia asked teasingly, a hint of laughter in her voice.

Tristan chuckled. "Aye, lass." He swept his arm in a wide arc across the ship. "This is what philanthropy looks like." They both laughed then sat for a time in silence, each to their own thoughts.

Tristan had been planning to wait until Ilia was stronger but decided it would be a good time to mention the binding ceremony. "The sooner we are set, the better I will feel about your safety. You are safe on this ship, but one never takes chances out here, and I can tell you some of the crew are superstitious about having a woman onboard. Having that woman as my wife will give them assurance. I like to do that for them when I can."

Ilia nodded. "Yes, I agree, sooner is better than later."

Nine

Ilia wore the moon scarf Anna sent her. She found a dress in the bottom of the trunk. Well, it was really a kind of shift. It was simple, straight, and hugged her trim body like a glove. It was silver and made of silk with strands of shiny thread shot throughout the material, making it shimmer when she moved. She found some white voile in the trunk as well. She cut a length of it and wrapped it about her. She wore no shoes.

Ilia looked at herself in the mirror. She had insisted on being married at night rather than the day. She felt stronger at night, could feel her magik humming the closer she was to moonlight. It was a full moon, and she knew she would be glowing, though with all her injuries she wasn't sure how much or what it would look like. She surveyed herself. Not bad for a woman who had been through a war just over a fortnight ago.

The bruises on her body were just about gone, though the damage to her cheek still showed a mottled bruise. She was able to walk easily enough. Her head was healing slowly. There was still no telling if hair would grow back. The scalp struggled to mend, and the healing process was extremely painful. Connor checked on it daily and added salves to help with the mending. For the ceremony, she had her head wrapped beautifully in the exquisite scarf. Her hair on the other side of her head she pulled loose from the scarf and allowed it to cascade down over her breasts and across her shoulder in soft shining silver curls. Her blue eyes shone in the mirror, looking back at her in anticipation. Was that it? Anticipation?

Yes. Ilia was excited for the first time in ages. This man to whom she was tying herself, who had so many fascinating aspects to his nature, who, under his intimidating exterior, cared for her so tenderly, was the one for her. She knew it from the start; had felt such a connection to him the first time they met, and now they would be making a partnership that would intertwine their journeys for the rest of their lives. Ilia drew a deep breath and turned to walk toward her future.

Tristan waited on deck. They agreed to have the ceremony on the upper deck of the ship so the crew could watch. Connor officiated, and Edmond stood nearby to lend moral support to either bride or groom. Tristan wore dark trousers, a crisp white linen shirt, and a light blue silk vest. He wore no overcoat, as the weather was balmy, and Ilia insisted he should put comfort before pretension. He wore nothing at the neck and a pair of black ankle-high leather shoes over dark stockings. His hair loose at Ilia's request and he cut his beard down so it hugged his face and jawline.

The full moon cast all the light on deck they needed, though they had lanterns lit to enhance the atmosphere. Down on the main deck the crew mingled, holding their own lanterns, as the moonlight wasn't as bright there.

Tristan wondered how the moonlight would affect Ilia, remembering what he witnessed before during a full moon. He wasn't kept in suspense for long though, for she came from his cabin with Dicken assisting her. The boy was completely dedicated to her, and Tristan couldn't fault him for it. She had a way about her.

As she came into the moonlight, it bathed her, and her whole body glowed with an iridescent light. She stopped in the fullness of it, and Tristan watched her draw it in like a swimmer coming up for a deep breath of air. Every moment she was in the moonlight, she glowed brighter. She looked up at the large globe hanging in the sky above the gently rolling waves of the ocean, and when she lowered her gaze to look at him, her eyes were glowing amber. She was filling up, and there was a healing deep within her, which he could only guess was her magik finally getting what it needed to mend within her.

She was breathtaking; an ethereal creature, more lovely than anything he had ever seen, and as her power shimmered around her, Tristan wondered if he deserved to claim such a creature. He heard the crew below draw a collective breath and emit noises of awe as she approached him. She reached him, and he took her hands in his as they faced one another. She smiled and he returned her smile, feeling that for the first time, she was the one reassuring him, letting him know everything was going to be fine.

The ceremony was simple. An exchange of vows promising to honor one another and the God of all creations with their lives and commitment to their union. Then true to the Celtic tradition, their clasped hands were wrapped in a cloth by Connor to represent the trinity of their union, man and woman united and blessed by God.

When they were presented to the crew below them, the men cheered. Tristan pulled Ilia into his arms, watching her face for signs of distress, as he kissed her, raising more cheers from below. Edmond and Connor gave their good wishes, as did Rudy, who had come up from below deck to stand in on the ceremony. Then they were gone, leaving Tristan and Ilia alone on the upper deck.

"Are they getting the branding ready?" Ilia asked.

Tristan chuckled. "I didn't think you would like to spend your wedding night in that kind of pain.

We can do it tomorrow."

Ilia smiled, turned toward the moon and, leaning against the railing, lifted her face to it. "This is the first time I have felt alive since all this began," she said. She flexed her hand out in front of her, and a surge of light moved down her arm, under her skin, and sparked out the ends of her fingers. She giggled and looked over at Tristan. "It's working again. I will recover more quickly now."

Tristan leaned in closer, taking her hand to examine her fingertips and behold the light flowing under her skin. "It's like there is a lantern inside you moving around," he said, his voice and face reflecting wonder.

Ilia nodded excitedly. "Yes. I will have some time to work with it before I must leave the ship.

It will feel good to be able to openly work with my magik. I can't remember when I was last able to do that. I always have to be so covert about it." She was still flexing her fingers and moving her hands and arms around.

Tristan leaned back against the railing watching her. After a time, he said "So tell me about moon children. What are they?"

Ilia paused in her movements then, carefully and slowly, extracted a glowing ball from her fingertips and began rolling the bright ball of light around on her hands and arms, expertly maneuvering with her fingertips. "Well," she said, "a long time ago there was a great storm in the heavens. Large pieces of debris hit the moon, creating a big hole in it. Slabs from the hole fell to earth.

A powerful sorceress watched the pieces falling and knew they would hit the earth and damage it right where she lived, so as the pieces were falling from the sky, she began to work her magik on them. It so happened that on that night the moon was full, and the beams coming through also hit the pieces of debris as the sorceress was changing them, and from the combination ethereal beings were born.

But the beings did not have form. They were made of moonspun, the silken strands produced by moonlight. But they had a bit more to them than that, thanks to the sorceress's magik. They needed, like most creatures, to create and advance their kind, so they found humans.

They were irresistible to humans, and it was not difficult to mate with them.

From that union, many of those unions, moon children were born. The first creatures did not have the physical presence needed to survive here, so most of them passed on. The moon child, as we know it, is a much more durable creature and will always exhibit the human side and have no special abilities. However, some retain more of the moon side and are gifted in one or more areas. Moon children, for the most part, are not able to pro-create. Yet, somehow, humans can have moon children. That part of the story is a mystery, but as you know that is where changelings come in."

"And then there is you," Tristan said.

Ilia nodded. "Yes. Then there is me. It appears I am an anomaly."

Tristan moved to take her in his arms. "You are exceptional, and though I never thought things would go this way, you must know, I am certainly glad they did, and I will protect and cherish you with my life."

Ilia looked up into his handsome face and knew he spoke the truth. "I never imagined I would find someone who would want me, much less accept all the strangeness, which is simply my normal way of moving through this life. I consider myself beyond deserving of what you are giving me, and I will honor you with my life. I am afraid of one thing though," she said, her eyes losing some of their tawny glow as she met his gaze.

"What?" he asked, with a look of concern.

"It is highly unlikely I can ever give you children, Tristan. I know that is an important thing for men. Women too, for that matter. It is something I learned to accept from a young age. I made my peace with it long ago, but you have not been afforded that opportunity with my messy life impacting yours in such a dramatic and permanent fashion."

He nestled his chin against her moonspun scarf. "I figured that out a while back, Ilia. It is of no consequence to me." Hurriedly, he continued when he saw the disbelief on her face. "I'm a pirate, Ilia. I am nomadic. I have never sat around thinking of the great lands and legacy I would pass down to my offspring. I have nothing to offer a child, and the fact that you cannot have one makes little difference to me." He released her, running a hand through his hair, an action she was quickly learning was a telltale of inner discomfort.

Tristan leaned against the railing again looking out over the waves. "I was in what you might call a relationship for a long time. It was probably closer to a captive/captor situation with Anne, but I thought it was a relationship, and though she had little hold over me like with other men, she still had some control over me in the sense that we shared a closeness I had not ever had with a woman. We made every decision together, and though, ultimately, it was she who made the decisions for her ship, I was given a say, and it was the most important relationship in my life.

She would not commit to me in a permanent way. We were not married, and I thought what we had was forever. At some point I realized this life is not always forgiving, and there are sacrifices, and I came to realize she wasn't the kind of creature to plan a forever future with."

He paused, giving Ilia a quick look before staring again at the sea. "I made the choice long ago. I chose not to have the stable life that included children, because I thought Anne would live forever, we would always be together, and I would always be a pirate. But things changed between us, and Anne did not live forever. But I am still a pirate, and I am at peace with this life I have chosen."

Night waves knocked gently against the ship. "So, I am not upset that this is something you cannot do. Though for your sake, I am sorry, if this is something you have wanted. But for me, well, I made my peace with all of it long ago." He paused again, turning to look at her, taking her in his arms again. "It is important you know why I feel the way I do, and that I am saying it is fine in earnest, not just to appease you."

Ilia nodded. "Thank you. I understand. I think you understand me better than I thought. I need explanations for things I don't understand in order to let them go. I suppose everyone is that way, but I appreciate you taking the time to explain."

He leaned down and kissed her. "We are joined now. I will not keep things from you, Ilia. It is simply not my way."

"I'm glad of that," she said, reaching up to pull him closer to her, his lips taking hers again and again, capturing and exploring until the moonlight that illuminated her surrounded and encapsulated them both.

At some length, they came back to their surroundings and Tristan said, "Madam, shall we retire?"

"Aye, sir." Smiling, Ilia put her hand in his and allowed him to lead her to their cabin.

When they were behind the closed door, Tristan watched as Ilia went to the desk chair and removed the gauze shawl that had been dancing about the silver satin dress all night. She did not remove the scarf from her head but touched it, turning to see him watching her. He was leaning against the door, his eyes hooded. Ilia suddenly felt a thrill shoot through her body, accompanied by a tendril of fear.

Tristan was not only watching her physical actions but also watching the moonlight that pulsed through her and saw it suddenly dim. He approached and placed his hands on her shoulders. "Ilia, I know you have been through something horrific. Do not forget I was there. I will never pressure you to do anything. You are still recovering, and that is only the physical aspect of this. You are not obligated to give me anything. I want only what you want to offer."

She looked up at the big, dangerous man in front of her who had so many aspects to his nature, yet seemed to sense what she needed. "I don't want to disappoint you, Tristan. I do not want to fail you."

Tristan snorted and walked away, removing his coat and vest, placing them on the chair by the gauze Ilia had discarded. "The physical act between a man and woman is about expression of what they feel for one another. It is not about obligation or an ideal that is expected to be fulfilled. You and I will define what we have and all its components. No one else, and certainly not some sort of mandate that hangs in the air between us put there by who knows. Am I clear?"

Ilia gave a small smile. "Crystal."

"Good. Now. We have plenty to explore about each other in a very short time. What we do and what we accomplish will need to be substantial and sustainable. I do not want this time we have to be cluttered with someone else's ideals." He walked back to her and kissed her. She melted into him, putting her arms around his waist as he tasted her mouth, kissing her neck as he held her to him.

"Having said that," he went on, "I will tell you I will live in this cabin with you, and I will sleep with you. I will not, however, take what you do not freely give."

Tristan released her and walked over to lower the lanterns in the cabin. He sat down on the edge of the bed and removed his shoes and his pants. "Oh," he said looking at her with a wicked smile, "I need to tell you I sleep in the nude."

With that he walked round to the other side of the bed, pulled back the blankets and removed the long shirt that hung nearly to his knees. He stood in the shadows with the bed between them obscuring his anatomy just below his hips.

Ilia started, realizing she had a naked man in her bed. Nearly. She looked at Tristan's face and saw a grin spreading across it. He was enjoying this! She smiled slightly, her sense of humor overriding her fear. Since he had set terms, she would comply.

Tristan climbed into the bed and propped the back of his head on his crossed arms, watching her. Ilia slowly removed her silver dress. She wore nothing under it, and as she pulled the dress over her head, she heard Tristan suck in his breath. She smiled to herself as she slowly removed the dress.

Tristan watched through half-hooded eyes. He had been curious to see how she would react, and he was pleasantly surprised on more than one front. He watched her lovely white body being exposed as the material fell away. She was lithe but still curvy in all the right places. Her skin was flawless and glowed with the inner light he was becoming accustomed to. He watched her pull the dress up over her full breasts and toss it onto the chair. Honestly, the way she carelessly tossed the dress aside was more of a turn-on than anything else had been. He swallowed and closed his eyes for a moment, regaining control of his faculties.

Ilia grinned mischievously and decided to put an end to the moment. She did not want to tease him, just give him a taste of the kind of tantalizing discomfort he had given her. She knew she would go no further; was not ready to take things further, and she respected him too much for making their first night together so safe for her.

She crawled into the bed, making sure to cover herself before rolling to face him. "Goodnight, Lord Pirate."

Tristan smiled. "Goodnight moon child."

*

Somewhere in the night, the nightmare came, as it always did. The men were taking her and tying her down, her sister standing by as they violated her, but this time when she cried out, so alone and scared, a voice said, "Oh lass. 'Tis okay. I will not let anyone harm you. Sleep wife. You are safe now." Strong arms curled around her and pulled her back against a solid warm chest while strong legs spooned about her. Ilia relaxed into the warmth and security, passing back into sleep.

Several days went by with a similar scenario each night. Tristan managed to keep his promise to wait for Ilia, but it was difficult for him. He spoke of their situation with no one, but it was one of the more challenging things he had done, or not done. After all, he was a healthy male with a beautiful woman in his bed every night. He did notice that after their first night, Ilia did not sleep in the nude. He suspected that was her normal, but she met his boldness that first night to let him know she was not afraid of him. He was thankful she modified her sleeping attire. It helped.

During the day they talked and walked. Tristan taught her about ships and the life of a pirate. Ilia told him stories of her training and her teachers. They laughed and bonded, sensing every minute counted as they drew closer to Marauder's Isle.

The only thing Tristan did not divulge readily was his ability to shape-shift. Ilia sensed it was something very private for him and not something he shared with anyone. She also got the sense that Anne, a woman he had dedicated himself to, had exploited his abilities and taken advantage of a young man enamored with her and their life. She hoped that one day he would open up to her about his extraordinary ability, and her only way of encouraging him was to be open about hers.

"I learned at a young age, among people who were supposed to be like me, that I was different, and my abilities were a cause of jealousy," she told Tristan one day. They were sitting on the top deck as they often did, looking out at the vast ocean. As she said it, she flicked a finger and a small globe of fire appeared at her fingertip. Then she dangled the fingers of her other hand over the globe and wiggled them back and forth. Water rained down from her fingertips onto the globe, extinguishing it.

Tristan's eyes widened in astonishment as he watched her. Ilia smiled at him, shaking out both hands, then placing them in her lap. "I have always had a strong control over the elements. Since Portsmith, however, I have discovered, and maybe it is because we are on the ocean, but I have found controlling water is quite easy for me. I'm not sure what has caused it, but somehow my magik has changed. It is stronger." She looked fondly at him. "Or maybe it is you in my life."

Tristan grinned. "So, you have all these teachers trying to make you, and all you needed was a pirate in your life?"

Ilia giggled. "Maybe that is the truth of it. I have never had instruction on what happens when a moon child pairs with a shapeshifter." At the mention of his ability, Tristan sobered.

"I'm not one to consider what I am a strength, Ilia. It is more of a curse."

"I do not agree. It is part of you, and something I am not afraid of. I hope you understand that. I don't think I could ever be with someone who was not unique. You possess a wondrous ability,

Tristan, and I honor that part of you as much as the human. You need to know that."

He looked at her for a long moment. "I don't become a tame little parakeet, Ilia. What I shift into is dangerous, and something that can be deadly. You have to know. I've never hurt this crew, but

I am not in possession of myself when I am my other."

"Then it would be valuable to introduce yourself to me. I am your partner. I need to know all of you." She replied.

His gaze captured hers. "I need to know all of you as well."

His remark hit the target. She realized he was struggling more with their lack of intimacy than she thought. She did not respond to his statement but spent the remainder of the day thinking about it, wondering if and when she could give him what he needed from her.

*

Tristan spent the afternoon with the crew and sequestered in the cabin with Edmond. Ilia lounged on the deck, reading. The feel of sun and spray coming off the ocean was better than any medicine she could have, and she took advantage of it. She couldn't sunburn, so having direct sun for hours only served in a healing capacity. She spent the time thinking about what had occurred, about Tristan, and about the uncertain future looming ahead of them. It felt good to be able to contemplate her life with someone else in it, and even though things were uncertain, she felt her ties to Tristan weren't.

That evening Tristan dined with the crew, and Ilia had a light supper in their cabin. She had gotten to know the crew over the weeks on the ship, and they were accepting of her and in awe of her. She couldn't blame them for that. Seamen were a superstitious lot. She looked unusual and knew she exuded the power that flowed in her veins.

After her dinner, Ilia took a sponge bath, changed the wrap on her head, and sat with a book to await Tristan's return. She soon fell asleep in the chair. wrapped in the fuzzy robe Dicken had given her, lulled by the movement of the ship as she so often was.

Sometime later, Ilia was not awakened by Tristan, but by a feeling of tipping. She jerked awake to find she was sliding toward the desk. She jumped up, grasping the bed, appreciating the fact that it was nailed to the floor. She quickly discarded the robe and reached for one of Tristan's shirts, pulling it on, and grabbing a wool shawl that lay on the bed. She wrapped it around her and, barefoot, made her way to the door.

The ship was in darkness. Gigantic waves were rolling, tossing the ship about like a leaf on a stream. She ran along the deck to see the crew scurrying about taking down the sails and securing what they could.

Ilia looked for Tristan and found him bellowing orders as he worked to steer the prow of the ship into the waves and at an angle to keep them from capsizing. As she watched, Ilia saw one of the sails tear before it could be taken down. The crew were fast but not fast enough for the storm.

Ilia could see they were losing the battle. She closed her eyes and felt her power. She just needed a little moonlight in the midst of this storm. Just a bit and she would be able to do what was needed. She had to get to the prow. She moved slowly, hanging on tight, watching to make sure she was not swept overboard. She looked back once to see Tristan yelling at her, but she ignored him.

She just needed a thread. Just one thread.

And then it happened. She reached the prow and looked up. The sky was covered in angry clouds, but the wind was moving them, and a small thread of moonlight filtered through. By that time, she was standing on the railing. She balanced precariously and waited. It only took a moment.

Tristan, Edmond, and all the crew were riveted to the spot, frozen in the fury of the mighty storm. All eyes were on what looked like a specter standing on the prow of the ship. She wore a long white linen shirt that billowed about her. Her shawl was tied around her hips. Her hands were raised and her silver hair, unbound, whipped about her as though static electricity held it in thrall.

She looked like a white statue, and just when they thought she would go over the ship, a small wisp of moonlight shot through the sky, igniting the statue. She began to glow, and an immense power emanated from her, along with a blinding light. She brought her hands together over her head, her palms together, then opened them and slowly lowered them toward her sides. The wind died, and a tremendous pressure descended. Everyone on board was pressed down onto their faces on the ship floor. As Ilia lowered her hands, the waves lowered. There was a tremendous shaking around them, as the water fought against the power, but it was suppressed down into gentle waves, as she touched her hands to her sides.

The sea was completely calm.

No one moved as they floated in the darkness. The clouds parted, and Ilia stood in the light of the gibbous moon. She felt it fill her and restore her power. She expected to feel drained but found she felt energized. The ease of it shocked her, but then she considered the connection between the moon and water and realized the act would be much easier than trying to do something on land that didn't involve water.

Ilia turned to see the crew slowly getting up. Tristan, she realized, had shapeshifted, and what came to her was not her handsome pirate husband but an enormous wolf. They stood facing one another, a few feet apart. His hair was black as night and his eyes shone a luminescent mossy green color. Edmond rushed forward and stood right behind Tristan.

Ilia put up a hand to prevent Edmond from coming closer.

She stood looking at Tristan. "I am yours," she murmured. "You are mine." She held up the wrist with the recent brand she had received. He stood looking at her a few moments longer, then raised his head and howled, moving to her.

Ilia stood waiting, and he came forward, his head level with her shoulders. He sniffed her, then nudged her hand, pressing himself into her breasts. Ilia giggled. "Aye, sir. You are something to behold in all forms."

She walked back to their cabin, the huge wolf right behind her. The crew stood in awe, hardly able to comprehend what they had experienced. Before she left them, she said, "You will need light to put everything back to rights." She opened her hands and blew on her fingertips sending little, tiny globes all around the ship, lighting it fully. "They will extinguish with the dawn," she walked quietly back to the cabin, nodding to Edmond, who was smiling broadly.

"Goodnight Ed," she said.

"Aye, goodnight then," he said, still grinning.

Tristan, still in his alter form, left her at the cabin. "I will wait up for you." She said, shutting the door without looking back at him.

Ten

He came into the cabin sometime later to find her sitting in bed. She wore a simple white shift that was an open V-neck in the front, plunging past the swell of her breasts. It was thin and he remembered it was what she'd worn the night she came aboard the ship, a physical wreck and unconscious. As he looked at her, the shift was the only thing that was familiar to that night. The woman in front of him was vibrant and actually glowing with a light he knew came completely from within her. She no longer covered her head where she had been damaged. Tonight, she wore nothing over it, and he could see she was losing her self-consciousness about her trauma and how she looked. To him she was beautiful.

She gazed at him, taking in every detail. He had his shirt over his shoulder, the rest of him bare to his waist where his slacks sat loosely on his hips. He was barefoot, and his hair stood out about him. He looked like a dangerous creature from the myths, half man and half something else altogether. Ilia sensed there was still something of the feral about him, and it made him even more dangerous and more appealing to her. His mossy green eyes burned in the dim light, and she knew she needed him as he needed her.

Ilia moved on her knees across the bed to him, and he came closer, wrapping his muscular arms about her waist, pulling her in as close to him as he could. She ran her hands through his hair and waited until he pulled his head back to look at her. "So, you have seen all the parts of me lass. It is what I am, and I will never be anything else."

He watched her, awaiting her response, and she raised her mouth to his with an answer, drawing him in with her lips, her tongue teasing his. He allowed her to tease him, but at length he pulled back. "Ilia. What are you doing?"

She smiled. She could still smell the animal on him, an earthy, otherworldly smell, and it drove her mad. She pulled her shift over her head and said, "What do you think?"

Tristan stood stock still, not sure who the nymph in front of him was, daring to believe it was his wife. He reached for her, and she pulled him onto the bed, rolling on top of him. "Lass are you sure?" he asked, reaching his hands around to grasp her bare backside.

She smiled down at him before taking his mouth with hers. She drew back and looked into his eyes, her world melding with his. "Absolutely."

*

Ilia could never explain why she was able to accept, so quickly, an intimate relationship with Tristan. What she experienced had been horrific, but somehow, where Tristan was concerned, her body and mind had made a bridge that allowed him to cross over to the intimacy that exists between couples who are deeply committed to one another. She suspected the healing that took place psychologically to allow her to have a man, in such a way, had a great deal to do with her magik and its impact on her.

Tristan was the man she wanted. He was her other half, and she had found a way to give him a chance to be that role in her life. She would not ever go back to who she was before she committed fully to him. It wasn't that she wasn't complete without him. Quite the contrary.

But Tristan accepted who she was without pause. He applauded all that was different and unique about her, and his complete acceptance allowed Ilia to show him fully who she was. By the standards of her kind, she was quite young, but by human standards, she was nearly 150 years old, and in those years many men had come across her path, but never had she been so involved or even interested until she met Tristan. Ilia had no doubt that had events not happened as they had, she would somehow still have ended up with Tristan as her partner. What had occurred only accelerated matters, and she was fine with that.

*

Tristan stood on the upper deck looking down on the lower deck, watching as Ilia practiced her sword lessons with Rudy using wooden sticks. He smiled as he watched her small frame dart back and forth. She looked like a nymph from the ocean's depths with her white hair flying out about her. He noticed she did not wear a covering over her head where her wounds were. He was glad of that. The crew treated her wounds as badges of honor, showing her scars of their own. Ilia took to their encouragement to leave the wounds unbound, and she was currently attempting to stab Rudy with her stick, her blue shift billowing out around her.

Since the night Ilia saved everyone's lives, the crew fully embraced her as their own and even insisted to Edmond they put Ilia's likeness as the figurehead of the ship. Edmond relayed the demand to Tristan, who smiled, "Well, she is the reason we are all still here to fight another day. Besides, I am the last person to insist my wife not be a symbol on my ship. I think it would finally dispel any presence of the previous commander of this ship."

Edmond grinned. "Yes. Ilia is a presence that could dispel any other." He nodded in the direction of the lower deck where Ilia let out something between a growl and a scream, throwing her sword to the ground in frustration and hurling herself at Rudy, jumping on his back and attempting to cover his eyes with her small hands.

Tristan laughed at Rudy's desperate look. Much of the crew was standing nearby laughing at the scene. Ilia was swearing a blue streak and was sitting piggyback on Rudy. Tristan heard him say,

"Lass. I'm not a horse. This is not how ye win a sword fight."

Ilia growled in frustration, not letting go, "I don't care. I will do it this way, or maybe I will just use magik."

With that Rudy bellowed, "Don't ye dare, ye demon. I will toss ye into that ocean. I will. I care not who your lord is!"

At this point, Tristan made his way down onto the lower deck and worked to extricate his wife from the back of his boatswain. "Lass, you can't harm my crew. I need them for the long journey," he said, still laughing as he hauled her away from Rudy.

Ilia was disheveled but he could see a gleam in her eye and a smile playing at the corners of her mouth. "If I can't beat them, I will just terrify them." She turned to face Tristan, as his arms came around her.

"Yes, I believe you can put the fear into any man," he said, lowering his mouth to capture hers. She sighed as his kiss deepened and she relaxed into him.

"I think you better come with me to the cabin," he said. "You are a mite disheveled and maybe could do with a change of clothes."

"Oh really?" she asked, pulling away from his grasp, straightening her dress and pushing her hair back from her face. "I believe you are correct. I shall go take care of that at once." She turned and started off toward their cabin.

Tristan looked after her for a moment, then around at the crew who were pretending to not watch the scene. He smiled and started after her. "I'll help."

*

The days leading up to their arrival at Marauder's Isle were full of sun, training, and loving. The crew spent much time sparring when it wasn't too hot, and Tristan sparred with them as well, while Ilia stayed on the upper deck practicing her magik. Her magik was flowing through her with no hindrances. Before, she had always had to push it through like hurdling a barrier, but now it flowed through her like a river.

The night Ilia calmed the storm, she assumed she would be exhausted after, but the opposite happened. She felt charged and ready to take on another storm. That revelation surprised her. One of her teachers, Vorna, told Ilia that one day the barriers, the natural human barriers that existed in her, would break down, and Ilia would have access to the full extent of her magik.

"Then we shall see what you are truly capable of. But remember Ilia, you need to use your magik all the time in everything. It is a part of your makeup, the very fiber of your being, so when that happens and those walls break down, do not hold your magik at bay. Let it flow."

Ilia had never feared her magik. Growing up where she did, being so alone and different from everyone, it had always been an invisible companion to her, her solace and comfort. Now she had Tristan, at least for a time, and there was room for both. Her magik was taking the role of life blood, flowing and surging through her every second of every day. She knew she glowed all the time now, but she didn't suppress it. It was just who she was.

One day while they were sitting on deck eating lunch Ilia said, "What do you suppose made you change forms the night of the storm? I mean, it wasn't an ideal time for you, so I'm guessing it wasn't intentional."

Tristan chewed a bite of his meal, reflecting. "Actually, I think it was your magik. It was so overpowering it compelled the magik in me. I remember just changing form. There was no transition, and it came spontaneously. Kind of like vomiting."

Ilia laughed. "That makes sense. I was just curious. I would hate for you not to have control over your phasing because of what I'm doing. That seems a bit unfair to you."

"It seemed a very natural reaction at the time. I'm always very conflicted when I phase, like I should be, or maybe I'm forgetting to take care of something before I go dark. I call it that because my normal view of the world, as a human, changes significantly as an animal. When I know I'm going to need to phase, I am always looking to make sure I have left everything in place before I go dark, and everything is situated for when I come back. This was so sudden and natural; I didn't have time to overthink anything. It was actually kind of nice, and the whole experience was, well, freeing for me." He shrugged. "I think that is the way it's supposed to be.

But over the years with my level of responsibility, I have somehow turned this integral, fundamental part of me into a sort of burden and something I shouldn't be doing. When I was first on this ship and everyone knew what I was, I stayed in phased form a lot. But over time I have moved away from doing so as much." He studied Ilia's delicate profile. "Yet, after watching you and how much you embrace what you are, I feel a real sense of need to connect more with who I am. All that I am."

Ilia turned to look at him, reaching out to squeeze his hand, "I thoroughly enjoy you in all your forms," she said with a teasing smile. "What is your favorite form?"

Tristan paused, thinking for a bit. "Well, the wolf is my easiest form to phase into, and probably the one I am most comfortable with. I do not have to concentrate when phasing to that form, but I have phased into a falcon at times and a hawk. I have also phased into a dolphin, but that is extremely uncomfortable, as I am not used to living in water. The ocean on the surface is something comfortable to me, for obvious reasons, but underneath is a totally different world. I have phased into a dolphin two different times when we had sharks around and a man overboard, but it was not at all pleasant."

Ilia's eyes widened in surprise. "Oh, I can imagine that would not be a comfortable choice! Just the incredible mass of water would be enough."

"Have a spot of Thalassa phobia, then?" he asked, grinning.

Ilia nodded. "I always have, from the earliest I remember. I'm not sure why it hasn't bothered me being on a ship, and even more standing in the storm in the midst of huge waves all around. I can only justify it with the idea that my magik was stronger than any of my mortal fears."

"I'm sure that was it," he agreed. "That night, you were greater than anything around you. I suspect the seas developed a healthy fear of you!" He laughed deeply, and his broad chest shook.

Ilia laughed as well. "Yes. Well. I would prefer to not have to do that again."

The rest of the day Ilia spent working with elemental magik, manipulating air, water, and fire, though with the fire she was very careful; not so much because she was worried about losing control of it on a wooden ship, but out of respect for the crew, who became nervous when she sparked. They had seen her abilities but had a healthy fear of fire on the ship in the middle of the ocean. Their sense of self-preservation was deeply entrenched and something she respected.

She found a way to make them feel safer by replacing their lanterns with globes that glowed brightly but would not catch fire. Ilia discovered that if she put the globes in place they would glow for days until put out. She suspected that if they were glowing after she was no longer aboard the ship they would continue glowing until put out. The knowledge of being able to provide such a contribution to the crew who had so readily accepted her and accommodated her presence made her feel as though she was able to give back a bit.

*

Tristan spent the rest of his day sequestered with Edmond, going over their plans for once they had deposited Ilia at Marauder's Isle. He said little to Ilia about where they were headed when she came into the picture. She knew it was dangerous, but everything they did had an element of danger to it. He left much of the planning to Edmond, as Edmond's navigational skills and map reading were unequaled.

Tristan knew they were behind schedule taking Ilia to the Isle, but Edmond pointed out that they made good time, and since they had not been hindered by the storm, thanks to Ilia, they would be closer to their timeline than they imagined.

"We can meet the Germain here," Edmond said, pointing to a spot on the map that showed open sea in between two bodies of land. "They will have made port at La'Janne and will have the cargo. It's a bit further up the alley." He pointed to the body of water between the two land masses. "But not much. And this spot is a bit more open than where we were originally going to board them. That will give us space to maneuver out quickly. It will be tricky, as I know you like less room for movement when we are doing something like this, but I think we can do it relatively easily."

Tristan looked at the map where Edmond was pointing, listening attentively to his captain. After a moment he said, "Yes. We will have to be on our toes so we do not allow them to maneuver away from us, but I agree, it should still be relatively easy. We are not taking all their cargo anyway."

Edmond nodded. "We slide up next to them in the dead of night. Climb up onto the ship, subdue their lookouts and send Nicola in to get the loot. Then back to the ship and on our way." Nicola had one job on their excursions. He had a nose for locating loot like no other.

Tristan and Edmond looked at each other and grinned. Tristan said what they were both thinking, "But then, when have things ever gone as they were supposed to?" He clapped Edmond on the shoulder, then seeing the look on Edmond's face said, "What?"

Edmond stood up, moving away from the large map spread out on the table. "Ilia is an extraordinary creature."

Tristan eyed Edmond. "Yes…?"

Edmond shrugged, "I was just thinking it is a good thing we are dropping her at Marauder's Isle."

Tristan gave a grunt of impatience. "Ed, subtlety has never looked overly good on you."

Edmond brightened. "Well, I was just thinking that if we were to have Ilia with us on a regular basis, it would open us up to a lot of attention, and it may not be too long before we were less the ones procuring treasure and more the ones with the treasure – being pursued."

"Edmond. I'm not going to spend my life without my wife," Tristan said, seeing where Edmond was heading.

Edmond waved a hand in dismissal. "I know Tris. I just didn't realize until the night of the storm how powerful a being she is. I understand better what happened in Portsmith, and I don't suppose for a moment whoever was hunting her then will stop until they have her."

Tristan nodded agreement, relaxing a bit. He ran a hand through the top of his hair. "I know. I haven't really talked to her about this. We just haven't had time. I guess I have been looking to the immediate. I need to get her to the Isle. I know she will be safe there, but after we finish this job, then what? I guess I haven't approached it with her because I simply don't know. This is new for all of us."

Edmond's face registered agreement. "Based on what I have seen, Ilia can take care of herself. I'm just worried about the crew. They didn't sign up for a war, and make no mistake, this will be a war, and you both will have to wipe out the enemy in order to have any chance at peace and to not have to live your lives on the Isle."

Tristan nodded, "I know. We have a little time yet. I will talk to her." With that he left the room. Edmond stared ahead for a moment, thinking about what might lie ahead of them on the horizon, then leaned back over the map to put his mind back onto their immediate task.

Eleven

It was the full moon. Ilia was excited all day, feeling the anticipation of it building within her. By the time the moon showed its lovely full shape, she was fairly dancing in excitement. She knew the crew would be watching her. By now they knew her connection to the moon, and while she did not see any of them except Edmond and Tristan, she knew they were watching.

If she felt self-conscious, she did not show it. Ilia's movements across the upper deck of the ship were less like footsteps and more like a glide. She stood in front of the gigantic globe consuming most of the sky as she raised her arms, her body beginning to shimmer and glow. She did not dance. She raised her hands to the sky and began to spider her fingers toward her as though inviting the moon to come closer.

Edmond moved to stand next to Tristan as they watched tendrils cascade from the moonlight and move toward her grasping fingers. She pulled the tendrils to her, taking more and more from the moonlight, as they spun around about her. The more she pulled, the more they circled around her, whirling in thin wisps.

Ilia walked across the deck to a pile of material, the torn sail from the night of the storm. Ilia moved over the long tear in the sail, pulling the tendrils with her, moving her fingers expertly in a dance that sent the moonspun weaving in and out of the material. Ilia worked the moonspun for some time until it had all detached from her body and was imbedded in the sail.

She walked back over and began the ritual all over again until she could carry no more, then went back to the sail to go through the entire process again. She continued the sequence throughout the night until the massive sail had been repaired with the moonspun.

Just before dawn, Ilia stood in front of the moon, swaying and moving in its embrace. She had finished her task and had just enough time to refill her energies and bathe in the moonlight. She danced and lifted her arms joyously to the light and energy it provided.

Tristan and Edmond remained riveted to the spot the majority of the night, utterly entranced by what they were seeing. As the dawn's first rays broke the sky, the trance was broken, and Ilia was walking toward them, her skin still glowing, the air around her shimmering. She collided with Tristan and leaned into his arms, kissing him deeply.

"The sail is fixed. It will never tear again no matter the pressure or how bad the storm," she said, smiling over at Edmond from within the circle of Tristan's arms. "It will shine in the dark night though, so if you are trying to sneak up on someone, maybe lower it." She knew how difficult it was to get sails fixed, and she had been planning for some time to spend her last full moon on the ship fixing the sail.

"Lass! What you have done is extraordinary!" Edmond cried.

"This is my home. You all. All of you are my family. I wanted to contribute to this life I have been so fortunate to become a part of."

She tilted her head and looked up at Tristan, who had not said a word. He kissed her gently and said, "I love you, lass."

Her eyes widened and she said, "For all the years I live, my heart will belong to no one but you." This was a monumental statement, for she knew she would long outlive him.

*

"Ilia, lass. We need to talk about some things." Tristan was lying in bed watching Ilia go through her morning ablutions. He enjoyed watching her graceful movements as she tidied up the room, stacking clothes to be laundered, folding those which were still clean, placing hers in the large trunk Dickon brought to her on the first day, and placing Tristan's in the wardrobe.

She looked over at him and smiled. Her heart flipped over. He was bare from the waist up, his tanned arms and chest bulging with muscles obtained from the physical labor of working on a ship. His chest had a thatch of dark hair, and the large anemone anchor tattoo on his chest stood out in the morning light. His dark hair, long and disheveled as usual, fell about his shoulders. His face was chiseled, tanned, and outlined with a closely cropped beard. Those mossy green eyes looked out at her, seeming to know what she was thinking, and his full lips curved into a lopsided smile.

"Keep looking at me like that," he drawled, "and we will get no further than this bed today."

Ilia giggled, drawing closer to the bed. "And how is that a bad thing?" she asked, climbing up onto the bed and into his arms. His mouth covered hers as he rolled over with her in his arms so that she was on her back, her arms around his neck.

He broke gently from her kiss. "Ilia, we need a plan for down the road."

"How far down the road?" she asked, her fingers moving across his brow to sweep his hair away from his face.

"Well, we know you will be on the Isle, and I will go do this job. But then what? What do you have in mind for the future? We have a serious threat from those who kidnapped you, and I always have people chasing after me."

Ilia pulled away and sat up on the bed, her legs crossed. She looked pensive as she fiddled with the fringe on the blanket. Tristan was looking at her profile and knew she didn't like to talk about what had happened. He didn't like to push her, but they had to come up with even a loose plan for the immediate future. Edmond's words rang in Tristan's head, and he knew that Edmond was right. They couldn't have her on the ship without the rest of the crew understanding the cost to them, and Tristan did not want to leave her alone on the Isle indefinitely.

He reached out and touched the creamy white skin of her shoulder, running his hand down, across her back to her waist. He gripped her there and pulled her back to him. She turned to face him then leaned in to give him a soft kiss, as she lay next to him, her skin flush with his.

"I know you have something to say. Don't try to find a way. Just say it. We can have nothing between us left unsaid, Tristan. We have too much uncertainty around us."

He inhaled and closed his eyes for a moment. "Okay. Here it is. If I put you back on the ship, the kind of power you have, and just the kind of unique person you are, will bring every hunter running to us to take a stab at getting ahold of you." He silenced her response by responding hurriedly, "I know. But it's not just about you and me. I have an entire crew who would be at risk, and they did not sign up for what you and I have signed up for."

He stopped for a moment then plunged on. "I love you, Ilia. You and I are bound for life, and that brand binds everyone else on this ship to you as well, but I cannot ask them to take on something they know nothing about."

"I know," she said quietly. "I would not want that for them."

"But I also will not leave you on the Isle indefinitely, and certainly not without me." He pulled her even closer, tucking her head under his chin. "So, we need to think about what we want, what we must do, and how we can achieve both."

She lay still for a moment, contemplating. "Well," she began, tentatively. "I need to find out about my lineage. I need to know if there is anyone else out there like me. I have been alive for nearly 150 years, and yet I know nothing of my immediate origins. I need to know what there is to know."

Tristan waited for a moment to see if she was going to continue and when she didn't, he said, "I expect you will be on the island a few months."

Ilia pulled back, her eyes widening "A few months? Why so long?"

Tristan shifted uncomfortably under her scrutiny. "Well, what we do is not an easy process, because we do it in a way that can't be traced back to us. Yes, I have a reputation, but other than Portsmith, I, me, the physical being is not associated with my name. I am, in most ports considered a gentleman tradesman, and I worked very hard to keep it that way for the protection of my crew and their families."

"You mean their families are not on Marauder's Isle?" she asked, taken aback.

"Ilia, the Isle is not a place to live a life forever unless you are from there and understand how it functions. Most of my crew have families all over the place, and the reason they do not have to take refuge on the Isle is because of how I handle what we do."

Ilia nodded in understanding.

"So, we have a job. It takes time to implement and do the job. Then we have to lay low for a while. But that doesn't mean we hide. That would draw attention. We are seen here and there carrying on with our lives. Then after things settle a bit, we fence what we need to, and that is done in various ports where we have contacts, which also takes time. This particular job has a specific object that needs to be obtained, but we will also loot the ship, as that is part of what we do and what pays the crew. It also helps with restocking this ship, thought with this particular job, what we take will be minimal. I don't want to prolong our time onboard with this situation."

He paused to sit up running a hand through the top of his hair. "So that is why it takes so long. I can't alter this process, as it would endanger us all. I am only hopeful I didn't draw too much attention to our departure in Portsmith. And then there is the need to figure out who has been hunting us."

"You mean by bringing me on board? And why do you think you are being hunted?" she asked,

sitting up to face him.

"Well, yes. I think we are fine. I was very careful, and everything was on a 'need to know' basis, but it only takes one person noticing something and then talking to just the right person, to get the ball rolling. As to the other. After our last job, we fenced some heavy loot. That's why I was able to get so many repairs done on the ship, but apparently one of our fences was not very discreet and sold us out. What I need to find out is why we are being pursued now, after we have gotten rid of all the loot."

Ilia's eyes widened in surprise. "You mean a fence sold you out? What will you do to him?"

"We won't use him again," Tristan said matter-of-factly.

There was a pause for a few moments, then, "I'm sorry I made things so difficult for you." It dawned on Ilia, just how much she had compromised the ship by being on board.

"I would never have left you, lass. Not in a million years," he said, looking into her eyes, smiling.

Ilia gave him a tentative smile. "So, what do you think should be our next step? You come to get me, and then what?"

"Well, I think we need to look very closely at this group of individuals who are taking people of magikal ability and either syphoning their magik or selling them as slaves, and if we ever want any kind of life, we are going to have to dismantle them."

Ilia nodded. "Yes. I keep getting this feeling that my past lineage and this whole syndicate thing are somehow connected."

"You mean like your family may have been involved with the creation of the group?" His voice quickened as he warmed to his theory. "I mean, they were the reason this group started. The whole point was to find moon children to give them a place, right? Maybe somewhere along the line things changed, and instead of trying to find moon children to provide safety, it became about hunting them."

"Something like that" Ilia said. "I know this group hunt all kinds of magikal creatures, including your kind, in case you haven't thought of that."

Tristan shrugged. "There isn't much shape shifters have to offer. We do not really have power other than changing form. I suppose they might like to collect some of us, but I'm guessing the real draw for them are the truly powerful creatures, including moon children, who are rare."

Ilia contemplated her thoughts as they unfolded. "You know," she said finally, "I think they did not have a clue how powerful I was. They would not have damaged me so much had they known. I know they thought they were going to pull magik out of me by removing my scalp, but that is a very antiquated method, is not very successful in accomplishing its goal, and rather often, ends up killing the victim." She paused then said, "Trissa would have had no idea my power range. I was very closed with her."

They both sat in silence for a time, each contemplating what the road ahead might hold. At length Tristan reached over and pulled Ilia up against him, saying, "Whatever we have to do, we will do it together. I will finish the job then come get you, and we will find out about your lineage."

Ilia said, "It's not comprehensive, but it's a plan." She smiled and kissed him.

*

Two days later, the ship moved into a fog so thick one could cut it with a knife. It was late at night, and there was little moonlight. A storm was moving in and the waves were beginning to roll. The ship pulled up alongside an area of the Isle that had an inlet, and the crew began to ready the boat in which Tristan would take Ilia to shore.

Ilia and Tristan said their official goodbyes in private. She was standing on deck looking out towards where she knew the Isle awaited her. She wore her heavy wool cloak and the long simple shift she had worn when she boarded the Anemone. She carried the scarf and letter from Anna in a small satchel.

Tristan gave her a huge opal ring. The wooden coin he had for her would fit nicely on the underside of the ring so she would always have it with her. She did not wear it for fear of losing it somehow on their journey, but she put it in the satchel, which she wore slung across her torso.

Ilia said her goodbyes to the crew. She hugged Edmond, Red Rudy, Connor, and finally Dicken before turning to Tristan.

"Ready?" he asked.

Ilia nodded. No need to prolong things. The weather was getting worse by the moment.

Before they climbed into the boat, Tristan pulled the wooden coin from his pocket. "You will need this. Show this to Reed and he will take you to my home on the island. Don't try to go anywhere on that island without Reed at first. There are many traps you could get caught in."

Ilia nodded, pulling her hood up over her head. Tristan climbed into the boat and held out his hand to help her in. They sat down opposite of one another as they were being lowered. Ilia looked up and waved at Edmond and Rudy, who were watching the boat ratchet down.

Once they were in the water, Tristan began rowing toward what Ilia assumed was the shore or a dock. She could not see anything, but this was Tristan's home, and she trusted he knew exactly where he " was going.

The storm continued to increase its intensity and the waves began to get rougher and higher. Ilia reached out a hand on either side of her and closed her eyes. She pulled from the small sliver of moon peeping through the storm clouds and generated enough power to calm the waves along their path. Once she felt her power stabilize within her, she was able to open her eyes, while holding the waves at a calmer level. Tristan was looking at her, his eyes filled with emotion she could not identify.

"Your eyes are glowing that amber color they were the first time I watched you dance with the moon," he said, his arms keeping a steady rhythm as he rowed.

"Really? I didn't know it was that noticeable," she said in surprise.

"Aye lass. And when I came to save you from your captors. I thought I would wreak havoc, but it was you, even in your weakened state. You sat up in my arms, and you punished every one of them. I have never seen the like. And your eyes were so tawny bright, I was afraid they would blind me."

He smiled at her. "That was something to see, but I knew I loved you the night you danced with the full moon, and I watched you create a wholly different world than the one I'd known. I knew then I always wanted to be a part of your world and a part of you."

She looked at him with her amber-colored eyes, and tears welled up, causing them to glow even brighter. The tears crested and fell down her cheeks as she looked at the handsome brave man in front of her. She didn't know what to say, to tell him how very important to her he was, so she said, "I love you."

He smiled. "Come over here to me. We are almost there, and I can row and kiss you at the same time."

Ilia moved over to kneel in between his legs. She kissed him, and as she did, she felt the boat shift and knew they were where they needed to be for her to get out. Tristan loosed his hands from the oars and put them around her, kissing her deeply, ravaging her mouth, the only indication that he wasn't sure he could be without her. Ilia clung to him, taking him in.

She had no idea how long they were locked in the embrace, but a heavy movement of the boat signaled that the waves were increasing. Tristan released her, saying, "There should be what you need in the cave to get started. Reed can help you. His wife will be good to you as well. Once they all know you are mine, they will accept you. Things move of their own timing here, Ilia, so be patient."

Tristan stood, taking her hand as she stepped out of the boat and onto the pier.

She turned to look at him. "I will hold the storm as long as I can."

Tristan nodded, winked, and blew her a kiss. She smiled and blew one back.

"I will be back for you lass," he said, then sat down and began to row back out into the blackness.

Ilia stood for as long as she could, holding the waves down, and even after she pulled her power back from the sea, she stood looking out into its black depths, lamenting what it had just taken from her. She felt a great sadness, and the heavy yoke of loneliness settled once again upon her like a mantle. She had not worn it since before she'd met Tristan, and now he was gone.

Part Two

Twelve

Ilia leaned against the closed door. She would not fall apart. Not yet. She would go a bit further. She just needed to get herself some comfort. Then she would sleep. Sleep always helped.

It was pitch black, but the room introduced itself to her through the scent. She knew it had not been inhabited for a time, as she could smell the mustiness. She also smelled dampness, but not as much as one might expect from a house made of a boulder in the middle of the ocean, if one expected such a thing at all.

She stood for a minute longer, smelling a whiff of leather, something akin to lamp oil, wood, and a few other scents she could not identify. Then she raised her hand, held out her index finger and blew. A light sparked at the end of her finger, and as she blew, it grew into an orb. She carried the orb with her into the room that was really more of a cavern. She was chilled to the bone; her heavy woolen cloak was soaked, as it was only able to wick away so much moisture before surrendering. She had to get some warmth from somewhere. Maybe there was a fireplace. She held the orb in front of her as she moved away from the entrance.

Off to her left, Ilia noted there was a room of sorts. It was more or less a cut-out section in the rock formation, but it was big enough to house a roughly hewn small table, a couple of wooden benches, a cupboard, and a wood stove.

Ilia did not go further into the cave, as she knew fire was a necessity. She began to look around, hoping for wood stores. There was no way she would find any dry fodder for a fire outside. She moved further into the small chamber and discovered a lamp sitting on a counter that was carved out of the rock of the cave. She pulled the small glass globe away and blew on it lightly.

Sparks jumped from the globe and, like tiny homing pigeons, found the wick. The wick ignited, sending light across the small room, illuminating a cupboard area to the right of the rock counter with several bags of dried goods stacked inside. Below the cupboard was a basin set in a wooden stand with a cloth towel lying next to it. There was a small pump for water positioned behind the basin. Ilia wondered how the pump could produce anything other than salt water. Where would fresh water come from?

She walked over, raised the handle and pumped it a couple of times. The mechanism hesitated then spit out water. Ilia stuck a finger in it and tasted it. Salt water, as she suspected. No matter. She put her finger back in the water, holding it there. Ilia closed her eyes in concentration as her finger began to glow. She held it there for a few moments then pulled it from the water. She reached down to cup her hand in the pooled water and tasted. Perfect. No more salt. No problem for her.

After she quenched her thirst, she pulled the tiny cork plug at the bottom of the basin and watched the water drain out. What a luxury after many weeks aboard the Anemone.

She turned back to her mission to find wood for the cook stove. The stove stood across the small space from the rock counter. The counter, wash basin, and cook stove formed a small U in the room, and though it was quite compact, Ilia found it served its purpose more than she had imagined. She opened the door on the stove and observed there were no ashes for her to clean away. It was ready to go. She just needed wood.

Ilia didn't see any in the small kitchen dining area, so she moved from the nook into the larger room. The wall curved out into the main area, and she followed the curve with her hand. In her other hand she carried the orb, leaving the lantern alight in the kitchen. The cavern opened up into a long room/hallway.

Somewhere, water was falling. It echoed in the open cavern. She stepped fully around the curved wall and stood stock-still, her mouth open in wonderment. To the left of her was another tiny room. It had a stone sitting area carved out and there was water pouring from a hole high up in the top of the boulder. The hole was small and there were small trenches that water ran through until reaching half the distance to the ground where the trenches ended, and the water ran over carved-out shelves in the sides of the small chamber. An indoor shower.

Ilia reached her hand out and touched the droplets that rained down then once again tasted the water. Salt water. So, the water must come from the spray from the ocean hitting the boulder. The boulder was pointed and tall enough that significant amounts of water could not reach a hole in the top, so the room had to have its ceiling and opening on the side of the boulder.

The floor had a lip on the outside she nearly tripped on as she leaned in to look up to the top of the chamber, her globe illuminating the small room. The floor of the chamber had what looked like a tunnel built into it where the water pooled and went… where she did not know. Something to explore later, she thought. Her hands were shaking from cold and fatigue. She must find some warmth.

Ilia moved away from the small room and realized right next to the room was a large fireplace cut out of the rock. Two sources of heat then. She moved the orb in front of the fireplace to see better and found another lantern sitting on a roughly hewn mantle. She blew a few sparks from the orb and the wick caught.

More light showed a poker and a metal frame inside the fireplace for hanging a cooking pot. In front of the fireplace was a large animal hide; a soft and pleasant addition. On the other side of the fireplace was a large stack of wood with a box next to it that held kindling.

Ilia knelt, and with shaking hands, she took several pieces of wood and kindling. She stacked them in the fireplace then held the orb close to her face as she blew sparks from it onto the kindling. The sparks found their home and ignited quickly, soon catching the larger pieces of wood.

Ilia kneeled for a few moments on the large rug then unfastened her cloak, setting it aside. She felt the heat permeating her thin shift dress. There was a chair and a footstool directly behind her. The space was narrow, and she could easily lean back and make contact with the footstool, but she didn't. She just sat kneeling for some time, letting the heat penetrate her chilled bones. She held out her hands and let the warmth thaw her ice-cold fingertips.

At one point, it occurred to Ilia there was no smoke in the room. That meant the fireplace had a chimney. She tipped her head back to look up towards the top of the cave but could not see the top. The ceiling was swathed in darkness. Ilia realized she may never see the top of the cave, as the light of day would not play a factor. There were no windows.

She slowly stood up and walked to the back part of the cave, carrying the orb to light the way.

There wasn't much distance from the fireplace to the bulbous carved-out area. She saw a bed and a small table big enough for a lamp to rest upon. There was a lamp sitting on the table and she lit it as she had the other two lamps.

More light showed a small stand holding several books, and off to the left was a water closet. Ilia determined not to think about how and where the water closet refuse went. There was also a trunk at the foot of the bed, and Ilia moved to open it. Inside she found a couple of heavy blankets, a pair of men's breeches, and a few shirts. There was also a long length of soft cream-colored fabric, a pair of heavy wool socks, and a few miscellaneous items at the bottom of the trunk she didn't bother to identify.

Ilia took the socks, the soft material, and one of the blankets, then closed the trunk. She removed her satchel and deposited it on the floor by the bed. She gathered the items she pulled from the trunk and headed back towards the fire. The fire roared, and the cave was losing the damp chill.

Ilia moved to the shower room and stripped down, removing her soaked leather boots, placing them by the fire to dry. She did the same with her cloak and the thin shift dress she wore. When she was naked, she moved to the shower room carrying the orb. She set the orb on the stone floor and reached in to touch each ledge where water poured down. The shock of the cold water jarred her concentration for a moment, but she regained her composure quickly and closed her eyes, concentrating.

The ledges began to glow hot, and steam filled the small room. Ilia darted back to her satchel and pulled out her small bar of lavender-scented soap, then headed back to the shower room. She sat down on the stone seat and let the now-heated water and steam envelop her.

From her body, her face, and what was left of her hair Ilia washed away the day. The feeling of the water running over her was decadent. Gingerly, she washed her scalp where her hair had been ripped from her head, still hoping the hair would grow back.

When she was finished, Ilia climbed out of the shower, shivering in the open room. She grabbed the soft fabric, which smelled of herbs she could not identify, and wrapped it around her shivering frame then slipped on the socks.

There was a thought about food, but it left her as she looked at the fire and felt its warmth. She added more wood, stoked the flames, and grabbed the blanket. She lay down in front of the fire on the rug, wrapped in warmth and softness, and slept.

Thirteen

Ilia awoke disoriented, a state of panic fully consuming her. Irrational, unrelenting fear rose within her, and she found herself in a state of panic trying desperately to catch her breath. Somewhere in the waves of panic, she heard a small inner voice coming through the ocean of fear. "You are safe. You are safe. You are safe," it chanted over and over.

She knew where she was. She was in the safest place in the world. An impenetrable fortress of a refuge, and she was going to be okay. She waited for Tristan's arms to close around her as they so often did when she woke panicked, but they did not, and she remembered where she was. And where he was.

As her rational self began winning over the paranoid one, her breathing stabilized, and she became aware of her surroundings. She sat up and looked at the fire. There were coals. Enough to get the fire back up and going. She needed a game plan for the day. Nothing helped with being and feeling displaced more than structure.

Ilia crawled out of her blanketed cocoon on the fur rug and stoked the fire, adding a few more logs to it. She stood, wrapping the blanket around her shoulders. Food. She must have food. She went to the kitchen area and began assembling a fire in the cook stove. She rummaged about in a wooden box she had missed the night before and found an iron pot.

Shuffling to the sink, she pumped some water into the basin, enough for breakfast and to drink, implementing the same process she used before to purify the water. She drank deeply, using her hands as a cup, then decided to look around for a spoon or a cup to dish water into the pot.

On the wall next to the cook stove, Ilia found several different cooking utensils and a pewter cup hanging on hooks embedded in the wall. She took the cup and scooped water from the basin into the pot. Setting the pot on the stove to boil, she padded to the cupboard, hoping to find something to boil that would satisfy her hunger.

She found oats in a tin inside the cupboard. Ilia thanked her lucky stars. She was so weak from hunger, she could hardly function. It had been a full day since she had anything substantial to eat. She poured a good amount into the pot and waited for it to boil.

Ilia looked about for something to season the gruel and found a small container of salt, a jar of honey, and was surprised to find a small container of cinnamon sticks. She broke a stick into small pieces and dropped them into the pot along with a pinch of salt and poured some of the honey into the concoction.

As she waited for the gruel to boil, she strolled around the cave. When she noticed tapers placed in metal sconces along the cave walls, she held up her finger, blew on it, and brought forth a small globe of light. She blew on it again, pointing in the direction of one of the tapers on each side of the cave walls and watched as sparks flew, one spark to each taper all along the cave walls. The cave glowed warmly from the globes sitting on the tapers.

Ilia walked back to the stove and stirred the gruel. Just about right. She began to look around for something to use as a bowl. She reached inside the wooden box and pulled out a small tin bowl she had noticed earlier. This would do. She reached for a spoon hanging next to the stove and wrapped some of her blanket around the handle of the pot, as she picked it up and poured a scoop into the bowl. She set the pot on the rock counter and cradling her swaddled bowl, walked back to the fire to sit and eat.

Gruel was hardly a fine dining experience, but Ilia had never enjoyed it so much. She finished one bowl and went back for another, taking another deep drink of the water in the basin. Once her belly was full, she lay back down in front of the fire, wrapped in her blanket, and slept some more.

The next time she woke, Ilia did not have the panic to accompany her as she drifted into consciousness. She stoked the fire and added more wood, then went to stoke the fire in the kitchen, placed the gruel back on the stove, added water, more honey, and stirred while it heated. She ate the rest of the gruel right from the pot and then set about washing up the dishes.

Once everything was back in its respective place, she looked at the small canisters sitting on the counter and in the cupboard where she found tea. She pulled a small kettle from the wooden box containing cooking objects of that sort and set to work making tea.

As she sat drinking her tea before the fire, Ilia thought about Tristan. He had referred to the Isle as his home, but she could not imagine he felt it was his home in the true sense of the word. No, the Anemone was his home. This was just a stopping point for him. Her life was as much his as hers now. She would not be alive had it not been for him, and she could no longer think of a future without him in it. Her home, now, was with him wherever he was, and the Isle was just a stopping point for her as well. She could be here as long as was needed, knowing it was, as Tristan said, just a place of safety. He would come back for her.

Ilia stood up and wandered to the back of the cave, carrying the globe. She stood in front of the oval mirror situated above the shelf. She still held hope her hair would grow back. She was not a vain woman, but she did not want to spend the rest of her days half-bald.

Much of her hair from front to back had been hacked away with a knife. At first, it was about an inch in most places and between two and three inches in others. But her hair had grown during the time spent on the ship and was beginning to form ringlets as it gained more length. On the right side of her head, her hair was intact, curling in two silvery ringlets to her waist. Ilia went back to the kitchen and retrieved the knife she had seen among the items.

She took it with her back to the mirror and began hacking away the long ringlets on the right side of her head, working to make the side that hadn't been touched match the length of the rest of the hair on her head.

Ilia stood back and surveyed her handiwork. Better. Somehow having the length gone balanced out the section where she had no hair at all. Maybe it was just that there was no longer a reminder of how long it had been.

She stared at the woman in the mirror. She was healthy despite all that had occurred. Her time on the ship had won her back her health and helped her deal with the emotional trauma. The face she saw in the mirror looked almost elfin with her short hair curling along her hairline. Clear icy blue eyes rimmed with dark lashes stared back at her. Aside from the obvious, there was a change in her. She stared a bit longer, trying to pinpoint what it was, and then she realized the fragility was gone.

Whenever she had looked at herself in the mirror, she always felt she looked somehow breakable, like a crystal object that, if dropped, would shatter into a million pieces. That was gone. Ilia saw no more fragility, because she had already been dropped, and had discovered she was not made of crystal but of something much stronger. While there may be chips and dings, there was no breakage to be found. She smiled at herself in the mirror. She was seeing the new and improved Ilia. How ironic. That which was meant to break her and take from her had honed her and made her much, much stronger.

Ilia turned from the mirror and began to search for something to wear. She had very little with her. She did have money, though. Tristan made sure she was well-funded so that she could provide for herself. She managed to tuck a few items in her satchel, as well. She opened it up and pulled out a few pairs of undergarments and a couple of chemises.

She dumped the rest of the contents of her satchel onto the bed. There was the small bottle of bubble bath she had taken on impulse, along with the bottle of lotion. She brought items from Connor to use on her head. She also had the opal ring and the coin. She picked up the ring and slid the thin coin into the prongs on the bottom of the ring. It fit perfectly.

She slid the ring on her finger and looked at it.

The setting was simple, as it should be for such an enormous and stunning stone; a precious metal called Allendar. Ilia had heard of the metal but had never seen it and had certainly never thought of owning any of it, as it was rare and priceless.

Tristan picked the ring up many years ago when the Anemone still belonged to Bonny Anne. It was a thing different from any he had ever seen and from foreign lands he might never explore again. He kept it for years, thinking someday he might have someone he wanted to give it to.

Ilia admired it on her hand. The white metal was smooth and fitted the icy blues and greens of the opal beautifully. Both fitted the tone of Ilia's skin and though the opal was large, the setting was delicate enough to offset the size. It was substantial on Ilia's finger but not enough to look out of place there. She smiled. She felt as though, in having the ring, she had a piece of Tristan with her. In a time when things seemed dark, this was something bright and beautiful to remind her better times were on the horizon.

Ilia pulled on a pair of underpants and one of the chemises, then moved to put on the only other item she managed to get into her satchel, a pair of breeches just small enough for her. She discovered them in the trunk Edmond delivered to her room, and she could not resist shoving them into her satchel.

They were made of soft gray wool and fit her perfectly. She pulled them on, put on one of Tristan's shirts, tying a dark red sash she found in Tristan's trunk around her waist to cinch the shirt. She pulled up on the shirt to shorten the length and blouse it around her. Then she pulled on her boots and grabbed her cloak. She needed some sunlight. She would have to be careful to make sure she balanced the outside world with the overwhelming darkness of the cave.

As she approached the front door, Ilia experienced a moment of panic. Did she know how to get out of the cave? What if she could not? What if she was trapped forever? Would anyone come looking for her before Tristan did?

Ilia stilled and calmed herself. She knew what to do. Mr. Reed explained what to. She walked over to the doorway, which was almost unidentifiable, it blended in so well with the cave walls. Ilia put a hand up on the same side she had the previous night and pressed. The cave wall lit up around her hand, and there was a scraping sound as the wall doorway shifted.

It was mid-morning. The sunlight glistened off water that had given up its tantrum from the night before and was lapping calmly at the edges of the boulder and the rock stairway in front of it. Ilia's spirits lifted, as she beheld the sight. She looked down and noticed a large basket on the step in front of the cave's landing. She began to put a foot forward to moved forward to get the basket when she heard a voice, thick with Celtic brogue, say, "I'd be careful of those steps, miss. Do not be fooled by the calm waters on the surface. If you step but just a little to the side, you will be swept under. I wager young Tristan would not be happy about that."

Ilia shielded her eyes to see a woman with a wild mass of curly gray hair that rioted down about her shoulders. She had it pulled back, but the curls were trying to escape at every turn. The woman was short, had an extremely ample bosom, and was round everywhere that mattered. She was not provocative but gave the impression of solidness and comfort.

The woman was standing on the edge of the water, awaiting a response. When she did not get one, she began trekking her way back across the rock path that protruded out of the water with each step she made.

When she was half the distance to Ilia she paused, shielding her eyes from the glare of the sun to better see Ilia standing in the shadow of the large boulder. "I'm Mrs. Reed, though everyone calls me Molly. What's the matter lass? Cat got your tongue?"

It may have been the fact she called Ilia "lass" just as Tristan did, or maybe it had been a long time since she had been around a woman. Ilia looked at Molly and burst into tears, covering her face with her hands.

Molly quickly made her way to the landing saying, "There, there, lass. 'Twill be all right. You are safe now and in good hands." She pulled Ilia into her ample bosom and held her until Ilia had spent all her tears.

At length Ilia's sobs subsided to sniffles, and Molly said, "Ah. There you go, lass. Better?" Ilia nodded, pulling away and accepted the lace hankie Molly pulled from her pocket.

Ilia wiped her eyes and nose, stammering. "I'm so sorry. I don't know what came over me."

"I expect you have had quite a time of it, by the looks of you. It is natural to let down a bit when you are feeling safe," Molly responded, then exclaimed, "Good heavens! You are quite a stunning creature! I can see why our Tristan would be taken with you. I suspect there is a story there. Come. Let's get this basket inside, and you can tell me over tea and some homemade bread."

Ilia turned obediently to open the door. Molly had not asked to hear Ilia's story. She just gave the command that Ilia would share, and for homemade bread, Ilia would have made up a story if she did not already have one.

They went inside, and Molly lowered the basket onto the rock counter. She then went around the counter and began pulling items out of the basket. Once she unloaded it, she set it on the floor then began making tea. Ilia noticed she was completely at home in Tristan's cave. The knowledge of that was somehow comforting to Ilia. Someone else knew Tristan and the life he had there.

"I see you found a way to purify the water," Molly motioned to the full kettle.

Ilia nodded but did not elaborate.

"That is a good thing. It will save you having to come into the village on a regular basis if you've a mind to be more isolated."

Molly stirred the coals in the cook stove and added another piece of wood from the floor next to the stove. "You will be needing more wood though. It helps keep this place warm and drives the dank from it. I will have my Wil see to that for you."

"I don't want to be any trouble," Ilia said, finding her tongue.

"Oh lass! No bother a 'tall! We are just so happy our Tristan has found someone he values so much, and from the looks of that ring, you are his wife!"

Ilia blushed, smiling at Molly. "Yes. It was sudden, but it was more than circumstances that brought us together."

Molly nodded, as she continued to prepare their tea. "I am glad to hear that. Sometimes things happen that force two people together, and they make the best of it, but it is not ideal. I am happy to hear that for the two of you, there is more." Molly paused, turning to pull the kettle from the stove and pour two cups of tea.

As she did so, Ilia took advantage of the moment to look at what Molly brought in the basket. There was a full jar of honey, a loaf of bread, some kind of fruit muffins, some dried meat Ilia couldn't identify, more tea, dried apples, an assortment of berries, a jug of water, and a flask of what Ilia thought might just be rum.

"I'm so grateful to you for all of this," Ilia said, motioning to the bounty on the counter. "I wasn't sure what to do for food. I made some gruel, but I was not looking forward to eating it long-term." She allowed herself a smile.

"Oh, it is no problem at all. I had Wil haul it down for me this morning before he went to bed.

He is on night watch, so he sleeps a good part of the day."

"Have you always lived here?" Ilia asked, as she watched Molly set up a small smorgasbord of food.

"Yes. Wil and I met when we were just babes, but I always knew he was the one for me, and I reckon he knew the same about me." Molly smiled to herself. "He went away for a time to serve in the Water Armament, but he wasn't like so many others. He had seen enough of the world. He wanted to come home to continue the job that passed from one generation of his people to the next. And he wanted to come home to me." She raised her eyes to Ilia, her countenance beaming.

And who wouldn't want to go home to such a woman, Ilia thought. She was rosy and healthy, full of vibrancy and passion for life. There was something inherently sensual about her comfort with herself and life. Ilia suddenly felt a desire to be like this woman who was content to live the life she had and squeeze every bit out of it.

Ilia started when Molly said, "We have five sons, and all of them have moved off the island save one, our Joshua. He will be following in his father's footsteps. But enough about our dull lives. Our tea is about ready. There will be time for you to tell me your story, and I canna wait. I know by the looks of ye, it's going to be a doozy!"

Fourteen

Tristan stared out at the water. Ever since the night he took Ilia to the island, he felt a part of him missing. He made a great effort to not allow the impact of having his wife gone show, but Edmond had known him a long time.

"Commander, you aren't thinking of jumping, are you?" came Edmond's voice from behind Tristan.

"If I haven't jumped from being tied down with you all these years, it's unlikely I will do so now." Tristan turned and smiled at his captain.

He then asked, "Have you any news for me?"

"No, sir. So far so good." Edmond folded and unfolded his hands. "Sir, are you alright?"

Tristan clapped Edmond on the shoulder. "I'm fine Ed. I just wasn't used to having a wife. Then I got used to her, and now she is gone. I find I'm not adjusting so well as I had hoped."

"Well, Ms. Ilia is not like any other woman I have met. And if it's any consolation to you, the crew are all rather mopey. It is like she brought her magik with her and covered us all in it, changing the color of everything, and now that she is gone it is back to gray. I confess I feel it as well, Sir." Edmond gulped almost imperceptibly.

"Thank you, Ed. I am hopeful we can wrap things up quickly and go get her."

"What then? Edmond asked.

Tristan's brow creased with lines of worry as he gazed back over the ocean. "Things are never so simple with people as they are just sailing the seas, Ed. I expect we will have to make some decisions as a crew. I have an obligation to find this network that is hunting Ilia and end it. It is not just an obligation for her but for all magikal creatures." He looked directly at Edmond. "Creatures like me."

Tristan turned his gaze once more to the ocean. "But I would never ask such a thing of my crew. I have no idea how far or deep this thing goes." Another pause. "And then there is the matter we have had dogging us since our last job. Someone is very interested in us, and it is not in a good way. I need to identify and nullify that situation as well."

"Sir, I can't speak for the crew, but I'm willing to wager, they will be with you in all things. They are invested in all of this as well; not just in you but for their families. Many of them have magikal creatures in their lives as well." Edmond responded.

"Well, we shall soon see. I want to get this job completed, and I need to focus on it. The jobs that appear cut and dried always seem to be the ones that get messy. I want to hit hard and fast and be done for a while. We don't need anything else on our proverbial plate right now."

They stood in silence for a time then Edmond said, "Sir, once this is all over, whatever 'this' ends up being, do you think you will give up the Anemone?"

Tristan was silent for a moment then said, "I don't know. I doubt it, Edmond. You saw her on this ship. She took to the life like a fish to water. I don't think Ilia will want to, but again there's the crew to consider." He turned and looked at Edmond. "And you."

“Me?” Edmond’s eyebrows rose.

“Yes you, you dolt. You have been my right-hand man for our whole lives. Don’t you want more? You sure as hell deserve more.”

“Maybe. One day. I have my plans. But, as you say, there are things to take care of first. Once that is done. I will take a moment to think about what I want. And maybe there will be some woman, somewhere, who is worth changing my life for, but that hasn’t happened yet. So, until then, I remain your right-hand man, and I’m the better for it.”

*

Two days later they reached the Germain. It was the middle of the night, and thankfully the moon was covered in clouds, so they could not be easily detected as they slid in beside the big ship. The job was unique, as they were only obtaining one item, a large golden egg. The egg had been stolen from the man who’d hired Tristan, and the man spent years hunting it down until he traced it to the Germain.

“Seems like a lot of hassle for one golden egg,” Edmond had commented.

“I know it’s quite large, and I expect it’s not solid,” was Tristan’s cryptic response.

“You mean there is something inside it?” Edmond asked.

“I can guarantee it,” Tristan answered.

“Like what?” Edmond asked.

“How about a very large diamond?” Tristan said, more as an answer than a question.

Edmond whistled. “That makes much more sense.”

Tristan nodded. “There is no angle that I can find. We have done other jobs for Neeman, and it has all been above board. Other than the fact he is not telling us exactly what we are obtaining, I have no reason to believe the job is anything other than what it appears.”

As the grappling hooks went into the side of the boat, Tristan stood waiting for Nicola, who materialized from the shadows, as though he was part of them. His role on the ship was specific. Nicola was a Camelox, a magikal creature who could sense treasure. He was especially equipped to blend in with his environment, whatever it might be. He had a human form, but when he wanted to blend in, he could change his appearance just like a chameleon.

Camelox made treasure hunting much easier and safer, as they easily identified the best treasure and were able to retrieve it quickly and fleetly. The crew on the Anemone kept Nicola's Camelox identity a secret, as his kind were incredibly valuable in the pirating world. The crew were sworn to secrecy and divulging his existence to anyone meant death. Tristan had not even told Ilia that Nicola was a Camelox.

Tristan met Nicola right after inheriting the Anemone. They were in the Borgeous Islands. The islands were a favorite stomping ground of Bonny Anne, and they often picked up lucrative jobs there. They were in the island town of Traipsana gathering supplies and taking a break before heading back out to sea when Tristan, Edmond, and Red Rudy encountered a skirmish in the town square.

Often those who dealt in slave trading gathered in the island towns and sold their human and magikal creatures, just as any merchant sells wares. Tristan had just come out of the local hotel where he'd had a bath, a shave, and his clothes cleaned, when he noticed a young man being dragged into the square. He had a noose around his neck, and the big burly man hauling him was yelling, "Change ya bastard! Show them what ya are!"

The young man was not complying, and Tristan could see the burly man was fully bent on strangling the young man to death if he did not obey.

Tristan stepped out into the street. "I do not hold with slavery for any reason," he began, "but putting my personal views aside, you do realize you are about to strangle your merchandise to death, don't you?" Tristan was still holding the coffee cup in his hand, his cutlass at his waist, as he calmly drew closer to the big man.

"If you aren't here to buy this ridiculous beast, shut your mouth!" the big man snarled. "And get out of the way." The man yanked on the rope again, and the young man sprawled in the dirt, choking, his face turning purple as he tugged at the noose.

Tristan could see it would only be moments before the lad expired. "Let him go, and I will talk to you about price."

The man sneered. "You couldn't afford him – pirate. He's a Camelox, and well out of your price range. Now mind your business or I will give you the beating of your life!"

Tristan didn't bat an eye at the threat. "Seems to me, he is just a lad you are choking to death. I see no indication he is such a magikal creature. I suggest you take my money for a crew hand before he dies, and you get nothing for him at all. No one around here will pay for a carcass."

"He's a Camelox, damn you! I have had enough of ya!" The big man dropped the rope, and

Nicola was able, finally, to draw in a breath as he lay in the dirt gasping and pulling at the rope.

Tristan watched the man come toward him, took the last swallow from his cup, tipped it sideways and hurled it with lightning speed at the man mid-advance. The cup hit the man in the throat, causing him to fall backward, grabbing his throat as he gasped for air.

Tristan was on him in a flash, extending a sweeping kick that hit him in the head so hard the "Thwak!" reverberated in the square. The big man crumpled to his knees then fell face-first into the dirt. Tristan stepped over to him, pulled out coinage and held it up to the crowd gathering in the square. "See this? I am paying this idiot 50 senta, which is the going rate for a servant lad." Tristan dropped the money on the ground next to the slaver and went over to the young man.

He held out a hand assisting the young man from the ground, then took the rope from around his neck. "You are free to go, lad. You may join us, or you may go on your way, but I would suggest you get as far away from this town as possible." Tristan turned and walked away.

The young man followed Tristan back to Edmond and Rudy. "I would work to pay you back the 50 senta you paid for my life, sir," he said.

"You owe me nothing, and don't ever let anyone tell you what your life is worth." Tristan eyed the young man. "Have you a place to go?"

The young man shook his head, "No. I was sleeping in the barn, when that man and some others snuck up on me. I can hold my own in a fight, but they got the noose around me before I could even get fully awake."

Tristan noticed the youth was well-spoken. "What is your name?"

"Nicola. I need work, and I would just as well throw my lot in with you as anyone else. I at least know you won't kill me, as you paid 50 senta for my hide." He mustered a lopsided smile.

"Well Nicola, you will need to read and sign a contract before you can join our crew, and we will need to get you cleaned up before you get on board."

Nicola had been living rough, that much was clear. He nodded "Yes, sir. I know what ship you have. I have been watching the ports. You have the Anemone. You are the Lord Pirate."

Tristan looked at him in surprise. "Yes. Well, let's not bandy that about, shall we? I have my own enemies whom I would just as soon not alert to my presence."

Rudy snorted. "Too late for that. Everyone and their brother will be talking about what just happened. We best get out of here. Where shall we take him to get cleaned up, Commander?"

Tristan gave Rudy an indulgent smile. "Take him to Lou's. She is discreet and will give him some clothes. Tell her we are on the move."

Rudy nodded and motioned to Nicola. Nicola followed, and Edmond brought up the rear. Tristan left them to quickly finish his business.

Once on board the ship, Nicola was taken to Tristan's cabin and presented with the contract.

Edmond and Rudy followed him in and shut the door.

"Can you read?" Tristan asked, and at Nicola's nod he said, "Read this, and before you sign, all secrets are revealed here. Do you understand? I will not have anyone on board my ship with secrets. It's deceitful to those who have your back, and if you have special skills, we will need to make use of them. Make your decision now."

Nicola stood for a moment, weighing the options, then he said, "I would show you." He suddenly turned from a young man wearing the attire of a crewman to attire that blended in perfectly with the room. The three men gasped. Nicola literally blended in with the colors of the room. A few seconds later he resumed his previous appearance.

"I am also adept in martial arts. Very impressive snap kick, by the way," Nicola said, smiling at Tristan.

"So, you *are* a Camelox," Tristan said. "Excellent. In the spirit of full disclosure, I will show you my special skill." And without any other explanation, Tristan transformed into an enormous eagle.

Nicola's eyes widened. Rudy and Edmond leaned against the wall; arms crossed at their chests.

"Usually, he is a wolf, but he is so big there isn't room here. Plus, the wolf is not very polite," Edmond said, grinning at Nicola's gaping mouth.

Tristan transformed back to his original form, taking a moment to regain his composure. "So," he said, "now we know one another's secrets. I do believe you will be a very helpful addition to what we want to achieve on the Anemone."

Nicola signed the contract.

The lad had been with Tristan and the Anemone ever since. He found a family with the crew, and somewhere in those years, Nicola met and married Meridee. They lived on Marauder's Isle. Tristan saw they were situated in the village where Meridee could never be used as leverage against her extremely valuable and unique husband. She had given birth in the last year to a baby girl they named Trista in honor of her godfather, Tristan.

*

The ships were hooked together. Tristan waited as Nicola moved across the ropes like a monkey. Once on the ship, Tristan lost sight of him as he changed to reflect his environment. It was several minutes before Nicola emerged, moving a bit slower. He was no doubt carrying a fair amount of loot on him, as the clothing he was wearing had special pockets for him to put items in and still be able to use his hands. To carry a bag would mean Nicola could change, but not the bag, and that would look odd. So, they had devised a special suit with pockets.

Tristan watched as Nicola moved back over the ropes and came back on board the ship. The crew silently cut the ropes loose from the Anemone and moved stealthily by the Germain. Tristan heaved a sigh of relief as they left the ship behind. There had been so many issues of late, that he had almost dreaded the job. But all was well. Tristan turned to follow Nicola to his own quarters, where Edmond joined them.

Once in the room, Nicola opened his pockets and spilled the contents onto the table. They decided that, for this job, they would not loot food and other wares. They were fine at present, and Tristan had an overwhelming desire to get in and get out of the job. There was just something deep down telling him it could seriously go wrong if they tried to take their usual loot. His feral side had a sense for trouble, and he never ignored it.

As he stood looking at the items on the table, he had a sinking feeling in the pit of his stomach. The treasure Nicola had procured was, in fact, real treasure, but the kind that was difficult to fence. Tristan would have to go quite some distance to be able to fence the items and get a worthy price. The egg was one thing. That was already accounted for in terms of reward, but the rest would need a special place, and that meant another long trip across seas to get the payout.

There were two large rubies the size of a child's fist. There were two emeralds and two sapphires the same size. There was a large pearl the size of a sparrow egg, and several handfuls of smaller diamonds.

"Not exactly easy to fence, Commander, but it was all together, and I couldn't leave it," Nicola remarked.

"You did well, Nicola. It is just the way things go. I'm certainly not disappointed in what you brought back. This is a fortune. We could all retire on this. We just need to get it off the ship as soon as possible if we can't fence it right away, and I think we need a break before we take on such a long journey. Maybe we can put it on Marauder's Isle until we are ready. I just don't want it sitting here. It makes us a target if word gets out."

Tristan and Edmond discussed later that night what their game plan would be. Tristan generally included Edmond in major decisions. The man had sound judgment, and Tristan learned long ago that the best decisions a leader could make often included the advice of others.

"I think maybe we should fence the diamonds," Edmond suggested. "They are small enough and usual enough to offload."

Tristan nodded. "I keep getting this feeling that we need to do some moving around before we deliver this egg. I wonder if we should offload these diamonds, as you say. Easy enough. Then head to the Isle, drop off the bigger jewels, and then head out to offload this egg. If we are being followed, we will lose them at Marauder's Isle in the mists. I think I will leave Nicola there. He has a new baby he should be able to see."

Edmond agreed and went to give directions to the crew. Tristan sat for some time thinking about why he felt so uneasy about the job. It wasn't that it was too easy. Having Nicola on board made most of their jobs easy. That was one of the reasons he didn't want Nicola on board all the time. He was as valuable a bounty as any, and while having him was an asset, it also put them at greater risk if anyone knew what Nicola truly was. That was one of the reasons Tristan made it very clear that if anyone divulged what Nicola was to anyone on the outside, their lives would be forfeited.

Tristan sat at his desk looking out the window into the darkness. The moon was peeping through the clouds, and as so often happened these days when he saw the moon, his thoughts moved to his wife. He wondered what she was doing. Was she out dancing in the moonlight? Was she pulling moonspun from the sky and glowing like a beacon? He felt his heart clinch. He missed her; missed her cheerful greeting in the morning. He missed her dancing in the moonlight. He missed their conversations. He missed her in his bed. He kept busy, and there was plenty to do to keep his mind off her, but she was never far from his thoughts.

He sighed, then caught himself. He didn't sigh. When had that started? He pulled back from the window and went to the door of his cabin. Maybe it was a good night for rum. He opened the door and headed below deck to find Rudy.

Fifteen

It took a couple of days for Ilia to conquer the floating steps to the cave. It was more a fear component than anything. Once she realized they would appear for her because they somehow recognized who she was, she quit worrying. The days were often rainy and full of mist on the Isle, but there had been a few days of sunshine, and while the mist never moved away from the outer edges of the Isle, in the interior, there was sunshine, and Ilia spent those days beach combing for shells and smooth rocks. Oftentimes she just sat on the sandy shore and watched the water move in and out and the birds diving and swooping for fish.

Molly showed Ilia how to scavenge along the seashore and gather scallops, clams, crabs, and mussels. They built a fire right on the beach, and Molly taught Ilia how to clean, cook, and eat all that she gathered. Ilia couldn't remember a time when she had enjoyed herself more. She felt she was beginning to adapt to her new life, and Molly was becoming a true friend.

A couple of weeks after Ilia had arrived at the Isle, Molly took her into the village. They brought with them a bucket of crabs they gathered. Molly explained Ilia could use them as barter for things she needed. Money wasn't always in demand, but seafood was always an item that could be bartered.

The village was situated in the interior of the island. The dunes on the island kept it from being seen by those on the shoreline. It was nestled covertly in a copse of trees serving not only as shade but as a shield from the ocean winds. There was no fog in the village, a fact Ilia did not miss. Anyone who made it past the fog most likely had a right to be there.

The village had cottages that were simple but durable, made of stone with thatched roofs. Most were one-to-two-bedroom cottages, but there were a few larger cottages with three or four bedrooms. The path from the beach wound over the dune, down an embankment, and straight into the main street of the village. At the front of the village were eight houses, two rows right off the road on either side of the main street and two on either side of the road behind the first row of houses.

As they moved into the village Ilia noticed a general store, a shipping building, a tavern, a smithy, a fishmonger's, and a workshop. The villagers had their wares out in front of their stores, and Ilia was fascinated with all the goods they had to sell. There were houses back behind the main street stores, and at the end of the main street there was a church, surrounded by houses. The village was clean and bright, seemingly untouched by all the elements that inhabited the shoreline.

Molly introduced Ilia to the merchants selling their wares. She was introduced as Tristan's wife, and while they seemed curious about the woman Tristan had married, they were polite and welcoming. Many were distracted by Anna's scarf, which Ilia wore around her head, often coming around their stalls to comment on the material and to touch the iridescent fibers – wondering where the material to make such a thing had come from.

"It's moonspun," Ilia replied. "I'm a moon child, and we are taught from an early age to pull moonspun." The villagers were amazed to find a moon child in their midst, and Ilia saw their estimation of her go up. She smiled to herself. It was the first time in her life that being a moon child elicited such a positive reaction from a group of people.

Ilia strolled through the village, trading her fare for some new garments to wear, as well as some wood for her stove. She had been gathering driftwood, but what she bartered for was already cut and ready to be burned, and the delivery was included in the price.

Molly took Ilia through the village and past the church, out a bit farther to a larger stone house with a fence around it. There were flowers of various colors growing around the house and chickens mulling about the yard.

"You have chickens?" Ilia asked. "However did you manage chickens here?"

Molly smiled. "You forget we have a lot of access to pirate ships, love. We probably have better options than most towns you visit, as a lot of the people who stay in the caves are from ships with all kinds of wares. They offer their goods for their stay."

Molly took Ilia through the yard and into her house. The house had a large picture window in the front filled with plate glass, yet another offering of a wayward soul staying on the island. The picture window faced the dunes and gave a lovely view of the grasses and rolling seascape leading in the direction of the beach. The sitting room was open, light, and airy with a large stone fireplace against one wall.

There was a couch and two chairs with a long squatty table in the middle. The couch and chairs were covered in neutral colors of tan and cream, with soft light blue woolen throws on each seating area. There were what appeared to be lamps hanging throughout the room, but Ilia knew after her first encounter with Reed, that they were resting spots for globes. She wondered how he managed to create the globes. He must have some magik to be able to conjure light, but she did not be comfortable in asking.

Molly led Ilia through the house and down a hallway. Off to the left were two rooms, one a bathroom, and the other a bedroom. Off to the right was another bedroom. They continued down the hall to the back of the house, which was where Molly spent most of her time-the kitchen and dining area. The space was one large room opening out to a back patio. The walls of the house opened up to allow an alfresco experience and could be shut during the winter months or during stormy days.

"This is an amazing space," Ilia marveled.

Molly beamed. "Thank you. It was my design. I have a stone oven outside and a cook stove inside. I wanted to have nature as much a part of what I make as possible, and when we have to close everything up, it still feels open.

I lived for a long time in a hut. It was terrible. Dark and dank. When we finally got a place to build, I knew what I wanted, and this is it!" she said, beaming as she gestured to her kitchen area.

Ilia sat down on a smooth rock stool in front of a counter, which also served as a place to eat in less formal times. She looked around the kitchen area. It was simple and spacious but also had everything Molly needed to create her culinary projects. Copper pots hung on one wall, just the height short little Molly needed.

"I wanted them in the middle of the kitchen, but Wil refused, as he said in order for me to reach them, he would be banging his head on them every time he came in the kitchen," Molly explained with a grin.

The dishes, including plates, bowls, and cups were on white shelves. They had little blue birds imprinted on the sides, and they gave the kitchen a lovely, beachy feel. The counter where Ilia sat curved around against the wall and a sink was situated down inside the rock. Ilia marveled at the masonry involved in creating a countertop from large rocks, no doubt dug from the shoreline, and then cut until they were flat. A hollow section was then created for a sink.

Molly noticed Ilia looking at the countertop. "Our nephew Mikael is a mason. When we built this house, he was just getting started in his business in the Bourgeous Islands, but he jumped at the chance to try his hand doing something like this. He did a fine job, and it was fascinating to watch. When all was said and done, it was exactly what I had in mind." Molly said, smiling. "But they are quite dark, so everything else had to be whitewashed and airy. Believe it or not, the most difficult part was getting wood for the inside of the house. We had to get it from one of the ships," she gestured toward the shoreline, "and it took some time to get enough." She paused for a moment then said, "But it was worth the wait!"

Ilia nodded in ready agreement. "I'd say! This is just beautiful!" The counter bottoms were made of smooth stones cemented together. On top, large black stones had been ground down until the tops were flat. They were smooth and shiny, creating the counter tops. The sink was also constructed from a large black stone that had been hollowed out, a hole cut through the center to drain water. A pump was stationed on one side of the sink, and seeing it, Ilia asked, "Is that fresh water or salt water?"

"Purified water," Molly said. "Come. I will show you what we do."

Ilia followed Molly out the entrance from the kitchen dining area onto the back terrace. The back yard was spacious and had green grass surrounding the stone patio area. They walked further from the house, and Ilia saw an area where there was a pump.

Near the pump was a large holding tank with a pipe running through it and over to another large clay container with a covered lid. There was a hole in the top of the lid, and the pipe covered the hole. The container sat on large flat rocks which were elevated above the ground enough to allow for a fire to burn under them.

"This is our distilling process," Molly explained. "Every house in the village has one, and we keep it going all day, every day. The water is heated as it goes through the pipe and is cooled in the holding tank while it is still moving through the pipe. It pours out of the pipe and into this jar." Molly pointed to a large pitcher sitting under the pipe. "We have to keep it going all the time or there will not be enough water. Then every day we pour the water from the pitcher into that container by the house and it pumps the water into the sink. It's not ideal, but fresh water is a necessity, and turning on a faucet to get it is a luxury I enjoy."

Ilia marveled at the ingenuity and said as much, to which Molly replied, "Well we can't quite manage the process you use." She grinned and headed away from the distiller.

As they strolled around the yard, Ilia enjoyed the soft, lush grass and trees spread out over the yard, creating a canopy of shelter from the hot sun. "It's so changeable, the weather here," she commented. "So much of the time it is misting rain and chilling to the bone, and then it changes to hot sun pounding down, bent on draining you dry."

Molly scanned the skies. "It is certainly more changeable in the interior of the island around the village. We have the benefit of a variety of weather patterns, but on the shoreline, it is mostly fog and rain, though you will get dry times but very little sun. That is due to the enchantment, I expect." She pointed off toward the shoreline, to what looked like a halo of low-lying clouds circling the island.

Ilia looked toward the shoreline. It was indeed a contrasting atmosphere inland to that of the shoreline. On the mainland, there seemed to be the possibility of some kind of normalcy, a life to be lived with love and community. She felt her spirits quicken when she was in the village. On the shore, in the caves, she found her spirits flagged. All was dark and dank with no light. She hadn't realized how low her spirits were until Molly brought her into the village.

Molly must have gleaned some of her thoughts because she said, "Are you unhappy in the cave, lass? I have no doubt it is somewhat oppressive."

Ilia looked up and smiled across at her. They were sitting on the grass in the backyard under a huge pincos tree. Pincos trees had lovely silver bark with light green leaves and produced the green pincos fruit. The fruit had a leathery outer jacket that could be peeled away to provide a luscious, sweet fruit with a little bit of tanginess, matching the color of the sky and tasting just as lovely. The branches of the trees spread out and drooped slightly with the fruit hanging towards their ends.

Molly reached up, gaining her knees for advantage, and plucked a piece of fruit. As she peeled it, revealing its juicy center, Ilia let her thoughts roll out.

"I do struggle," Ilia began, carefully. "I hadn't thought it bothered me so until you brought me here, and I realized just how much I have been missing beauty."

Molly nodded. "I can see it in you. You have perked up quite a bit this day." She paused for a moment concentrating on disposing of the last vestiges of the outer shell of the pincos fruit. She then split the fruit and handed half to Ilia, who bit into it with gusto and sighed with pleasure.

"I have something to show you, Ilia. I don't know what you and Tristan discussed in terms of where you would stay or how long even you would be here, but I want to show you anyway."

They finished the fruit, licking their fingers to free them from the stickiness of its juice. Molly stood and Ilia followed suit, walking behind her as the sturdy woman moved across the grassy backyard that was fenced with roughhewn logs. She looked at Molly's back, thinking just how very dedicated the woman was, and her family as well, to persevere in creating something so beautiful and personal as Molly's home.

They walked to a gate on the back side of the property, closest to the ocean. Molly opened it, allowing Ilia through, then closed it. As they walked on, approaching the dunes flanking the back of the house, Molly said again, "I'm not sure what you and Tristan discussed about you being here, but I want to show you something that might be a better place to stay if you are going to be here for some time. Tristan has only stayed in the caves for short periods. It is tolerable in the short-term but not for an extended stay." She looked, searchingly, at Ilia.

Ilia smiled back at her, saying nothing, as Molly turned to lead them on. They climbed up and over a small dune and dropped down onto the beach. There, a short distance in front of them, was a small cottage made of stone with a thatched roof. There was a fence around it containing what at one time looked to have been a beautiful garden but had become overgrown with a riot of flowers, ivy, and weeds.

The stone house was covered in ivy, and as they moved around from the back to the front, Ilia could see a gate sagging on its hinges. Molly pushed it forward, and it protested greatly at being moved. They walked through the mass of vegetation, and down the stone walk, which was barely visible through the overgrowth.

The house had two shuttered windows in front, walled with ivy. Ilia stood staring at the building, absorbing its presence. There was magik all over it, so powerful, and familiar to her. "What is this place?" she asked, turning to Molly, who moved forward to pull some of the ivy aside to reveal the window better, then tugged at a shutter and pried it open slightly.

Molly turned to look back at Ilia and gasped. "Ilia! You are glowing!"

Ilia looked down at her arms and then back at Molly. "This place has been lived in by someone incredibly powerful. The power is rolling from it like water off a duck's back."

Molly did not answer but moved to the door and pushed her weight into it as she turned the handle. The door came open grudgingly, reluctantly giving up its secrets. Molly motioned to Ilia who stood rooted to the spot, taking in the magik flowing around and over her.

Molly did not wait but went in, and Ilia soon followed. Even in the dim light, Ilia could see the cottage was perfect for her. It was round and open. In the middle of the big room was a large stone fireplace open toward the back, facing the kitchen and dining area for cooking, and open in the front for the sitting room to provide heat. There was a table on the right of the room towards the back. To the left, cupboards hung on the wall above wooden counters, between which sat a stone basin in the middle for water. There was a pump directly over the stone basin. The wood was in good shape considering the amount of moisture and salt coming in from the ocean not far away – another indication there was magik about.

Ilia noticed there were two smaller windows on the back wall of the house she had not seen before, as they were completely covered in ivy. The floors were stone and in good shape. The living room had a wooden rocking chair and several shelves with books in varying degrees of decay.

To the left of the circular room was a small hallway, and as Ilia moved down the hall, it was dark enough to require the small globe she conjured from her fingertips. Molly followed her without showing surprise at Ilia's use of magik.

At the end of the small hallway was a bedroom housing a brass bed, tarnished from years of neglect and the elements. There was a small window also covered in ivy, and a trunk at the foot of the bed, as well as a wardrobe. Everything was covered in a thick layer of dust.

They moved back through the house to the other side, where there was another small hallway. There was a room containing items for laundering, another stone sink with a pump, and a large copper tub, tarnished and covered in dust. There was a door leading out the side of the house, and Ilia found a privy just beyond it.

They were silent throughout the exploration, until they made their way back to the open living area. Ilia extinguished the globe with a flick of her wrist and said, "Molly, who owned this house? It is vibrating with magik, and by the looks of it, no one has lived here for some time."

"It was owned by a great sorceress, and when she died the house lay abandoned. Everyone was afraid to live in it. The magik has a mind of its own in this place, and it is strong. The ivy began to grow after she died, and this ivy on the house is not indigenous to the island." Molly shrugged. "But I thought you might be able to live in it. You are every bit as magikal as the sorceress."

At Ilia's surprised look, Molly smiled. "I can smell it on you. Oh yes, it has a smell. Earthy and old. Very old, but yours is different than hers. Yours smells like the sea and the sand after a lightning strike, but hers smelt of rich soil and green growing things; ancient and powerful."

Ilia stood, face upturned, looking around the house. She closed her eyes and reached out to see if it would welcome her. She let her magik fill her up and move out past her to touch the magik in the room. When Molly gave a muted cry, Ilia opened her eyes.

Ilia's magik danced about the room, a slivery swirl in the dim light. As they watched, a green wisp formed and moved tentatively about the room, circling the silver swirl, moving ever closer. The two colors twirled about each other in an ethereal dance then finally, after some minutes, they touched. A bright collision of energy exploded around them as they combined, continuing to swirl and dance. The colors coalesced into a silvery green that weaved and bobbed about the room.

Ilia felt the magik. Though it was foreign, there was something familiar and ancient about it that matched what she already knew about her power. The shape continued to move about the room, and as it did so, the ivy on the windows parted to let the sunlight through the windows.

On the outside of the building, the ivy pulled away from the doors and the weeds in the yard sank into the ground as grass emerged. Flowers sprang up all around the house, all colors, shapes, and species. Ilia went to stand in the open doorway and laughed with glee, clapping her hands together as the swirl continued to pull back an enchantment that held the house since the sorceress left it.

Finally, the swirl made its way to Ilia and shyly approached the outstretched hand she offered, then touched and disappeared into her fingertips. Ilia felt the surge of new power as it sank into her, finding a home with her magik.

Ilia turned to look at Molly who stood transfixed, mouth agape. Molly shook her head and muttered "I would never have believed it had I not seen it. I guess you have your answer."

Ilia grinned. "I guess I have. I think I best go back to the cave and bring my things here. I will also need to figure out what items I need to make this home." Home. Her home. The thought of it made her want to jump up and down with glee.

*

The next few days Ilia spent cleaning the little cottage. She intended to take only a few things from the cave, but at Molly's suggestion, she decided to bring most of the items from the cave to the cottage. This would be their home; hers and Tristan's. The cottage was well situated. No one could get onto the island from the side it faced, not only because of the enchantments protecting the isle but also the natural barriers. The beach wasn't as expansive on the cottage side, and it was layered with large rocks and the reef. No ship would be able to sneak in on that side of the island regardless of enchantments.

Ilia spent some of her time beach combing to find crabs and other creatures to barter for items she needed for the cottage. By the end of her first week there she managed to obtain a small table and a couple of mismatched chairs. Molly gave her an old rocking chair, and Reed found a couple of lads to help move the mattress, trunk, bookshelf, and wardrobe from the cave. Ilia made several trips to the cave to remove most of the contents in the kitchen, bedding, wood stock for the fire along with the poker, lamps, and the large fur rug.

Ilia stood looking at the nearly barren cave and hoped Tristan would not object. But then she reminded herself she was his wife. He told her his home was hers no matter where it was.

She smiled to herself. She had upgraded their home, and that should count for something.

As she made her way across the waterway between the cave and the shore, she breathed a sigh of relief. It was the last time she'd have to deal with those stone steps. She was always nervous when crossing them and couldn't blame the village lads who helped carry the furniture. They were scared to death of the cave, not only because of the mystique surrounding it but the very real peril of navigating the stone steps.

Ilia, Molly, and Reed had to trundle the furniture across the steps with a cart, and even then, moving the bulky items was both difficult and hair-raising for them. Once they cleared the water, the boys were willing to manhandle the furniture through the village and out to the cottage. But when they arrived, the boys balked at stepping foot near the cottage. So, once again, Ilia, Molly, and Reed maneuvered the items into the house, and through much grunting and many breaks, they got everything moved in.

That evening Ilia set a fire in the fireplace and lit globes to hang in the air about the room. She was exhausted, but it was a good exhaustion. The cottage was sparse but clean and would serve her needs. The mattress found its way, along with the wardrobe, into the bedroom, and Ilia put the bedding on it, smiling in pride at the freshly polished bedframe. The bedding was crisp and smelled of ocean air from being dried outside in the sun and sea breezes.

The kitchen was scrubbed, and the table had a bouquet of flowers from outside the cottage sitting on it. The utensils from the cave were in the cabinets along with the dishes. The kettle sat on the stone hearth and the cooking pots hung from hooks imbedded in the fireplace on the kitchen side. On the living room side, the large fur rug lay in front of the fireplace and the rocking chairs sat nearby.

Ilia opened the shutters to the windows for a view of the ocean and shoreline. She sat on the floor in front of the fireplace looking out the window at the sunset, as she ate cheese and a thick slice of bread Molly sent home with her. Next to her sat a lovely red wine Molly packed in a "Welcome home" package.

It was perfect. With one exception…

Tristan wasn't there to enjoy it with her, and she had no idea when he would be. She looked out at the vast ocean and wondered where he was. What was he doing? Was he safe? Was he thinking of her?

Ilia closed her eyes and reached out to him. She had never attempted such a thing, but somehow it felt natural. She knew she had the strength to do it. Maybe it was the new house or the magik that lived there. Maybe it was because, for the first time in her life, she felt she had a place of her own. Whatever the reason, she knew she wanted to try.

Ilia shifted her position to lean back against the hearth, feeling its warming comfort as the cool breezes from the coming night brought a chill with them. She closed her eyes, stilled her mind, and connected it with her heart. Her breathing grew rhythmic and mists of magik swirled lightly about her as the moon rose above the horizon. Blue and green tendrils danced slowly about the room as Ilia moved deeper into her heart, allowing her longing to pull her further into her need. She did not move or speak. Deeper and deeper she went, pulling at the dark veil of separation until she could do nothing more than call to him. "*Tristan.*"

Sixteen

Tristan shot bolt upright in bed. He shook his head, trying to clear the sleep, but being awake did not dispel the dream. He had heard his name. Ilia had called to him. He rubbed his eyes and went to light a lamp but stopped when moonlight filtered in through the open window, casting enough light for him to see thin threads of mist moving around him, silver-green and fine. He watched them move, dancing and intertwining. "Ilia" he said tentatively. Nothing.

Then a whisper, "*Tristan…*"

Tristan closed his eyes, purposefully slowing his breathing, calming his senses, and stilling.

"*Tristan it's me…*" came the whisper.

This time he was ready, "Ilia? How…Why...?" Tristan found he didn't know what to say.

"*I don't think I have long. I missed you. I needed to hear you. I didn't know if it would work, but it does…*" Ilia's voice faded then came back again. "*Are you well?*"

Tristan watched the threads pulse as Ilia spoke, then responded. "I am well. Finishing up. Hope to see you soon." He abbreviated his thoughts, fearing they had little time.

Her response was faint, "*Good. I am well. Staying on the island now near the village.*"

Tristan frowned, "On the island? Not in the cave?"

"*I'm…cottage.*" Ilia's voice faded out, not allowing him to catch all her response.

"Ilia? Ilia? Can you hear me?" Tristan spoke aloud, as he tried to reach her.

She responded, "*It's fading. Can't…hold…it. I love you,*" and then she was gone.

Tristan sat, watching the threads slowly evaporate. He felt a tightening in his chest as he watched the last bonds of communication slip away. He sat back in his chair, lost in thought. He needed to get to the island.

He felt uneasy knowing Ilia wasn't staying in the cave. It wasn't that the island was dangerous. There was protection all around its shores, and he knew every person on the island, many of whom were in as much danger to outsiders as Ilia, but he rested easy knowing that the cave was doubly protected, and Ilia would be sequestered away in it.

Tristan shook himself. He was being overprotective. She would be fine wherever she was on the island, and maybe she would be able to develop her skills further than she would be able to in the cave. Still, he felt a sense of urgency, stronger than before, to get to her.

*

Edmond sat across the table from Tristan. They were below deck, seated at a dining table, tankards of ale in front of them, and a large map on the table between them. They had gotten rid of the diamonds and had a tidy sum to show for it, but it had taken longer than planned. Their usual contacts were nervous. Edmond and Tristan were trying to pinpoint why, but so far, they could only ascribe the reluctance to rumors of unrest between the islands and the mainland.

"But that has been going on for eons," Edmond said. "Why so much concern now?"

Tristan shook his head, "I'm not sure, but having to sit on this loot makes me uneasy."

They eventually found a fence, one they had used on occasion, who was willing to take the diamonds. When asked about the reluctance the response was, "Things are changing and those of us in the business are thinking we better hang onto our currency rather than gems. If we end up in a way, the islands will need currency."

Tristan understood the explanation. "Makes sense. But damned inconvenient for us," he said to Edmond.

As Edmond watched Tristan, he sensed there was something else on his Commander's mind.

"What is it?"

Tristan looked up from the coin he was spinning absentmindedly on the table. "I don't know. I guess I'm wondering if somehow, some of what is going on has to do with the Syndicate chasing magikal creatures. I know it seems farfetched, but I keep having this nagging feeling that there is a connection." He gave a huff of frustration, dropping the coin, and sitting back in his chair to stare off into space. "I just can't shake the feeling there are a lot of loose threads, and whether I see them or not, they are going to come together and have a big impact on us."

"Let's head out to the island," Edmond suggested. "Maybe you just need some time to think. We can all use a break,"

Tristan nodded. "Inform the crew. They will be happy to be on land for a bit. We will regroup and then get this package where it needs to go." He flicked his gaze toward the golden egg, and whatever it held.

"Aye Commander," Edmond said, smiling at Tristan as he stood to obey orders.

Tristan smiled back briefly, but his smile faded to a frown as he stared at the map. What was going on? What was happening? It was as though there was an ill wind blowing through their world, and he couldn't figure from where it was coming. He only knew there was something on the horizon, and somehow, some way, they had to be prepared for it.

*

Ilia sat on the beach in front of her cottage. Molly was teaching her how to make pottery. The process took a lot of preparation. A place was set up to fire the pots, then clay had to be gathered from around the island, and just the right flat stones had to be gathered to use as a surface for turning.

Once they had all they needed, Molly showed Ilia how to smash the clay dirt into small pieces and then add water to make a moist clay mixture. From there they took a lump of the wet clay and shaped it into a flat pancake on their turning rock. Then they took strips of wet clay, rolled them into coils, and placed them on top of the flat clay all the way around the circle. They continued building the walls of the pot by stacking the coils of clay on top of each other.

Once they finished with that part, they used water and smoothed the outsides and insides of their bowls. Then they dug a large, long pit, and lit a fire setting the pots along the edges to preheat. After the coals burned down, they placed the pots in the center and built the fire up around the pots, allowing it to burn down again to coals.

Then Molly showed Ilia how to build the fire up around and over the pots, adding to it several times. A few hours into the process, they moved the fire over the pots, let it burn down to coals, then covered the entire pit with sand.

The next morning Molly and Ilia began the slow process of carefully uncovering the pots, pulling them from the pit. Molly tapped on one of them, hearing a tinny sound, indicating the pots were successfully fired. Ilia made two small pots to use as cups and a small bowl. She made a larger pot to use for storing grain so critters wouldn't get into her food stores.

By late afternoon the pots were ready to use, and Ilia was able to put the clams she found early that morning into the pots to boil them over the open fire. Reed made her a metal stand which allowed her pots to be suspended over the flame of her beach fire, preventing them from getting too much heat.

As the sun set, Ilia sat on the beach eating the dinner she'd made with her own hands from start to finish, only using her magik to produce fire. She felt a sense of satisfaction deep within, and she sighed in contentment as she watched the sunset.

The fire burned low as the night sky emerged in the dying light. The moon rose enormously in the sky, and Ilia felt its power pull her as a magnet. She rose from her place on the beach and moved toward it. She danced and pulled the moonspun from the giant orb. It flowed around her as though alive. She pulled and pulled, gathering the shining threads about her like a cloak.

The power that had waned within her filled as a cup with water, and Ilia began to glow as she raced up and down the shore. The freedom to fully experience her connection to the moon was there for the taking, uninhibited, and Ilia danced and flew up and down the shore.

*

The huge black wolf stood poised on the edge of the clearing. He melted into the night, his eyes gleaming a bright green. He was mesmerized by the glowing creature moving up and down the beach, her feet only touching the ground briefly as she whirled and moved, bright strands of moonspun encasing her. He stood, rooted to the spot for a long time, his eyes never leaving the figure on the beach.

Ilia stopped moving and began gathering the strands of moonspun wrapping around her. She walked over to her fire and stooped to pick up a small bag. Gently she tucked the strands into the bag. The sun was beginning to light the sky, and Ilia quickly pushed the remaining threads into the bag. It wouldn't do to have them exposed to sunlight. They would keep as long as they did not come in contact with the sun. She had plans to use the strands to make merchandise to sell at market. She needed every strand she could collect. When she made the items she had in mind, she would treat the material, and it would then withstand exposure to sunlight.

She had just finished her task, when she saw an enormous creature coming toward her on the beach. The dawn just outlined its shape. As it drew closer, she could see it was a huge black wolf. Her breath caught. "Tristan?" she said, tentatively daring to hope.

The big wolf moved slowly toward her, his pace quickening as he heard her call. She stood as still as a statue as he approached her. He stopped a few feet away, eyeing her.

Ilia called softly, "Tristan is that you?" The question was simply to fill the space, for she knew it was him. He stood unmoving, except for his big tail, which flicked back and forth.

Ilia smiled. "Come here." She put a hand out to him and beckoned.

He stood a moment longer, then made his way toward her, his green eyes glowing in the moonlight. When he was next to her, Ilia reached down and placed a hand on his head. She wasn't afraid of him. She knew he would never hurt her, but she felt the need to respect his caution and let him dictate the contact.

She need not have been concerned. When she touched his head, she felt his muscles relax, and he leaned into her. The top of his head came up to her chest, his big body moving in front of her in a protective stance. Ilia put her arms around his neck and hugged him close.

He gave a primal growl and licked her face. Ilia laughed. "It's nearly sunrise. Would you like to come back to the cottage with me? I have a cottage now. It's my first real home, Tristan, yours and mine." Ilia turned and began walking back to the cottage, her satchel heavy with moonspun, which she was eager to tuck away from the rising sun.

They walked toward the cottage together. Ilia opened the door and allowed him to enter first, then followed. She shut the door and moved to put the satchel in her room where there was no light to compromise the strands.

Ilia went back into the living room and Tristan stood near the fireplace looking about the room.

His human form was just as impressive as the canine, and Ilia's breath caught in her throat. He seemed to fill the room. His long hair lay loose and in disarray about his shoulders. He was dressed in a white linen shirt tucked haphazardly into a pair of trousers, which were tucked into a pair of boots. His face wore a substantial beard, adding to the dangerous look of his strong features. When he turned to look at her, mossy green eyes glowed with intensity. Ilia wondered if it was because she had just seen him in his animal form.

He seemed to read her thoughts. "Are you going to stand there all-day lass? It's me. You know it's me." As he grinned, his perfect white teeth shone from the dark beard around them.

Ilia giggled and hurled herself into his arms. He caught her up in his embrace, his mouth claiming hers as he scooped her up in his arms and carried her to the bedroom.

*

Tristan lay back in bed, propped up on pillows as he watched his wife pull moonspun from her satchel. She had the look of a woman who was loved and content, her hair, now falling in short ringlets about her head, gave her an elfin look. The area of her head that had been wounded had healed nicely, the scalp regenerated, but he could see no hair. He hardly noticed anymore.

She saw him looking at it and said, "I don't think the hair will grow back, but I'm used to it now.

And as my hair grows in around it, I think it will cover." She smiled in return for his smile.

"You are beautiful either way, and I have to say, it makes you look dangerous, love."

Ilia laughed, glancing at Tristan reclining back, watching her. He was bare to his hips where the bedclothes covered him. His arms were raised behind his head, and he seemed completely at ease.

Ilia felt an electric shock run down her spine. She dared not look at him too long or she would not get the moonspun treated. She blushed, and Tristan laughed, reading her thoughts. "Are you sure you want to work on that now? I think we can find other things to occupy your time," he said, enjoying the effect he had on her.

She sat with her legs off to the side, knees bent. She was using her magik to treat the strands of moonspun, and they glowed as she ran her hands down each strand. The picture was enchanting, and he wanted to reach for her and do all over again what they had been doing most of the morning.

"I have to treat these strands, Tristan. If I don't, they will disintegrate."

Tristan smiled, then asked, "What exactly are you doing?"

Ilia looked up as she ran a hand down another strand. "Well, they are very fragile, you see. There are other methods for coating them, but I have never been good with mixing elixirs. Anna is very good with those, but fortunately for me, I can use magik. I just coat them with it, and it strengthens them so that they can endure sunlight. See? Feel the difference." She handed him a treated strand, then one that wasn't treated.

"Wow. There is quite a difference. They feel almost like touching a cloud." His face softened in wonder. Then, "What do you plan to do with them?"

"I want to make garments with them. It takes quite a few, but with this batch, I can get several scarves, and I will keep some to add to the pile every time I can get more. Eventually, I will be able to make larger garments. When I have enough."

"And what are you doing this for?" he asked.

"I want to be able to trade with the village people. Molly taught me how to make clay pots and how to hunt for crabs and lobster, but I want something of my own to offer; something they don't have here."

Tristan's eyebrows lifted. "You have been busy. And here I was worried you were wasting away in my cave without me," he teased.

Ilia finished the last strand and tucked her work back into the satchel. "I would have, I think, but Molly and Reed took an interest in me. They have helped me so much. It was Molly who showed me this cottage."

Tristan nodded. "Aye, they are the best of people. I'm surprised about this cottage. Everyone is afraid to come here."

"That is why she thought it would be good for me. It's private, and the magik that lived here before likes my magik." She said, a pleased smile lighting her face.

"And who wouldn't like you or your magik," he said, reaching for her, his eyes twinkling as a smile played on his lips. "I know I sure do."

*

They sat on the beach, a fire blazing, as they watched the sunset. It was a cloudy evening allowing little view of the night sky. There was the smell of rain on the breeze, but it wasn't chilly. Ilia sat cross-legged while Tristan lay on his side, his head in her lap, looking out at the rolling waves.

"So, what else have you been doing with yourself in my absence?" Tristan asked.

"I was just about to ask you the same thing," she responded sweetly. "I wasn't sure where you were, but I had no idea you would end up here so soon," she said, adding quickly, "Not that I mind at all!"

Tristan laughed. "Let's first talk of that night when you came to me." He sought her eyes with his own.

Ilia blushed. "I wasn't sure I could do it. I have been trying to stretch my magik a bit. Just to see my limits, you know?" When he nodded, she continued: "And I was missing you so much. I just decided to see if I could reach you."

She raised her hands and shrugged. "And it worked. I don't know how long I can maintain it. I was sort of startled that it worked and startled you responded, but I would like to keep trying. It might be helpful when we are apart."

Tristan nodded. "Aye. It was a surprise to feel you so close and hear you. But I agree it is something we should develop. T'would make the time apart a bit easier." He rose, pulling her head down for a kiss.

"But to answer your question," she said, "I have been learning how to make things. I have been learning how to dig for sea creatures for food. I have been making pottery, and I have been making a home for us." She smiled down at him. "Whatever may come, we need a place to escape, and I just couldn't keep living in that cave."

"Aye," he agreed. "It's a depressing place to have to spend a long period of time. I never thought of this cottage. It's protected by the magik that stayed behind when Andora passed, and it is protected by the magik she placed around the island."

"It looks different on this side than over by the caves," she commented.

"Most ships will try to come in over by the caves. It's hard to get 'round to this side, and the reef is a natural deterrent, but should anyone get past that, they would walk into other traps much like those set by the stairs leading to the caves and never return. It's not advisable to enter from this side, as there is really no way to get through it like there is by the caves. Reed is equipped to maneuver through it, but not here," he explained.

"It isn't foggy here, though. No one would even know the same thing is here on this side." Ilia said.

Tristan smiled, chuckling, "I think Andora did that so she would have a view, to be honest."

"I bet you are right! And what a view!"

They looked out to sea for a few moments, then Ilia said, "Now, for you. What have you been doing?"

Tristan sat up and crossed his legs, running a hand through his errant mane. "Well, we had a spot of trouble after we got the loot. Everything went fine when we were retrieving it. but I had a funny feeling about the whole job. I couldn't understand why all the bother for a golden egg.

So, when Nicola brought it back, I got to looking at it and inside the egg was the biggest diamond I have ever seen in my life, and I have seen a lot of diamonds. That's when I started to get nervous.

Nicola also brought back very large gems and a bunch of smaller-cut diamonds. I knew we could fence those smaller diamonds, no problem, but those bigger gems were going to be a problem. Trying to offload those would draw too much attention, especially since we hadn't dispensed with that egg and its contents."

So, we took care of the smaller diamonds, and decided to come back here to leave those big gems. We will be heading out to take that egg to the contractor soon, and the sooner the better. I just have a bad feeling."

Ilia saw the strained expression on his face. "Why are you so worried?" she asked. "It seems you have a sound plan. What is making you fret?"

Tristan paused for a moment to think, using a stick to trace patterns in the sand next to his leg.

"Well, I keep having this overwhelming sense of being followed. I can't shake it. It's like the feeling of being watched, you know? That sort of cumbersome weight of observation."

Ilia's brow creased in concern. "So, who do you think it might be?"

Tristan looked at her a moment, his mind lost in thought. "I can think of two possibilities. The job we did just before I met you was messy. There were a lot of details we didn't know; more moving parts than I had expected. We planned well for the intel we had, but we barely got out, and Nicola just about got nabbed. It was like they knew we were going to be there, and they knew about Nicola. You know what a priceless gem he is. More valuable in the pirating world than any jewel."

Ilia nodded. Tristan had explained Nicola's abilities. He was the reason the Anemone was as successful as it was, with little brutality on either side. "So, do you think this is a case where someone is actually after Nicola and not the treasure you loot?"

Tristan nodded, "I keep coming back to that. When we docked in Portsmith, Edmond and I were careful about not letting word get out we were there. We had to get supplies, and the ship had taken some damage in a storm," he smirked as he looked at her. "We didn't have you to calm the storm back then."

Ilia smiled. "And then you got involved with me, and that no doubt helped advertise the fact that you were there."

Tristan nodded. "A bit, but we had to leave very suddenly with you, so that put paid to any plans someone might have had to get up to trouble with us. Rudy made a few inquiries about new additions to the area, but he had to be careful. You can't stay incognito and then go about asking questions, drawing attention to yourself.

The last night we were there, the crew went out, but that was the only time they were out and about; and that night we were all onboard, so it wouldn't have been a good time to get up to any mischief."

"Do you think the Syndicate has something to do with it?" Ilia asked, giving an involuntary shudder.

Tristan reached over and took her hand, giving it a reassuring squeeze. "That was the other possibility I considered, though I didn't even realize they existed to the magnitude they do. I think they are far more organized and far-reaching than anyone realizes."

"And now they most likely have new members, like my sister and whomever she recruits," Ilia supplied.

"Very likely, and they will know now that there is a moon child alive who is more powerful than any to exist in a millennium." He watched her gravely. "More valuable than Nicola could ever be."

They were silent for a time, enjoying the sea air, until Tristan broke the silence. "Ilia, I need you to stay on this island. I know you want to go in search of lineage, but until I can find out what we are up against, I need you to stay here."

Ilia couldn't hide her disappointment. "But surely if I'm with you, and I have abilities to protect myself…" She groped for an argument.

"I know love, but you are still learning. I know you are enjoying adjusting to village life, and all these skills are beneficial, but you need to really delve into understanding your power and what you are capable of."

Ilia pulled her hand from his, a defensive look spreading across her face. "I am, Tristan. I have been working on it. I just don't know what to try. It's like being placed in the ocean with no map, expected to get to land. I just don't know what I should know."

Tristan watched her pull back from him and wanted to pull her into his arms, but they had to have this conversation. "I know you are, but I'm saying, maybe you need to immerse yourself in trying to figure out what is possible. Maybe there is something in the cottage, in Andora's books or journals, that would help you."

Ilia looked at him in surprise, "How did you know about her journals?"

Tristan smiled. "You forget I was her pupil. I know she had journals. She documented everything."

Ilia crossed her arms over her chest, contemplating, as Tristan continued, "I wouldn't want to take you with me right now anyway, as we have to finish this job. I brought you here to keep you safe, and as long as we have no intel about whether you are being pursued, who is pursuing me if that is the case, and if they are one and the same, I can't take you away from the only place I know for certain you are safe."

Ilia listened. She wanted to be angry with him. She wanted to rail against having decisions made for her, but the rational part of her brain knew he was right on all counts.

Finally, she said, "Okay, Tristan, but we have to come up with a definite game plan before you leave. I refuse to be tossed about on the decisions of others without any say, even if the one making the decisions is you." She looked at him, her chin up, eyes blazing into his.

Tristan suppressed a smile. She was well. The wounded woman was gone. This woman was confident and ready to take on life again. He gazed at her, her eyes aglow in righteous indignation, her magik coursing through her veins making her skin glow. She was magnificent, and she was his wife. "Okay. Let's come up with a plan both of us can live with."

Ilia nodded, the glow ebbing from her skin. Tristan stood, brushing sand from his clothes before holding out his hand to her. The sun had set, and the fire burned to embers. The overcast sky prevented light from the moon, and he knew tonight would not be a night for her to dance under the stars. She stood. He picked up the blanket and shook it, then took her hand and they walked back to the cottage.

*

Their first disagreement, Ilia reflected. It wasn't something that had caused a rift. They were taking steps to create a solution, and she hoped all their disagreements could be answered in such a manner. They had not had enough time to learn each other's nature. Granted, they had been trapped on a boat for some time, but she had been so weak, and he had been in his role as Commander. This was new for both of them, this sample of domestic life.

Ilia sighed as she looked over at the sleeping man next to her. He was without guile. He truly wasn't looking for a "win" except for a solution to their joint problem. He was methodical in their discussions about what to do, exacting every detail and possible outcome from their predicament. Ilia marveled at his ability to stay on track with multiple scenarios presented to find a plan that suited them both.

They stayed up into the wee hours of the morning carving out a plan. They decided Ilia would stay on the island and work on her skills. She would also do some investigative work with the villagers to see if she could get any information from them on what they might know about the Syndicate and how it worked. They were from all corners of the world, many of them, and a large majority were transplants, seeking refuge.

Tristan would finish his job, then head to Portsmith to see what he could find out about anyone who might have placed a contract on him. He didn't have any immediate jobs on the horizon and could focus on helping Ilia in her search for information about her past. There were other fine details they needed to hash out, and issues they knew would arise, but they now had a way to communicate with one another which hadn't previously existed, and that would help them meet challenges in a timely manner.

Tristan, who was lying with his eyes closed, body in a relaxed sleep state, hands crossed on his bare chest, suddenly reached up and pulled Ilia to him. She gasped and then giggled as he peppered her neck with kisses. His mouth moved to claim hers as he rolled her onto her back, the weight of his body holding her in place and his teasing kisses becoming altogether more directed, as he moved down her neck, pushing the thin chemise aside, exploring in earnest, until she was wriggling and gasping, demanding more.

He rose up from the task at hand and smiled at her, allowing her to pull him down to her in a deep kiss. "Something I can do for ye lass?" he said, grinning at her, the teasing look in his eyes not hiding the heated passion behind it.

Ilia's eyes were glowing that odd amber color they took on when she was powering up from the moon. "Let me show you the way," she said, smiling like a mischievous cat. And she did.

*

While they spent most of their time at the cottage, and most of those hours in amorous abandonment, they did manage to spend some time with Reed and Molly as well as Nicola and Meridee. They enjoyed the conversation and catching up.

Meridee and Ilia had a little time to get to know one another, and Ilia felt she'd made another friend. Like her gifted husband, Meridee had magikal gifts. Meridee was able to read thoughts, a powerful gift with a price of never being able to shut them off. They moved to the Isle as much for her as for Nicola. On the island, there were fewer people and less to filter.

"Do you think it might be possible for you to create a barrier, so I am unable to read your thoughts?" she asked Ilia. "I would so like a friend, and it is difficult to have one when I can read the other person's mind."

Ilia thought for a moment then said, "Let me try." Tristan and Nicola sat and watched the exchange with interest. The petite, dark-haired woman with dark round eyes and a sweet face, watched as Ilia worked her magik to create the barrier.

After a few moments Ilia said, "Now try."

Meridee closed her eyes for a moment to single in on Ilia, then opened them in surprise. "I can't hear anything." She grinned. "I can't read Tristan's either. Shape shifters have some sort of natural barrier that prevents it, so now we can have regular conversations. Oh, I'm so glad!" Her small hands fluttered together in silent applause.

Ilia smiled at her. "I will put it in place every time we come together."

Tristan stayed with his decision to leave Nicola on the island for the next journey. "Until I get some answers, you and Ilia are both in a lot of danger. For all I know, I could lead that danger right to you, and until I know who the players are, I can't take that chance with either one of you."

Nicola was happy to be home. "I could use a little time with my family," he said, indicating the infant nestled in his arms. "I should like to be around for a bit, Commander."

Tristan nodded, wishing Ilia accepted the directive in the same way, though there was no infant to look after. He looked at her across the table. She was dressed in a white gauzy shift dress, simple in its cut, but it moved with her every curve. Her skin did not tan but there was a glow to her that had not been there before.

He watched her laugh at something Nicola said and wondered again about her inability to bear children. There were exceptions. He wondered how such a thing would impact her, and he knew, though he would never share it with her, he wanted a child with her. He wanted to give her that gift, he realized, as he watched her take the infant in her arms.

She looked up and caught him watching her. Their eyes locked and she flushed, her eyes taking on that iridescent glow they did right before they changed color from a power surge. She wanted it too. He could see it, as though it were written on her face. They sat there locked in desire and longing for a moment until it was broken when the babe moved and began to cry. Ilia looked down at the child and spoke softly to her as she handed her back to her mother.

They left with Ilia's promise to Meridee they would meet up soon. As the couple walked back to the cottage, hand in hand Tristan said, "Something else I forgot about. And it may play a factor. There are rumors of war."

Ilia looked up at him. "War? With whom?"

"The mainland and the islands. The islands are railing against the tariffs on trade and the fact that many of those living on the islands are magikal folk. The mainland is slaving out a lot of the island inhabitants. I know there is a lot more traffic on the seas than there has been in the past. Yet another reason I do not want to take on any more jobs at the moment, until I get some updated intel. Edmond is working on that. I left him at Enchara before coming here, just for that reason. Some of the other crew have families there so I have a few stationed there to dig up what they can. He will make his way through the other islands to figure out what he can."

Ilia nodded, losing herself in thoughts of what war might mean for their world and the two of them. They reached the cottage, and Ilia lifted a finger, blowing a globe in through the door to light the way, something she hadn't often had to do, as Tristan spent a fair amount of time in his other form while on the island. She appreciated his developed senses at night, especially the ability to see in the darkness, which he did not possess in his human form. They tramped all over the island at night, needing no light to show the way.

They entered the cottage and silently moved about their nighttime ablutions, each keeping silent counsel. The air was heavy with all they had learned that evening and the knowledge that their time together was coming close to an end.

Tristan built a fire. The breeze blowing through the open windows was decidedly cool, and there was a chill in the air. The fire came to blaze in the large stone fireplace and warmed the room, the wood heat dispelling some of the moisture in the cottage.

Ilia came from the bedroom wrapped in a large fuzzy wool sweater for which she had traded one of her moonspun scarves. Tristan went outside to bring in more wood, then went to the bedroom, coming out a bit later wearing a long, white linen shirt. Ilia giggled when she saw him.

"What?" he asked.

She continued to giggle. "Sorry. You just look funny in the big shirt, like you are dressing up in your big brother's clothes."

"It's a night shirt," he said, grinning at her amusement. "You haven't seen me in one, because I usually go to bed in nothing but my skin" he said, adding, "as you well know."

Ilia flushed with enjoyment, watching him as he sat down next to her on the big white fur rug in front of the fire. They stared into the flames for a while, enjoying the warmth. After a time, Tristan got up to go to the kitchen. He returned to the fire with a plate of cheese in hand.

Ilia giggled again. "What?!" he asked in mock exasperation. "Are you going to laugh at me every time I move around?"

Ilia's giggles launched into peals of laughter. "I…Sorry…Must be… tired. You just look…funny!" she gasped between snorts of laughter.

At that, Tristan set down the plate and whipped the shirt off. "Fine woman, I will wear what I wear every night!"

Ilia's eyes grew large at the site of him. He advanced on her and then tackled her on the floor. She shrieked in laughter as he tickled her.

"Oooooh," he said, as he realized the only thing she had on was the sweater. "So, it's like that, is it?"

Ilia continued giggling, trying to pull the sweater back around her as he maneuvered her hands above her head then brushed his scratchy beard up and down her skin. They were both laughing, and Ilia's eyes ran with tears as she tried to control herself.

Tristan looked down at her as she struggled to regain her composure, a hand still holding hers above her head. "I love you, wife."

Ilia stilled, looking into his eyes. "I love you, my husband."

Tristan pushed the sweater away from her and lowered his lips to hers. Ilia's arms came up around his neck and pulled him closer. The room suddenly warmed, and they were lost in loving well into the night.

*

He left before dawn some days later. They lay awake talking and loving most of the night, taking every moment and spending it to the fullest. She followed him out the front door and stood in his embrace, his mouth on hers for an eternity, his hands memorizing every curve of her.

She clasped him to her, trying to take him in. Their eyes met and locked, saying everything.

Tristan finally pulled from the embrace, touching two fingers to his lips as he turned back to her and then sent his fingers out toward her. "Be seeing you, lass." Then he turned and walked down the beach toward the village.

Ilia smiled to herself, placing her fingers to her lips. It wouldn't be long, and they would be together. Tristan promised this would be the last time they were apart, and they would be able to work on finding out information about her parents.

She turned and went back into the house to stoke the fire. She reached out lightly for him and felt him there, a warm presence just beyond the physical boundaries, but firmly within reach of her magikal abilities. "Tristan?" she queried.

She felt the warm pushback from him. "I'm here lass. No worries."

Ilia smiled and went about her day. She had so much to accomplish before he came back. From the bookcase in the living room, she pulled out one of the journals. No better time than the present. She had a lot to get through.

*

Ilia was standing on the beach. There was a storm brewing; she could feel it. The electricity in the air pulled on her magik, making her fractious. She had been digging for clams for some time and had just reached down to pull another from the wet sand and rocks when she caught a movement from the corner of her eye.

She looked up and saw a figure coming toward her. For a moment her heart leapt, thinking it was Tristan. She knew he would be a few days yet before making it to the island. He was gathering intel, but he suspected most of the needed information would come from Edmond. Edmond had a way of pulling information from people without them even knowing he was doing it.

Ilia watched as the figure came closer. Her eyes widened in surprise. It was Edmond. She looked around in confusion. That meant Tristan must be there as well, but she didn't see him.

"Edmond?" she asked. "Where is Tristan?"

As he drew closer, she saw the look on his face, and she knew.

She put up a hand to halt him.

"Ilia…" he started.

"No." She said, then "No!" she screamed at the look on his face.

"I just talked to him a few days ago. He can't be." She said, her eyes welling with tears at the look of anguish on Edmond's face.

Ilia reached out into space for Tristan and his warm presence, but she could not feel the warmth of him on the other end. She began to shake. "No. No. No. No!" she screamed, her power blowing out of her in distress, sending a huge ripple through the ocean that caused the waves to shift and rise.

Edmond shrank back. The water rose and towered over the land. "Ilia. No! Stop it!"

She turned a blank amber stare to him then turned back to the water, realizing the imminent threat. She motioned the water to flatten out, and it did. Ilia stood staring at the dark waves, uncomprehending.

Edmond heaved a sigh, then moved toward her. "Ilia," he said gently.

Ilia turned to look at him. His eyes were red-rimmed, and his grief snapped her back to reality. Edmond grasped her arms and she fell into his embrace, sobbing. They both went down on their knees in the sand, holding onto one another, as two lost in a storm, crying their pain out into a world that had taken what they loved.

At length, she pulled back, wiping her eyes on her sleeve and said, "What happened?"

Edmond shook his head. "I don't really know much. He brought the Anemone to get me. I am thinking, he was looking for me and went down an alley as a short cut. Someone came up behind him and stabbed him from behind. Someone else saw him lying there, knew we were connected, and they came to get me."

Edmond wept again, his body shaking. "He wasn't there! He wasn't there when I went to get him, Ilia. Who would do that? Who would take him? I had no idea he was being hunted. He kept saying he felt he was being pursued, but I didn't take as much stock in it as I should have. But you know he had that sixth sense; that canine sense, and he knew." He shook his head. "I just can't believe it. I…"

"Wait! His body was not found?" Ilia interrupted.

Edmond nodded. "When I got to the alley, there was only a pool of blood. I guess I kind of lost my mind and ran all over trying to find him. Rudy found me and took me back to the ship. I'm ashamed to say I don't remember much about it." He looked at Ilia, a stricken look on his face.

Ilia bobbed her head, understanding. She squeezed his arm saying, "There was no body."

Edmond stood slowly and said, "You will get a chill."

She looked up at him with an empty stare. He reached down and gathered her in his arms, half carrying her to the cottage where he placed her in the rocking chair near the fireplace as he worked to start a fire.

He moved to fill a kettle with water and placed it on the hook above the fire to boil then set about making tea. Eventually, he presented Ilia with a cup of tea to warm her, as he went to the bedroom for a blanket for her and wrapped another around himself. Taking up his own cup of tea, he sat on the floor in front of the fire. He shifted and pulled a parchment from his pocket, handing it to her.

"He left this for you. Said I should make sure you got it if ever something happened to him."

Ilia took the paper from him with numb fingers. She opened it and read through the contents then looked up at Edmond. "Do you know what is in it?" she asked.

Edmond shook his head. "That is between you two. But I'm hoping it provides some direction.

With his death. We have a crew to think of."

Ilia stared into the fire for a moment then said, "I can't read it to you. I'm sorry. But you are welcome to read it, as some of it pertains to you."

Edmond took the letter and read through it, skipping anything that did not have his name attached. The Anemone would pass to both Ilia and Edmond. Edmond would be commander and Ilia could be either an active or silent partner as she chose.

After some silence Edmond said, "I know you must need some time. I have days on you, and I am still struggling with disbelief. But eventually I would like your input on what we should do."

Ilia looked up from the fire and met his eyes. Hers were almost translucent. "There was no body, Edmond. That is strange, is it not? Why would you kill someone in cold blood and then take the time to pick up the body? It doesn't make any sense."

Edmond stared at her in disbelief. "No Ilia. No. You can't do that. Tristan is gone. "

Ilia shook her head, interrupting him: "I will not accept that until I know where his body is; until I know there is only a body." She closed her eyes and reached out again to Tristan. There was still something there. That something gave her a small glimmer of hope.

Edmond was staring at her, as though she was delusional, a look of sympathy etched on his handsome face. "Ilia…" he started, but she interrupted. "I can feel him still. I don't know what has happened, but I can't believe he is gone." She jumped up and grabbed his shirt with both fists. "I can still feel him, Edmond!"

Edmond looked at her for a moment, then seemed to make a decision. "Okay. We need a plan then. If you are saying there is hope,

I'm willing to hang on to it with you." He pulled her to him and held her as she cried once more.

After a time, she pulled away and said, "I need you to go find Anna and bring her here."

Edmond looked at her in surprise. "Anna? Why?"

"I need her, Edmond. I am going to need her in more than one capacity. She is a historian. I need her knowledge of the Syndicate, and I need her knowledge of my background. Tristan feels everything is connected somehow, and I agree. Once we make some connections, I have a strong hunch we will also know where my husband is." She stopped, swallowing back a sob.

She burned with anger, the power of her emotion turning her eyes amber. "Go get Anna."

Part Three

Seventeen

Ilia stood on the pier, a solitary figure, oblivious to the ocean waves breaking all around her. A month had passed since Tristan was attacked, and she made the trip to the pier daily. She couldn't help but look for him, even though she knew he wouldn't come. She reached out for him often, and while she did not feel a void, she did not have the connection to him she once had, and when she tugged on the invisible chain that connected them, he did not respond.

She went to the pier every day, because the ocean by her cottage was calm and ordered, waves rolling in a leisurely fashion, the water a cerulean blue lapping sparkling sand. But the water by the pier was angry, despairing, and forbidding, seeming to recognize all was not well in the world. This part of the island she connected to. This made sense to her. She felt somehow equalized, standing there within moments of being swept into the dark waters. It was the time in her endless days that everything made sense.

Eventually Molly and Meridee would find their way through the mist and call to her. "Ilia? Ilia! It's time to come back, lass."

The same thing every day. They would wait for her to float back to them, dripping with the salt spray from the waves. They would pull her to them and walk her back through the mist, over the dunes, through the small village, and back to the cottage where they would dry her off by the fire, then put her to bed.

They never chastised her or suggested she quit going. They understood it was her way of coping, and even though she believed Tristan was still alive, the hopelessness of how to find him left her grief-stricken.

They never left her alone. Molly stayed with her through the night and much of the day. Meridee had the baby to care for, but they made sure someone was there to be near her, to tend her garden, and see to daily chores that kept up the house. Ilia never spoke; never cried. It was as though she had climbed into a space within herself and walled herself in.

In the second month, Anna arrived. It was late in the night, but Edmond helped her find her way to the cottage. Molly greeted her at the door, a worried expression on her face. "You'll be Anna, then," she asked. "Welcome. I could wish it was under better circumstances."

Anna nodded. "It is a pleasure to meet you, Molly." She paused to allow Edmond brief conversation with Molly, as he deposited Anna's luggage, then asked, "Where is she?"

Molly pointed to the bedroom and watched Anna's retreating form as she walked to Ilia's room. She put on the kettle, then sat down in the rocking chair, a book lying untouched in her lap as she stared at the bedroom, lost in thought.

⸸

Anna walked quietly into the room. The windows were shuttered, not allowing any moonlight into the room. There was a dim orb hovering above the nightstand. Anna walked over to the window, opening it to allow moonlight to stream in, then looked over at Ilia, who flinched when the moonlight hit her.

Ilia was much paler than normal. She looked small and frail in the bed, and Anna got the impression she was wasting away. She walked over to the bed and sat down next to her.

"You are almost drained of magik," she said.

Ilia opened her nearly colorless eyes slowly. "Anna?"

"Don't sound so surprised. You sent for me, and now I am here. Did you think I wouldn't come?"

Ilia looked at her for a moment as though trying to determine if Anna was real or a dream, then her face cracked with emotion and she cried, "Oh Anna, how will I ever find him?" It was a wail wrenching from deep within her.

Anna, as small as she was in personage, seemed robust next to the fragile figure in the bed. She reached down and gathered Ilia to her as a mother would a despairing child, stroking her hair as she crooned, "There. There. Let it all out." Anna rocked her back and forth, as Ilia sobbed and moaned in pain.

When the sobs subsided, Anna said, "Okay. I'm going to help you, and we are going outside.

There is a full moon, and you must refill."

Ilia shrank back, "No!" she exclaimed. "I don't want it. I can't."

Anna grabbed her by the shoulders giving her a hard shake, "Ilia you must. This is part of you. You are starving. Tristan would not want this, and if he is still alive, as you believe, this is not the way to get him back! You can't give up!"

Ilia tried to pull back, but Anna held her in a vice grip, not allowing her to retreat. "I know it doesn't feel right, but I promise you, once you have done this, you will feel stronger and better able to cope. It's a full moon. You must refuel."

Ilia wanted to continue to resist, but she didn't have the strength. She nodded in acquiescence, and Anna helped her slowly move from the bed. They carefully made their way into the living room where they met Molly.

Molly quickly jumped up, placing the book on the chair, as she moved to assist Anna. They made their way out the door, to the garden gate, and onto the sandy beach. Molly ran back to grab a blanket then spread it out. They all sat down on the beach, facing the huge orb that seemed to cover the entire sky.

Ilia resisted at first. She felt anything that made her feel better was somehow unfair to Tristan and what he must be enduring. But as the moonlight worked on her, she felt a stirring deep within her; a quickening.

She did not dance. She sat next to Anna and Molly, her face lifted toward the moon, and she remembered how much Tristan loved to watch her moonlight rituals. She felt the power of the moonlight seeping into her very bones. Like a dry plant being watered, she felt life coming back to her. In all her lifetime, she had never been so depleted of energy. The rush of it left her with a heady, disconnected feeling, but she relished it.

"Where is Edmond?" Ilia asked, her sudden question breaking the spell the moon seemed to have cast over them all.

Molly caught Anna's eye over the top of Ilia's head before responding cautiously, "He's on the island, love."

"Where are the rest of the crew?" Ilia asked.

"They are all here staying on the island," Molly responded. She did not elaborate, but Ilia sensed there was more Molly wasn't saying, and like a good bloodhound, she continued to probe.

"Where are they staying? Not all of them have families here to go home to. Are they staying in the caves?"

Molly shifted a bit uncomfortably, sharing another glance with Anna before responding. "Well, some are in the caves. Some are on the ship. Edmond, well, he…uh…well he…"

Anna jumped in to save Molly from her discomfort. "Ilia, Edmond is in pretty bad shape. He was in his cups when he came to get me, and I don't think he has stopped."

Ilia looked at Anna. "Did he deliver the egg?"

Anna shook her head. Ilia jumped up, shouting, "Bloody hell! They will put a bounty on us all!"

She was pacing back and forth periodically flailing her hands in exasperation.

Finally, she stopped pacing and asked, "Where is Edmond now?"

She stood with her hands on her hips, her body now alight with the magik recharge she had just experienced. Her eyes glowed amber in the moonlight, her short curls standing out wildly all over her head, her cheeks hollow from weeks of little food. She looked like a spirit from another world.

Anna smiled. "You go see him looking like that, and it might kill him."

"Serves him right, the fool," Ilia said, a small smile playing about her lips. She reached up and touched her mouth. She didn't think she would ever smile again; didn't think her face would remember how. Yet here she was doing just that.

"Ilia,' Molly said softly. "In your conversations with Edmond, please do not forget he is grieving as well. Tristan was as close to a brother as any man could be, and they spent their whole lives together." She saw Ilia's eyes widen with something akin to hurt. Molly rushed on, "I'm just reminding you where he is at, lass. He is grieving in his own way. That is all I am saying. You may need to go a bit gentle with him."

Frustration and disbelief overrode understanding. "He believes Tristan is dead. All he has done has been lip service and indulgence for me! He does not believe Tristan is alive, and neither do you, Molly!"

"I'm sorry, Ilia. I do not have the connection to Tristan you do, and neither does Edmond. It is hard to believe Tristan is still alive when we don't have the assurances you do." Molly said.

"I can't spend my energies trying to convince everyone. I will not grieve him, as he is not gone," was Ilia's emphatic reply.

"Isn't that what you have been doing?" Anna's soft voice questioned.

Ilia whirled away from Molly to look at Anna. "That's not fair, Anna."

"Ilia, no one blames you for grieving. Even if he is still alive." Anna paused to put up a hand, as Ilia moved to interrupt. "Yes, I know you feel the connection is not broken, and I believe you. But you cannot rail at Molly and Edmond when you have not acted on your knowledge.

Your behavior has done nothing to reassure them. It looks more like denial than the assurance that you know Tristan is still alive. Make up your mind. Is he alive, or is he dead?" There was a moment of silence, as Ilia stood staring at Anna. Then she turned away and began pacing back and forth.

After a few moments, she stopped in front of Molly. "My apologies, Molly. You have been nothing but a kind and true friend. Anna is right. I have not been acting on what I know. I have been wallowing in self-pity. And I have knowledge none of you have, but I am requiring you to act as though you have it."

"There is nothing to forgive, love," Molly responded. "No one has a blueprint for behavior in such situations."

Ilia gave a small smile and began to pace again, then looked up suddenly. "How is Nicola?"

"He is grieving, of course, but he has Meridee and the baby. He will pull through fine," Molly said.

Ilia nodded. "Red Rudy?"

"He is staying with family here," Molly said. "He is taking it pretty badly as well, but he has people to help him through it. I think for Rudy, it's a matter of getting back to work. That will help him more than anything. Idleness does not suit him." Molly paused for a beat then continued, "Neither of them know what you know. That might give them some hope."

Ilia agreed. She knew where Edmond was without being told. He would be in Tristan's cave.

"I need to get to the cave. If you would come with me, I would appreciate it," she said.

They agreed and stood to join her. Ilia produced a globe, gently pulling her hand away to leave it hanging in the sky next to her to give the other two women light to see, though she glowed so brightly that neither really needed it.

They moved across the island in silence, each woman lost in her thoughts. When they reached the cave, Ilia paused to explain to Anna how they would get to its mouth. She turned towards the cave then turned back again to look at Anna, "How did you get through the mist? You can't get through without a coin or a bond?"

Anna gave her a mischievous smile, "Rudy had me climb on his back and he put Edmond's cloak about us, and we tricked the enchantment."

Ilia gave a sharp laugh and Molly shook her head, "Fortunate for us all those who have tried to enter the island have not been so clever; though no one who has leave to enter the Isle would try to sneak another in anyway."

Anna moved between Ilia and Molly so she could be caught if her steps faltered across the water. Ilia glided over the water confidently and placed her hand on the massive stone face. The door slid open, and they entered.

The first thing that hit them as they entered was the odor. They pulled back and exclaimed in accord. The cave was in darkness save for a lamp at the back of the room. Ilia blew sparks from her fingers that lit the lamps throughout the cave.

They could see the cave was barren save a few empty jugs of what Ilia determined was strong brew.

As they moved through the cave the stench became stronger. "Well, it stinks, but not of death.

That's a mercy." Molly quipped.

They could hear heavy breathing that confirmed the lone inhabitant had not expired. As they passed the fireplace, Ilia quickly lit the half-charred wood in the fire and added more, the flames immediately leaped to action to remove the dampness and cold from the air.

She led them to the back of the cave, where Edmond lay on the thin mattress Ilia had supplied when she took the original mattress to the cottage. The three stood for a moment staring down at the man in the bed. In the dim light, he looked small, his face hidden by a riotous beard.

Ilia spoke softly. "Edmond?"

There was no response. She increased her volume and reached down to shake his leg.

"Edmond?"

Edmond snorted at the touch and jerked awake. "Huh? Wha…?" He opened his eyes, and then let out a high-pitched scream at the sight of the glowing figure at the end of the bed.

"I told you, you would scare the life out of him," Molly admonished Ilia, as she moved quickly to Edmond's side to place a comforting hand on him. “It’s okay lad. It’s just Ilia. Come now. Sit up.” She helped him gain an upright position, and he shrank back against her as he stared at Ilia, transfixed like a small boy emerging from a nightmare and needing comfort.

“Edmond. It’s me.” Ilia murmured, looking at the young man who was so obviously wrapped in grief. He looked up at her, still shaking, his red-rimmed eyes brimming with tears as they met with amber eyes filled with concern.

“It’s my fault, Ilia. He was looking for me. If he hadn’t been looking for me, he would still be here.”

Ilia’s eyes filled with tears, as Edmond wept, and Molly pulled him closer. “There, there lad,” she said, patting the head that lay on her shoulder.

Ilia sat on the edge of the bed, making a quick adjustment to the wave of alcohol and unwashed man that assailed her senses. “Edmond, you and I both know Tristan does what he wants.”

“But he had been saying for a while he felt like he was being followed, and I just ignored him!

He was right!”

“Yes, and he should have taken precautions. He didn’t. But whatever happened, you drinking yourself to death out of guilt over something that could have happened anywhere but on this island is not going to help our situation. We need to find him,” Ilia said.

She reached out and touched his arm, allowing her magik to flow through her and into him, warming him and purifying his body from the effects of his drinking. He looked up at her in wonder as he felt it.

“I have been lost in my own grief, indulging myself as well,” Ilia said, as she heated his skin and purified his blood. “But we have work to do, and we have people we need to protect. And we need to find him.” She tried to soften her gaze. “It’s time to get back to work Edmond. We need to figure out where he is and go get him.”

Edmond sat staring for a moment, then nodded slowly.

*

After a warm wash, courtesy of Ilia's shower-warming abilities, and clean clothes, Ilia coaxed Edmond back across the island to her cottage. He sat in the rocking chair in front of the fireplace staring into the flames absentmindedly, as Ilia made coffee and handed him a cup. She sat on the fur rug across from him.

She waited until they both had a sip of their brew then asked, "Where is the crew, Edmond?

"The crew? Well," he paused for a moment as he wrestled out the thoughts to answer a difficult question. "Rudy is here. He has a daughter here. Nicola is here." He paused at her nod. "Aye. I guess you would know that already. There are a few others with people here in the village. The rest are in the caves. I don't even know how they have been feeding themselves." A look of alarm appeared on his face.

Ilia gave him a reassuring smile. "Don't worry. Reed made sure they were tended to."

Edmond gave a heavy sigh, nodding his head. "Well, that's a relief."

Ilia waited for his breathing to return to normal, then said, "Edmond, we have to make some plans. We need intel. And we need to get that egg delivered before it is unsafe for any of us to leave the island."

Edmond looked at her blankly. "Intel?" he asked finally. "Oh yes. I have some information. I was going to tell Tristan, but then…" he trailed off, his eyes filling with pain as he looked at a past only he could see. He seemed to have missed the second half of her statement about the egg.

"What were you trying to find out?" Ilia pressed. "And what *did* you find out?"

Edmond sat back in the rocking chair, taking another swig of his coffee. "Well. We weren't looking for anything specific. I had been there for a while, as you know, and I managed to meet up with people we know, but everyone was pretty tight-lipped. That was information in itself pointing to there being enough fear of something to warrant not discussing anything with others, even those considered friends. So, I didn't really feel my time there was all that useful.

Tristan wanted us to just move around and listen. We picked up a lot more information just hanging out in drink houses and such than I did trying to work people we know. People get to drinking and tongues start wagging. It's the quickest way to get information when you don't want to have to hunt down a source, and you don't know what you are looking for.

So, Rudy and I and a couple of the other boys were just moving about the islands gathering what we could hear. Tristan didn't want to have both Rudy and me off the ship, but he knew, knows…" He gave her a quick glance as he corrected his tense, "Rudy and I are the best at ferreting information without drawing too much attention. As I said, I had been nosing around, but with Rudy, well Rudy is good at finding the right people to prod." He stopped to gather his thoughts.

Ilia waited patiently as he assessed what was worth telling.

"It takes time to get intel without being noticed. You can't ask questions, or you draw attention to yourself. We never got to the asking questions part, because of what happened."

Ilia nodded, both in agreement and encouragement to continue.

Edmond's eyes took on a glassy stare as he reconstructed the past. "What we did learn is that there is a war brewing. Tristan thought there was something up along those lines, but it's closer than even he suspected."

"Between the islands and the mainland?" Ilia asked.

Edmond nodded. "Yes. And what I've been able to piece together, based on the bits of information we received, is that the Syndicate is helping the mainland. They are hunting and capturing those individuals with special abilities, and either extracting their magik or slaving them out to the highest bidder, and the demand is through the roof, because the mainland is looking for a way to not just win over the islands but break them. They want complete control."

Ilia sat staring. "Why? Why does it matter so much what is happening on the islands? They are separated from the mainland by a huge ocean. Why does it matter?"

"It matters because the islands have it all. They have multiple ports. They are rich in bounty and mainly export. The pirating network flourishes because of those islands. The mainland can't shut down the pirating unless they have control of the islands and the very healthy business done there.

And then there is the magik. The islands have the highest concentration of magikal creatures of anywhere else in our world. There is some speculation there is a source or something on or around the islands that fosters the magnitude of magik, producing all the creatures."

"Except moon children," Ilia stated.

"Except moon children," Edmond repeated. "I understand a little better what happened in Portsmith. My best guess is someone knows about you. Someone knows you are not from the islands, and I would wager they are not going to stop with you. They will want to find all the moon children.

They will want them to extract their powers, and they will want young ones, changelings, to train and use."

Ilia sat contemplating the thought, then froze, as her eyes widened. "Senza!"

Edmond watched her, realization donning only moments after her exclamation.

Anna came out of the bedroom at the sound of Ilia's cry. Ilia looked at Anna, alarm registering on both their faces. "Trissa knows where

Senza is. We have to get her. And we need to find as many moon children as we can, declared powers or no."

Anna shook her head. "Ilia that is an insurmountable task. They are all over the world. Places we don't even know of, they have gone to. I don't see how we can do this task as completely as you are suggesting."

"We have to try. We have to get them to this island. It's the safest place for them," Ilia said.

"But we would be putting a spotlight on this island. Can the spells in place withstand such a barrage?" Edmond asked.

Ilia nodded. "Yes, I believe so, and I can reinforce them."

"You? You can do the kind of magik that surrounds the island?" Edmond asked in surprise.

Ilia glanced at Anna, sharing a confirming look with her before continuing. "I have not been idle while staying on this island, Edmond. I was going to go in search of my heritage to see if knowing the past might aid the present, but I was also going to try to find out information about my own abilities. That will have to wait now. But I believe I have information about my magik."

Ilia paused for a moment, warming up to her topic. "You see, I have been reading the journals and books the sorceress left here. That information, along with the encounter I had when I first came to this cottage, leads me to believe her magik and mine are very compatible."

Edmond gave her a questioning look. "What happened when you first came here?"

Ilia explained about magik living in the cottage, and the premises accepting her magik. Edmond leaned into the rocking chair. "So that means her magik will marry yours?"

"Yes, I believe very strongly it will. When and if I need to reinforce the spells here, I am confident I will be able to."

Edmond pondered her response for a moment then said, "And what if the magik in the spells rejects yours? What will happen?"

"Well, I don't know for certain, but I expect it will put up a barrier and not allow my magik to penetrate. But the integrity of the spells will not be compromised. I would only strengthen the spells with my own magik."

"We need to test this, Ilia," Anna put in.

"Actually, I already have. The spells put on the cottage were nothing like what is around the island, but they were spells, nonetheless, and when I offered my magik to them, the magik in the spells intertwined with mine, creating a bridge to me.

When I am in this cottage, the garden is lush and beautiful, the vines pull back, and the place looks inhabited. When I leave for any length of time, it covers back up, and the garden looks overgrown and full of weeds. It is the acceptance of my magik that pulls the spell back."

Anna nodded. "Yes, that is significant. I think we need to discuss this with the villagers and get their acceptance of what we want to do. It is one thing to bring those seeking refuge here, but I wager this is something different from anything the island has sheltered in the past."

Edmond commented. "Yes. I agree. Plus, we only have so many caves, and I know the village will not be accepting of being overrun with moon children."

"I don't know that there are large numbers of moon children out there, Edmond," Ilia responded.

"Anna, do you have any idea what we are looking at for numbers?"

Anna calculated silently, then said aloud. "Moon children live for a very long time. So, depending on how many we can find, we are talking between 50 to 100."

Ilia's eyes widened. "That many?"

"Well, keep in mind many are without power like Trissa, and of those left, it is likely only a tiny portion have powers that rate as significant, and none like you," Anna said. "Regardless of abilities, I agree we need to find as many as we can. They will be tortured like you were, Ilia, to see if their magik will be revealed."

Ilia nodded. "Yes. The Syndicate will not take a moon child's word that he or she does not have magik."

"So, what now?" Edmond asked.

Ilia looked at Anna as she said, "I desperately want to get Tristan, but I feel we have a more pressing matter at hand. We have to get that egg delivered, and then we go get Senza."

*

Portsmith seemed unchanged in the year since Ilia had seen it. They made port late in the evening. To Ilia's mind, they could not have timed it better. The trip from the island to deliver the egg had been remarkably uneventful. Edmond delivered the egg to their contact and received payment. The contact was content, and the contract fulfilled. The Anemone was on its way to Portsmith. There were no storms to delay them, and there was a nice tail wind to push them along their way.

In bringing Anna onboard the Anemone, not once, but twice, Ilia had broken the by-law for having a woman on the ship. The fact that Ilia was a woman was addressed with Tristan's punishment, but the price had not yet been paid for bringing Anna onboard. No one came to her to point out the fact, but Ilia knew it must be addressed. She would never violate the laws that governed the Anemone's ability to function in harmony.

So, once they were settled on the ship, Ilia approached Rudy, as she knew Edmond would never listen to her. At first, Rudy recoiled at the prospect of having to whip her the way he did Tristan for the violation, but when Ilia presented her reasons, Rudy acquiesced, suggesting they inform Edmond, as he was acting commander.

Edmond responded much the way Ilia anticipated, but with Rudy on her side, providing sound reasoning, Edmond finally gave in. Secretly, Ilia hoped they would not have to go through with the punishment, but she was prepared to do so. She steeled herself for what she knew could be a very uncomfortable and humiliating experience.

Her hopes were realized when she was standing with her hands on the ship railing looking out to sea for courage, clothed only in her chemise, as she awaited Rudy to provide the first lash. She waited for what seemed an eternity, finally turning to see Rudy with the whip lowered to his side.

"I canna do it, lass. I would challenge any of our crew to do the same to you. To my mind, ye have enough scars to carry ye through this this life and the next, and wee Anna is onboard to help us get back our commander. I don't believe it would be just to punish you for it; bylaws be damned. I won't do it." He crossed his arms at his chest the whip clutched on one hand.

"If there is anyone who feels differently, I encourage you to follow through with the bylaws of this ship." Ilia proclaimed, turning back to the railing to brace herself for one of the crew to finish what Rudy declined. She waited for several minutes, turning her head slightly to look at Edmond who was standing in her line of vision. He raised his eyebrows and shrugged.

Ilia turned to see all the crew had left the area. The whip lay on the deck where Rudy dropped it. Anna was standing behind Edmond, a look of combined horror and relief on her face as she realized what might have happened just to allow her to be onboard the Anemone.

Ilia gave a heavy sigh of relief and turned away from the railing, scooped her dress up from the deck, and walked toward Anna, taking her by the elbow and guiding her into Tristan's cabin.

It took Anna a few days to get her sea legs, but once she had, there was no keeping her off deck. They enjoyed the sun and sea as much as possible but under the shadow of fear cast by the possibility that they might not arrive in time to wrest Senza from the clutches of the Syndicate or, more likely, from Trissa.

"How much does Senza know about what happened to me?" Ilia asked Anna one morning as they sat staring out to sea over a cup of strong coffee.

"I told her everything before I left. I felt it was the right thing to do. She is so naïve about the world, and I was afraid to leave her without giving her a heavy dose of reality," Anna replied.

Ilia inhaled deeply the sea air. "Good. How did she take it when you told her Trissa's role in all of it?"

"She was shocked, of course, and appalled, and maybe a bit disbelieving, but coming from me, she had no cause to disbelieve what I told her. I begged her to guard herself, stay away from strangers, and above all, to stay away from Trissa, should she come around."

Ilia could only hope the young woman had listened. Senza was sweet, a good-natured soul, but she was far too trusting, and she rarely thought beyond her next new outfit or the next opportunity for mindless entertainment.

*

It was sunset when they pulled into the harbor. Ilia watched as the ship sailed smoothly into the cove, then listened to the sounds of the men preparing the ship to dock. She had become familiar with their different calls, and being on the ship gave her a sense of safety. It was also the place where she felt closest to Tristan.

Edmond insisted she and Anna keep Tristan's cabin. "I'm used to my digs," he'd stated. "And it was your first home together anyway." Anna was reluctant to share the cabin with her. She didn't want to impose, but when Ilia pointed out that there was no other place to stay other than on deck, Anna relented.

Ilia smiled at the memory of his generosity and the first time she'd entered the cabin. It still smelled of Tristan, and she found tremendous comfort in his belongings. She felt the connection between them was stronger when she was on the ship. She often reached out to tug on the invisible chain that connected them. There was no tug back, but there was still a presence on the other line.

"Rudy and Nicola will do some looking around to see who is in town. I already sent them to check things out. I will see about getting us a conveyance to Ella's. We can take horses from there for our journey," Edmond said, coming up to stand next to her on deck.

Ilia nodded, "We will be ready."

She watched Edmond stride to the gangway. He seemed to be doing better. Anna suggested men could not sit idle in their grief, as they were more likely to work through it while having a task. Ilia agreed. Being back on the ocean and having a mission had done wonders for him, and while she knew Edmond was still skeptical when she proclaimed Tristan to still be alive, he seemed more willing to at least entertain the idea.

It wasn't long before Edmond was back with a carriage. Ilia saw the silhouettes of Rudy and

Nicola join Edmond. Edmond turned to face the ship and waved, and Ilia waved back, then went to get Anna. She found her sister in the cabin, gathering the small satchel they packed with a few necessary items. Ilia walked over to Tristan's desk and picked up his cutlass. She tucked it into the dark red sash tied about her waist. It was the only thing Edmond found near where his body had been. When she looked up, Anna was grinning.

"What?" she asked.

Anna giggled. "Look in the mirror," she commanded. "You look like a ruffian."

Ilia turned to the mirror and laughed at what she saw. She wore one of Tristan's linen shirts tucked into the pants she found before, when she was on the ship. The shirt was bloused around her hips and the neckline was open nearly to her navel, though it was difficult to tell, as she wore a long coat that reached to the floor and buttoned up from the waist, with long sleeves capped with large, open French cuffs. The coat split open at the waist to reveal the red sash into which she had just tucked Tristan's cutlass; the wool pants that encased her slim legs disappeared into knee high leather boots.

"Just one more thing," she said, as she pulled the hood on the back of the coat up over her head, covering the silver locks of her hair that were now touching her shoulders. "Better cover my head.

Not a full moon, but it is a cloudless night, and I am likely to glow like a beacon." She glanced at Anna. "You will too." She tossed Anna her wool cloak. "Here. Put this on. That should do the trick."

Anna caught the cloak and put it on. Her sliver hair, smoothed into the elegant French roll she always wore, disappeared into the cloak's depths. She silently followed Ilia out of the cabin and into the cool night air. The season was changing. The sultry nights of summer had given way to cool evenings. So, wearing coverings in the evening was completely appropriate.

They descended the gangplank and climbed into the waiting carriage. They joined Edmond and

Nicola in the carriage, while Rudy drove. "How did you get a carriage at this time of night?" Ilia asked.

"I have quite a few connections in Portsmith, luckily," Edmond replied. "I called in a favor. We will leave it at Ella's."

Ilia nodded. She lay her head back against the carriage, disappearing into the comforting darkness. It had been a long day, and the anticipation of what was to come had her magik humming. Still, she would need to refuel as much as possible before she encountered any opposition.

*

Ella came out of the house to wait on the front stoop as soon as the carriage pulled up. When Anna and Ilia alighted, she moved quickly down the steps to embrace both women and pull them into the warmth of the house.

"I am so delighted to see the pair of you!" she exclaimed, her lovely face alight with happiness. "Even if it is for just a night." She hugged Ilia to her again, saying nothing more as they held each other.

Ilia finally pulled away and smiled at Ella. "I know he is alive, Ella. We are going to find him and bring him home." Ilia saw the look of disbelief and pity cross Ella's lovely face and said quickly, "No. Don't. I know he is alive because I have a connection with him. When I pull on it, he is there. If he were dead, I would pull on it and it would trail back to me with nothing but void in its wake. I know he is alive, but it is different. I have my theories on why that may be, but I am not certain."

Ella nodded. "If you say it is so, Ilia, I accept your word. We can all use a little hope."

Ilia smiled in response as Anna said, "And we have a mission to accomplish, which diverts all of us. It gives action and purpose, as Ilia continues to try to make a better connection so we may discover where he is."

"Let me take your coats," said Ella, "and I will put on the kettle. Take yourselves to the fire in the sitting room. I'm sure the lads will join you soon."

Ilia and Anna, divested from their outerwear, moved to the fire and sat down to enjoy its warmth.

"I feel as though I am thawing for the first time in ages!" Anna exclaimed, leaning in closer to the fire.

The sea travel had been hard on her. She was unused to living so near the ocean and traveling on it. Every time the air cooled, as it so often did as the seasons changed, Anna was chilled to the bone and struggled to get warm.

Ilia watched her sister soak in the warmth of the fire. The air on the mainland was not as damp. She smiled to herself, thinking how much she enjoyed getting to know Anna better. Anna had a calmness about her that belied great passion underneath. She was extremely analytical, something Ilia assumed came part and parcel with being a historian, but she was also capable of great depths of passion and cared deeply for others.

Ilia lamented that she'd been in close proximity to her sister in her younger years and had never gotten to know Anna's keen mind and curious nature. When she mentioned the fact to her sister,

Anna shrugged and said, "I was to keep my distance. That is part of the role of historian, but events have changed that with you, and I find I am unwilling to go back to the way things were. I don't even think it is possible between you and me. We are what we are now, and frankly, I prefer it."

Edmond and Rudy came in just in time for some tea and a sit by the fire. The wind had come up, and the temperature dropped. "We are in for a storm," Edmond said, taking a seat next to Ilia on the sofa.

Rudy, looking a little displaced in the more elegant surroundings, stood until Ella encouraged him to take the empty chair next to the sofa, while she sat on the settee next to Anna.

A hush followed, interrupted only with the sounds of them all sipping their tea.

It was Ella who broke the silence. "Right about now," she emitted a chuckle, "Tristan would have been telling us what needed to be done on the morrow, making sure we all knew our roles and barely giving us time to finish our tea before sending us off to do his bidding."

They all laughed in unison.

"Aye. He wouldn't even give Rudy and I time to drink our tea before he had us on some errand," Edmond said, with a nostalgic smile.

"What is the plan for the morrow, then?" Rudy asked.

Edmond looked at Ilia and shrugged at her.

"Well," said Ilia, realizing Edmond was nudging her to respond, "we need to get to Luna. I suggest we leave as early as possible. I am concerned Trissa has managed to wheedle her way into the house and get to Senza. Senza is very impressionable, and no matter what we have told her, Trissa will find a way to spin it to her advantage."

"Aye," Edmond said, nodding. "But it will be harder for her, being as she can't talk anymore."

Ilia gave a choked laugh, a look of surprise registering on her features. "I had forgotten about that. No doubt she has found a way round that as well. She is nothing if not resourceful."

"Will you be needing the horses, then?" Ella asked, getting down to brass tacks.

"Yes, we will, if that is fine by you?" Edmond asked. "We will come back, hopefully, with the girl, and we would ask to impose on you again for the night before getting back to the ship.

'Twould make it easier for the ladies to have a night before having to get back on board the Anemone. I know Ilia will not have a big adjustment, but it's Anna and Senza I'm thinking of." "What will you do then?" asked Ella.

"My intel, what I have gotten thus far, tells me the Syndicate is not doing much in Portsmith. I think they are spreading out to try to find magikal folk, and I am thinking they are focusing on moon children at present. I think they want Ilia," Edmond said, glancing at Ilia. "But they will take any they can get. We will need to be looking in other towns to make sure households of moon children are safe."

"Ilia, Anna and I feel that the best course of action right now is to look for as many moon children as we can, make sure they are safe, and then go after the Syndicate; always keeping in mind they will be looking to set a trap to get Ilia," Edmond finished, looking to Ilia for agreement.

"That is an ambitious task," Ella said. "Where will you put all these children once you have found them?"

"We haven't gotten that far," Ilia said. "It's a concern. We cannot keep running them back to Marauder's Isle. For one thing, there aren't enough places to house them, and the travel time would prevent us from getting to others before the Syndicate."

Everyone was silent for a moment, then Ella said, "Bring them here."

"No. We could not do that Ella. It would put you in danger, and you have no defenses to protect yourself and them," Ilia countered.

Again, there was silence. Finally, Anna, who had been silent during the exchange said, "Ilia can put a protection around the property."

Ilia and Edmond responded with resistance, but it was Rudy who spoke up. "You can lass. I've seen you pull the waves out of the sky and back into the ocean. This will be a small task for you."

They looked at Rudy in surprise, and Ella said, "That's proof enough for me. When do you want to do it?"

Ilia bit her lip in contemplation. "Well, it would be best on a full moon. I'm fully charged then."

"That is two days from now," Anna said.

"So, we need to get Senza and get her back here before then," Edmond stated.

Ilia nodded. "That will give me the night to recharge, and I should be able to do the work that night. I can pull tremendously from the moon. I have learned it's not really about me learning skills. It's knowing exactly what I want to do. With the power I get from the moon and my magikal abilities, I can do just about anything."

They all sat looking at her in awe until Edmond broke the silence. "Well! It's nice to see you becoming confident in your abilities." He continued hesitantly. "I know Tristan would...will be proud of your growth. He often said...says he knows you are capable of great things, but you have been trapped in your insecurities."

Ilia smiled. "Yes. He would be proud of me, but he will be prouder of me when I am able to use what I have to stop this vile group of individuals from destroying our beautiful magikal creatures."

They sat up making plans into the wee hours of the night. Ilia and Anna left them after a time and went out into the moonlight, pulling energy from what little remained before sunrise. When they entered the house, everyone else had gone to bed.

Having refueled their energy resources, sleep was not necessary for either of them, so they made another pot of tea and sat discussing their plans until dawn. Ilia found Anna's company as comfortable as what she shared with Tristan. As she sat across from the tiny lady, listening to her talk of coming events and those of the past, Ilia once again lamented having missed so much time getting to know Anna. She would not have felt so alone in life if she'd had Anna's friendship.

Eighteen

The town of Luna was comprised of one main street. There were houses and farms dotted all around it, but the town itself was quite small. Still, it had all that was needed for a small bustling community.

The group slunk quietly through the small town, hoping not to be seen. The less attention they brought to themselves, the better. It was just after dusk. They traveled some distance from Ella's that day, stopping as needed for those less familiar with riding horses.

They cut through the small town and up, over a hill, then dropped down into a valley covered in thick forest. There was the sense of something ancient in that forest, and Ilia smiled to herself at the feel of things long past still lingering. Townsfolk were afraid of the forest, and it provided a natural barrier to their home. The forest was a labyrinth. One had to know how to get to Ilia and Anna's home before venturing there. Plunging in without having directions would only get a visitor hopelessly lost.

Ilia took the lead, as they neared the forest. They forayed into its murky depths, the night in combination with the moon peeking through the clouds periodically, providing long eerie shadows that seemed to follow them. Ilia was not bothered by them, nor was Anna, but Rudy and Edmond were unnerved.

Ilia broke the quiet. "Not much farther now. Don't worry. Anna and I know this forest like the backs of our hands. It blusters, but it will not harm." She grinned to herself, as no one could see her. She thought of how Tristan would enjoy the experience, and her heart gave a thready jerk. She reached out to him again, feeling that presence on the other end, something to which she was growing accustomed. It was different, but it was still him, and she clung to that, sending him her love and longing through the line. She felt a small twinge come back to her, and she nearly exclaimed out loud, but she held her excitement inside. He was responding. This was progress.

Anna looked over at Ilia, sensing a change in her mood, her expression questioning. Ilia could see her face illuminated by the moonlight and shook her head quietly saying, "Later." Anna tilted her head slightly in acknowledgement, and they continued forward.

Finally, the forest opened into a clearing. The house was a good-sized building made of wood with a stone base. There were windows on either side of the large front door and a wisp of smoke came from a chimney atop the house. Ilia always thought their home large, but now, looking at it after being away for so long, it appeared more of a cottage than a large house. The roof was gabled and extended over the side of the house, the thatched roof looking like a pointed hat hanging jauntily over its owner's face.

Ilia smiled as she looked at the building. It looked charmed and fit in exactly with the enchanted forest they had just cleared. They rode into the front yard and dismounted. They tied their horses to the corral railing that lined the driveway and headed for the front door. It wasn't so late yet that everyone should be in bed, but the occupants would be settling in for the night.

Just as Ilia lifted her hand to knock on the door a voice spoke from the darkness, "Who are ye and what do ye want here? No funny business. I have a shotgun trained on the lot of ye."

Ilia whirled around and Anna said, "Jenz?"

"Miss Anna?" came the shocked voice. Jenz materialized from the corner of the house. He stepped into the light, and the group could see an elderly man wearing a long coat with the collar standing up, a slouch cap, holding a shotgun. He lowered it as he saw Anna and Ilia. His eyes widened. "Miss Ilia! You look like a creature of the forest! Scared me half to death."

By that time, the door opened, and Madra stood in the entrance, proclaiming both her excitement and welcome into the house. They all gathered into the light and warmth of the house with Jenz bringing up the rear.

Sometime later, after all introductions were made and everyone was sitting around the living room with cups of hot tea in their hands, Ilia asked, "What was Jenz doing outside with the shotgun?"

Mena sighed. "Well, we have had some strange things happening around here. We are trying to figure out what is going on."

"What kinds of strange things?" Edmond asked.

Madra took up the conversation. "Some of our animals came up missing. Our cat just disappeared, and then one of our goats…" She trailed off.

Jenz picked up the thread. "I found the cat, dead, just this side of the forest, and I found the goat out back, behind the house. Dead as well."

Anna put her hand to her mouth in dismay. She loved the cat, Patches. Tears ran down her cheeks, and Ilia reached over to squeeze her arm.

"We had a letter about a month ago…" Mena paused for a moment, stealing a glance at Ilia, "from Trissa. Actually, the letter was to Senza, but Senza brought it to us as soon as she saw the handwriting."

As if hearing her name, Senza materialized from the back part of the house. "I don't care if she is, technically, my sister. After what she did to you, Ilia, you, who have always been so kind to everyone, well I have no interest in talking to her at all. Did she honestly think I was that stupid?" Senza strode forward and hugged both her sisters.

After greeting Emond and Rudy, she continued. "Did she think that I wouldn't know what happened and would just go to her with open arms?"

"What did the letter say?" Ilia questioned. Senza went over to the side table by the door and opened a drawer. She pulled the letter from it and took it to Ilia. Ilia opened it, read it, then paraphrased for the rest of the group.

"She says she is near Luna and would like to meet Senza. She has some exciting news to share that she thinks Senza will want to hear." Ilia looked up from the letter. "Did you respond?"

Senza shook her head and looked over and Mena and Madra. "I didn't know what to say. We talked about it and decided we couldn't encourage her, but we didn't want to do anything to provoke her. So, we did nothing. Then these terrible things started happening."

"No doubt punishment for not taking the bait," Rudy replied.

"What are we to do?" Senza asked.

Anna took Senza's hand and said, "Senza, we are in perilous times as moon children. We are worried about your safety. There is a group called the Syndicate, and they are stealing magikal creatures like Ilia, and most likely you. They are trying to extract magik or sell moon children as slaves."

Senza looked over at Ilia and the smooth patch of her scalp where no hair was visible under the mass of silver curls. "Like what they did to Ilia?"

Anna nodded. "We would like you to come with us where we can better protect you. This way, Mena, Madra, Jenz, and Sam will all be safe, because they are not magikal creatures."

Senza's eyes lit up. "You mean I get to go on an adventure on the ship? Will Tristan be meeting us?"

Ilia's countenance clouded for a moment. "No Senza. Something has happened to Tristan. We don't know where he is, but we are going to find him."

Senza's eyes filled with tears. "Will he be okay?"

Ilia looked at her little sister and gave her a small smile. "We aren't sure, but we hope so."

Senza held her sister's gaze for a moment and as she did, a warm sensation moved through Ilia. She felt, from head to toe, as though someone had just wrapped her in a warm fuzzy blanket. The sensation was almost decadent in the moment, and she knew it wasn't from her.

Ilia's eyes widened, as she realized it was Senza. Senza smiled, and Ilia heard a voice in her head say, "I want to do my part in this. I am not a little girl anymore."

"No, you are not," Ilia responded aloud.

*

Ilia's sleep was filled with dreams of Tristan in his wolf form, running back and forth down the length of an invisible fence. She knew she was the one on the other side of the fence, and he was trying to break through to get to her. His green eyes shone through the darkness, and she could sense his urgency. She kept trying to find a way to break down the fence but couldn't figure out how to do it.

She became more and more agitated the longer she watched Tristan running up and down the fence.

Just when she was at the point of waking where she always awoke, a warm sensation washed over her. She felt comfort and safety, as a voice said, "You have more than one kind of magik in you."

Ilia lay between sleep and awake, pondering what the voice had said. Tristan was still running up and down the fence, but this time she was able to think without panicking. Her magik. The magik of the Isle. Ilia reached down inside herself, past her own familiar magik, and touched the magik from her cottage on the Isle. The green threads danced as she touched them. She pulled lightly and encouraged them to glide up and over her own magik. She stirred them together, and this time, unlike times in the past, silver and green threads stacked on top of one another in a three-dimensional snake. It paused to look at her, and she whispered, "Break the fence."

The snake hissed, baring long, silver fangs, and slid toward the fence where it opened its jaws and sliced through the barrier, then slithered through to the other side where the wolf paced. He saw the snake coming and froze in place. The snake slithered up to him, climbed up his leg, wrapped around his neck opened its jaws once more, then drove its fangs deep into his back.

The wolf cried out and collapsed. Ilia cried out, but again, she felt the warmth overtake her, calming her. She watched as the snake moved over the still wolf, and before her eyes she saw the wolf change shape. There, with the snake wrapped around his neck was her husband.

"Tristan!" she cried out, weeping as she viewed him through tears.

"Ilia!" he said. "Thank God you got to me. I haven't been able to shift, and I have been trying to get through this fence. I thought I might be stuck here forever." Tristan approached the fence, and Ilia moved in her dream toward her side of the fence. Their fingers intertwined. Ilia felt a jolt at the joining and sobbed openly.

"My love," he said. "I'm so sorry I have caused you pain. I don't know what has happened, but it has obviously been devastating for you."

Ilia said nothing, her relief overwhelming her into speechlessness. She intertwined her fingers with his through the fence.

Tristan looked at her with love and compassion, saying again, "My love. We don't have much time. I need to know what you are doing."

Ilia pulled herself together, wiping her nose on her sleeve and calming herself before she explained quickly what had happened and what their plan was. She finished by saying, "I need to know where you are, Tristan. I don't know how to find you. I think you are physically still in wolf form, and you can't change back. I have been trying to find a way to change our link to reach you, and it seems now that has happened, but I still don't know where you are."

Tristan thought for a moment, then answered, "For some reason, I can't tell you." He shook his head as she began to protest. "No. Stop. We are wasting time. I don't know who has me. I believe it is because I am not conscious, have not been conscious since I was stabbed. I shifted and have not been conscious since, but I have my senses as a wolf. I'm going to share them with you." He reached for a better grasp of her hands then said, "Let's try this. Close your eyes.

Ilia did as he asked, and it was only moments before Ilia was inundated with blurred images, overwhelming scents, and sounds. She pulled her magik in tightly around them and commanded it to record every single moment.

When it was over, Tristan smiled at her. "I love you. Come find me."

Ilia touched her lips to his through the fence. "I love you too," she whispered. She would have asked more, but he touched his fingers to her lips and said, "Ilia wake up."

"Wake up. Wake up, Ilia."

Ilia jerked awake to hear Senza's voice saying calmly, "Ilia, wake up. Wake up."

Ilia stared at her sister for a long moment. As realization dawned, she said, "It was you. You were filling me with the comfort and talking to me."

Senza nodded. "Yes. It was me. I have discovered my magik takes me into dream worlds, and I can also talk to certain people without speaking out loud. When they are open." She said, smiling at Ilia. "I hope you were able to be there long enough to get what you needed."

Ilia was still staring at her sister. "Ye-es," she began. "I think so. I will have to spend some time sorting through it. But one thing I do know: Tristan is alive!" She smiled at Senza, relief and joy brimming on her face.

Senza hugged her. "I'm so glad this worked. You will have plenty of time on the ship to do that sorting."

*

Ilia sat near the prow of the ship watching the waves roll. The sun was out, and the heat felt good. She was mentally going through, yet again, the images Tristan provided her. She tried again to reach him but was only able to feel his presence. It was different than before. She could feel him more solidly now, and she hoped they would be able to connect again on a more substantial level so she could get more information from him if possible.

Ilia sighed. It was no use. She would have to wait until night when the moon was up. It would be easier for her to focus then. She rolled to her side on the blanket where she lay and let the waves lull her to sleep.

She awoke to a gentle shaking. "Ilia come have some dinner. You have been asleep out here for some time." Anna's voice cut through the fog of deep slumber, and Ilia stretched and sat up, taking her sister's hand to stand. The sun was beginning to head toward the horizon. "I must have been tired," Ilia said.

Anna nodded, "I checked on you a few times but didn't want to wake you. You have been so tired and have had little sleep. Edmond has done the same." Ilia looked at her questioningly.

"I just mean he was so tired he could hardly function. We sent him to bed, and he slept nearly as long as you," Anna said.

Ilia studied Anna for a moment then said, "Edmond is a good man." She smiled at Anna's blush then added, "And smart!"

Anna laughed. "You are chasing shadows, sister. I am hundreds of years too old for him."

"But you don't look it," Ilia replied, reaching to clasp Anna about the shoulders for a hug. "Just don't begrudge yourself some happiness if it comes your way. You deserve it."

Anna smiled. "Thank you."

*

Senza was growing up. There was an awareness about the things around her she had not previously had. She was curious about the ship and how it functioned. Edmond was patient with her, showing her how things were run. She watched the crew working at their various tasks, and Ilia was glad Senza did not suffer from sea sickness, though she wasn't surprised, as moon children tended to be comfortable on the water. Even Anna, who did not favor being on a ship, did not struggle with the water. She struggled with the humidity and staying warm.

Tristan's cabin had grown crowded with three women. Edmond offered the use of his cabin, but Ilia insisted he keep it, as it would also serve as a place for him to work and for them to plan for what was to come. She wondered if the presence of three women on the ship was too much for the crew, but Rudy assured her the crew was willing to make an exception for the voyage and the circumstances. Ilia still made a point of letting Anna and Senza know they were on the ship against the rules and regulations. She admonished Senza to stay clear of the crew and remain above deck.

Ilia stood leaning against the railing as she had so many times before with Tristan. The moon was creeping out of the horizon into the night sky. It was a cloudless night, and while the moon was waxing gibbous, not yet full, it gave off plenty of light and energy. Soon Senza and Anna joined her, and for the first time she could ever recall, Ilia danced with her sisters under the gibbous moon.

*

As the morning sun peeked over the horizon, the three women sat down on the deck with cups of hot coffee and biscuits in hand. They were all energized from their evening in the moonlight and decided it was time to sort through Tristan's memories. Senza felt she could connect all three of them, and they could sift together. She sat in the middle of Ilia and Anna; her hands joined with theirs. She allowed her magik to flow over them, and Ilia felt the soft blanket cover her, pulling her toward relaxation.

Ilia heard Anna inhale, as Senza began to work, and smiled to herself. This was Anna's first experience with Senza's abilities. A small exhalation came from Anna's lips, and there was a sudden mental snap, as though there were links that had finally clicked together. Ilia didn't need direction, she pulled on the mental box holding Tristan's memories and opened it. She felt her sisters watching the memories, living them as Tristan had.

After several minutes, the memories were done, and the three women sat in silence.

"I smelled ocean," Senza said at last.

"And a musty odor, like a room that has been closed up for too long," Ilia said.

"I smelled Andolgias," Anna said.

Senza and Ilia jerked to attention to stare at Anna. "You are kidding," Ilia exclaimed. How do you even know what they smell like?"

Anna gave her an indulgent smile. "You forget I have lived much, much longer than either of you. I was alive when Andolgias were everywhere. When I was a girl, I wore them in my hair." She smiled at the memory, her mind far away from their present situation.

Andolgias were a flower produced by the Andolgia tree. The tree bark was the color of sapphires, and the flowers were ruby red. The flowers provided a strong perfumed scent that drew out passion and desire in those who spent much time inhaling the tree's scent.

The trees were used to make aphrodisiac potions, and the bark had healing properties on a potency level that was unlike any other elixir or ointment. They had been cut down without replanting until the trees became nearly extinct. There were only a few areas in their world where Andolgia trees still grew. Those areas were protected, and there were efforts in place to grow more.

"That was the scent I couldn't identify," Ilia said, excitedly. With that one identification, they had very nearly pinpointed where Tristan was. "Let's go tell Edmond, and maybe he can show us the areas on the map where habitats for these trees exist. From there, maybe we can use some more of what Tristan shared to narrow things down a bit further."

Edmond, too, was excited by the hint. They looked on the map and discovered there were three places where Andolgia trees grew. One of the locations was on the mainland and two were on the islands.

"I think we can eliminate the mainland location. They would have wanted somewhere close to haul a wolf that size, and since most of the slave traffic is in the islands, it would make sense to have a site there," Edmond stated.

"But isn't the trafficking happening due to the mainland demand?" Anna asked.

Edmond bobbed his head. "Yes, it is, but they would need a hub on the islands to hold creatures until they can get them shipped to the mainland. So, in looking at these two places, which is more protected and has easy port access?"

Senza pointed a finger at one of the marked areas on the map. "I think this would be a good location. It looks on the map to have good access but limited vulnerability, as the shoreline does not allow for more than one vessel at a time."

Senza looked up from the map to three pairs of eyes staring at her. "What? I've been watching and learning all this time. Did you all assume I was just play-acting?"

Edmond was the first to recover. "No, no. Great deduction, Senza. I think you are correct. If we started there, I don't think it would be a waste of our time."

"I have one question about all of this," Ilia said, her eyes steeling as she contemplated the map, "This looks ideal for moving creatures around. In and out, and then they are on the mainland to supply demand." Everyone nodded at her assessment.

She continued, looking at the group, "Then why has Tristan not been moved? He is still there, has been for quite some time. What is the holdup? He is a specimen to behold in either form. Why haven't they moved him?"

No one responded. They stared at the map, considering the reasons. Then there was a collective gasp, and Anna said what no one wanted to articulate. "He's bait." She looked up and met Ilia's eyes.

Ilia felt her blood heating, her magik flooding her body, the anger threatening to explode from her. She stood up and left the cabin to stand at the railing and stared out at the vast ocean. She drew in a few deep breaths and stilled herself.

Anna came to stand next to her, saying nothing. She did what she had always done, offering support and reassurance in her calm, inconspicuous manner.

Ilia turned to look at her. "It's because of me. My husband is a captive somewhere out there, having who knows what done to him, and it's all because of me!" She choked on a sob and allowed Anna to gather her in her arms, as Ilia cried tears of anguish and anger.

At length, she pulled back and accepted the handkerchief Senza, who had joined them, gave her.

She wiped her eyes and blew her nose, then took in a deep breath. "I'm sorry for that outburst," she said, looking at her sisters a bit sheepishly.

"Crying is good for the soul," Senza said. "Everyone needs a good cry now and again. You have lots of reasons to cry, so it is good to get it done and over. Now we can come up with a plan."

Anna smiled. "She is right. And it is not your fault Tristan was taken. It is and always will be the fault of those who took him."

"Who could have taken him?" Edmond's voice came out of the shadows as he walked toward them. He stood in front of Ilia, who was leaning with her back against the railing, Senza and Anna on either side of her. "Who knew he was connected to you, and who knew where to find him?" Edmond asked.

Ilia pondered his questions, but it was Anna who answered. "Who knew you all were going to be in the islands? This wasn't by chance, if whoever took him determined to use him as bait to get

Ilia."

Edmond nodded. "I think we are going to have to look at our contacts to determine who might have sold us out. I know it is no one on this ship, but past that, I can vouch for no one."

"And then there is Trissa," Senza said. "She would have been able to divulge the connection between Tristan and Ilia. I know she was actively looking for Ilia, and I think I was her first choice as bait."

They all turned to look at Senza. "Why do you say that?" Ilia asked.

"She contacted me some time ago. She sent a letter," Senza's eyes flitted from person to person. "One I… haven't shown you yet. She invited me to meet her in Luna. She said she wanted to explain what really happened with Ilia, and she said she wanted to have a better relationship with me." Senza snorted. "I think you all have underestimated me, especially her. I am not the ninny you all seem to think I am."

Anna reached out a hand to pat Senza. "We did not think you a ninny. We thought you young, sheltered, and naïve."

Ilia smiled and nodded.

"Well, I decided to see what her game was. I responded and told her I would meet her. She wanted to meet at the stable yards." Senza paused. "So, I went, but I didn't go at the designated time. I went a bit early and hid. I waited to see who would show up, and I saw Trissa with two other men. They were talking. Not her, of course," she threw a sly smile Ilia's way. "She was gesturing to them, and they were saying they would hide and grab me. It was at that point I had what I needed, and I got out of there."

"I can't believe you didn't tell us this sooner, Senza!" Anna exclaimed.

Ilia tried to hide a smile. "Well, that is pretty definitive," she said. "I'm glad you were savvy enough to know when to get away."

Anna was not amused. "They could have found you, Senza. They could have taken you! You took a terrible risk." Her voice was a steely calm, a sure indication of her anger.

Senza reached over and put an arm around her. "I'm sorry, Anna. But you and Ilia were gone. I knew what Trissa had done to Ilia, and I had to know what she was up to. I found out, and she never knew I was there; just that I never showed up. She tried again later, and that is the letter I showed you at the house."

There were a few moments of silence, then Edmond said, "So what do we do now?"

"We go Nicola. Then we go get my husband," came Ilia's steely response.

Nineteen

They made anchor at Passmore, one of the outer islands, part of the Bourgeous Islands. Passmore was where one of the preserves for the Andolgias was located. They disembarked, leaving the crew on board. Ilia, Anna, and Senza went with Nicola to find lodgings, while Rudy and Edmond visited a nearby pub to see what kind of news they could pick up.

Ilia, her sisters, and Nicola found lodgings near the port in a small Inn run by an elderly couple. The women were happy to have their own rooms with connecting doors, and the men had a matching situation. Once Nicola had them settled, he went off to notify Edmond and Rudy of their location.

Finally, bathed and readied for bed, Ilia found she was too tired to do anything but sleep. She enjoyed a deep and dreamless sleep, awaking the next morning to the aroma of coffee and sweet rolls, which Anna carried in to tempt her out of bed.

Ilia stretched and sat up. "You are up and ready early," she said, as Anna set a tray on the bed and started pouring coffee into cups.

"I slept well and awoke feeling refreshed," Anna replied. "Maybe it was not being on a rocking ship that did it. But I found I was ready to start the day." She took a bite out of a sweet roll and said, "So I did."

Senza came in through the adjoining door on the other side of the room. "I thought I smelled coffee and something bready!" She plopped on the big bed beside Ilia, reaching for the cup of coffee Anna handed her.

Ilia bit into a roll and almost felt guilty at how much she enjoyed the taste and how good she felt when they were on such a terrible mission. She sat for a moment; her eyes closed as she tasted the roll. She reached out again for Tristan and felt his presence. Then a jolt as he pushed back against her.

"I can feel him, and he is responding," she said aloud without opening her eyes. Anna and Senza stared at her, waiting to see if there was more.

Ilia touched him again. "Tristan, my love," she emoted, "Are you there?" Again, he pushed back but did not speak. She was not surprised, as she knew he was in his animal form, but she tried again. "Tristan, we are in Passmore. I think you are near Andolgia trees. I know you do not know exactly where you are, but do Andolgia trees sound familiar?"

She held her breath. Then he pressed gently twice. She nearly broke the connection, she was so excited. But she managed to hold it together and said, "And the sea. Can you smell the sea?" Again, she waited, and again he pushed twice.

They were on the right track. Ilia had one more thing to impart before she broke off. "Tristan, they are holding you as bait for me. I am not alone, and I am coming to get you. Please know we are coming to get you, my love." She waited until she felt him push back, and then she broke the connection.

"We need to get the others to make a plan," she said after she regained her footing on the physical world.

"And we need to find out what they learned last night," Anna replied.

"We also need something to wear that does not draw attention to us," Senza said.

Both women looked at her with blank stares. She sighed patiently. "We have to find a way to disguise ourselves. We look too much like moon children, especially Ilia. She pretty much glows all the time, but after the full moon we had the night before last, she is positively shimmering."

Ilia had to agree. She filled her tank, and her capacity for holding lunar energy had grown. Now her entire being emanated with energy, and her eyes glowed an unsettling amber even in broad daylight.

They finished their breakfast and went their separate ways to get ready for the day. Anna was already dressed, so she went down the hall to find Edmond, Rudy, and Nicola, whom she knew had been up for hours.

Anna knocked on the door to Edmond's room and found him at work, looking at a local map of the island. He informed her Rudy and Nicola had gone to get a few supplies and check on the crew.

"Come over here and look at this map, Anna," he said, motioning her forward. "I think we can find a way to get into the general area where we think Tristan might be held."

"Really? How?" They had been trying to figure out a way to get all of them across the small island without drawing attention to the fact that they were there.

"I guess these trees are such a big deal they allow people to go in groups to see them." He paused and shook his head. "Strangest thing I have ever heard. People going to visit a bunch of trees."

Anna smiled. "The fruit of the trees is used in many curative potions. I'm betting Connor would love to have some."

"So, people go and pick the fruit?" he asked.

Anna nodded. "If it is not harvested, it falls on the ground, and when it rots it stinks to high heaven."

Edmond looked at her in surprise. "You have done your studying!"

Anna shook her head. "No. I have lived 500 years."

Edmond pulled back in amazement. "500 years? I had no idea."

Anna grew an impish grin. "Yes, yes, I'm the granny of the group." Sobering, she said, "When I was a young girl, Andolgia trees were everywhere."

Edmond was fascinated by her revelation. "You don't look 500 years old, and you certainly don't look like MY granny! How does that work? Do you just age very slowly?"

Anna smiled. "No, we age like everyone else, but at some point, in the adult time span, we stop aging for an indeterminate amount of time, then we start aging chronologically once again. Some of us will only live, say, 100 years. Some of us much longer. Even after 500 years, I have not begun what we call the descent. It's that chronological aging process that takes us to death. But then, I am a historian, and we tend to live long lives."

Edmond sat down on the bench in front of the desk. Even seated, he was nearly at eye level with her. He stared at her until she shifted uncomfortably under his gaze. He started. "I'm so sorry,

Anna. I didn't mean to make you uncomfortable. I was just thinking of all you have seen. Such a long progression of time and changes. And you have completely altered my view of a little old woman. I have never seen one as beautiful as you." He melted into a grin.

Anna blushed and, to her own horror, giggled. "Thank you, Edmond," she stammered, trying to regain her equilibrium. "We are trained, as historians, to weather the many years we are on earth.

It could become overwhelming if one were to not have tools to progress through the ages."

Edmond nodded, then looked back at the map. "So, have you been to this island before, in the past?"

Anna nodded. "Yes. Once. But it was a long time ago, and a lot has changed since then. I'm not sure I would be much help to you. I can tell you it is fruit-picking season for the Andolgias. That means we have a way into that area. What we need to find out is if there are out buildings or someplace where someone might be able to hold an enormous wolf."

Edmond agreed and was just about to comment, when Ilia bustled through the door, followed by Senza, Rudy, and Nicola. "It's getting crowded in here," Edmond said without irritation. "I haven't had my breakfast and neither have Rudy or Nicola. Maybe we can see if the good owners of this establishment will let us take over a sitting area, if they have one, and we can perfect our plans with some comfort."

They agreed, and Edmond left to find an area for them to work.

The rest of the day the group spent sequestered, perfecting a plan for reconnaissance. They had to know the lay of the land and if, indeed, there were facilities in the area where Tristan might be kept.

It was determined that for the recon mission, Nicola, Edmond, and Ilia would go. They argued heavily about whether Ilia should go, but in the end, Ilia insisted she needed to be there to see if any of the memories Tristan gave her matched with the surroundings. "There is absolutely no reason to continue on with this if we are in the wrong location," she said, happy to state the obvious.

"Aye lass, but you stick out like a wee beacon in the dead of night," Rudy said, eyeing her skeptically.

"I know," Ilia said, shrugging her shoulders, "I will just have to wear my heavy cloak with the hood. It covers me adequately."

Edmond snorted. "Yes. Except it is warm here. People are not wearing outer coverings this time of year."

"We shall have to hope for a storm, I guess," Ilia responded hotly, then eased her temper under his gaze. "All right. If there is a storm. I will go. If there isn't a storm, I will stay here. I don't want to endanger anyone."

"But then there will be no tours for us to use as cover if there is a storm," Nicola put in.

"I have an idea." Senza, who had been observing quietly up to that moment, said, "I can go. I remember Tristan's memories."

Everyone sat, contemplating this new option for a few minutes until Ilia broke the silence. "It's a good idea. Let's go with it."

"We can move to another inn closer than this one, and that might help," Anna said.

"I like that idea," Edmond said. "That is quite a distance from where the Anemone is anchored, but if Rudy will check in on the crew, I will feel easier about being farther away."

"Aye Captain," Rudy replied.

*

The small group joined the tour the next morning. Nicola, Senza, Anna, and Edmond masqueraded as two happily married couples looking to see the wonders of the amazing trees on the island. They joined the group at the last-minute, so as not to draw attention to themselves.

Ilia waited until later in the day when Rudy, having taken care of matters on the ship, made his way back to the inn to join her so they could find accommodation on the other side of the island. Ilia gathered her belongings along with her sisters', in a satchel, while Rudy gathered those items belonging to Edmond and Nicola.

They asked the innkeepers about other reputable places for lodgings on the other side of the island. The old innkeeper gave them the name of an inn his brother owned. "It is reputable, clean, and safe," he said, smiling proudly at Ilia and Rudy. "Our family has humble establishments, but they are good, and the food is as well."

Ilia and Rudy thanked the innkeeper and his wife for the information and the hospitality, then left to follow the directions the innkeeper gave them.

As soon as they were on the street, Rudy hailed a carriage turning to look at Ilia, "I think the less exposure you have to the people on this island and they to you, the better for all."

Ilia nodded. She knew she drew attention even within the recesses of her hood. They had already taken great risk in letting the innkeeper and his wife see her. But there was little they could do about it.

They traveled in the carriage, down the main road that wound through the middle of the island. The island was shaped like an unshelled peanut. The main road traveled through, narrowing to one lane in the thinnest part of the island. Ilia was thankful for the carriage, as she was able to sink back into its recesses and travel unnoticed.

They reached the inn recommended to them, and Ilia waited in the carriage, while Rudy went in to check the place for availability and security. Mainly, he wanted to make sure there wasn't a lot of traffic in and out of the inn. A busy inn meant a lot of eyes looking and watching.

Ilia leaned out of the carriage when Rudy came from the inn. "This will work just fine," he said, reaching forward to help her from the carriage. Ilia gave him the fee to pay the carriage driver, as she grabbed her satchel and made for the entrance.

She was just reaching for the door when a commotion down the road a small distance away drew her attention. A woman dressed in a beautiful dark green dress was motioning wildly to two men standing nearby. The woman had white hair covered almost entirely by a large black hat, and her face was covered by a veil. The two men were trying to explain something to the woman, and she was not liking what they were telling her.

Ilia sucked in a breath, frozen to the spot, as she watched Trissa flailing her arms in displeasure at the men. Rudy nearly ran into her when she did not move to open the door. "What?" he asked then followed her stare. He quickly reached around her to jerk the door open, "Don't stare," he hissed. "She will feel it."

He pushed Ilia through the open door and guided her to the desk, where the innkeeper stood waiting to finish their reservation. Rudy dropped the rest of their baggage on the floor and relieved Ilia of her large satchel, as she fumbled for the funds to pay for their lodgings.

She finally managed to make the exchange, then she led Rudy, who was carrying all their belongings, down a corridor that opened into a sitting area. There were three rooms on one side for Ilia and her sisters, and three rooms for Nicola, Edmond, and Rudy.

Rudy delivered Ilia's big satchel to the room she chose then went back to drop the rest of the bags in one of the other rooms. When Ilia returned to the sitting room he said, "I'm not used to living so nice. These rooms are better than those we had last night. I'm getting spoiled with all this luxury." He sat down in a comfortable chair, taking his ease, his hands clasped behind his head.

Ilia gave and indulgent smile then said, "I think I need a drink."

"How about a bit of brandy?" Rudy asked.

Ilia nodded. "That would just about hit the spot, but let me get us some glasses, and I think I shall also order tea with something to eat."

Rudy shook his head in agreement. "I could do with a bite."

Ilia pulled a light shawl from her baggage and wrapped it about her head and shoulders. Seeing

Trissa had shaken her to the core, and she didn't want to take any chances by drawing attention. She met the innkeeper's wife and put in her request. The woman was a rosy, plump woman with a ready smile. "Here are two glasses, dear, and I will see to tea and a bite to eat for you."

Ilia thanked the woman and went back to the sitting area, where Rudy was sitting in one of the deep-backed chairs, smoking his pipe, lost in thought.

Ilia sat down in a chair across from Rudy and said, "I know this island is rife with magikal creatures. I can feel it. I wonder if they know they are being hunted. They seem to be just going about their daily lives. You would think they would know there are predators right under their noses.

Rudy contemplated this through his pipe. Then he looked at her and said, "Well, I don't know.

You are pretty savvy, lass, but you didn't know, did you?"

Ilia realized the truth in what he was saying. "No, I suppose I didn't. People don't pay attention, and I suppose that is what these predators are counting on. People go about their daily lives not bothering about anything around them, and then one day they are snatched and never make it home."

Rudy bobbed his head. "Who was that woman you were staring at earlier? Was she your sister?"

Ilia nodded. "I didn't realize you hadn't met her." She waited for him to shake his head. With some effort she met his gaze. "I didn't know how I would react seeing her again. It came upon me rather suddenly."

"Aye, and to be sure it was a shock. I nearly fell over you trying to get in the door." He grinned, and then a moment later said, "It seems your, er, alteration of her speech abilities has been successful."

Ilia gave a small laugh. "Yes. She apparently doesn't bother about drawing attention to herself.

She was flailing her arms at those two men as though she was drowning." She sobered, saying,

"Those were two of the men who were there that day."

Rudy nodded. He learned enough from Tristan to have an understanding about what had happened to Ilia. "Eye on the prize. We keep track of them, and maybe they will lead us right where we need to be." He paused, watching her face. "But you must not leave this inn."

He waited for her agreement. It came a bit slow for him, so he added, "You have the ability to ruin all of this if you are seen. Is that what you want?"

Ilia's expression became defensive. "I am aware of what is at stake, Rudy."

"That is not what I asked," he responded, blowing smoke out of the corner of his mouth, as he studied her.

Ilia leaned back in the chair. "I am committed to getting my husband back by whatever means possible. You need to know what that means to me. I will follow whatever plans we have implemented to get him, but if that does not work, I will take matters into my own hands and raze the building – and all the knaves trying to steal both of us – to the ground. I will do absolutely everything in my power to stop this."

It wasn't so much what she said that made the hair stand up on the back of his neck. It was the calm and precise manner in which she delivered the information; cold and calculating. Rudy was reminded of the glowing form on the Anemone's prow, pulling the raging waves back down into calm seas, and for the first time, he found Ilia frightening, as he looked at her sitting back in the deep-backed chair, her silver curls covering her pale face, her eyes like amber orbs, the only display of the intense power she held in check deep within.

Rudy cleared his throat, "Well, I can't find fault with your logic. Hopefully, we can get in and get out without anyone the wiser."

He put his hand up as she prepared to refute his statement, "Please, lass. I agree we have to take this organization down, but what if annihilating everyone in this faction prevents us from having access to the bigger group? Then what? None of you will ever be safe."

Ilia leaned back into the big chair once again, sighing. "You are right, of course. But you must understand one thing this Syndicate does not. There is little they can do now to contain me.

Last time, I was taken off guard and so very new to my magik. I thought I needed my hands to work, but it turns out, a flick of a finger would have sufficed." She paused, flicking her index finger to watch sparks fly from it, as she gently blew and then put them out before they could cause mischief.

"You see, Rudy, for me, it's not just rescuing Tristan that drives me, though that is the core. It is also the fact that, unwittingly, I put all of us on the radar of the Syndicate by leading them to think they actually could catch me and anyone else connected to me.

I did that by being so naïve and not understanding of what I was capable. Now they are operating under the assumption they can take my mate and somehow lure me in and manage either to take me or have me make a trade. Had I known what I was doing, I would have been able to show, easily, they cannot contain me." She sighed again. "But I suppose they would have to try, regardless."

Rudy watched her, forcing himself not to cower at her intensity. "So, you have a plan to get in and get Tristan? Some sort of covert operation?" he asked.

Ilia turned her glowing amber eyes on him. "Oh, no. There will be nothing covert about it." She saw his confusion and smiled. "You all have made your plans for how this will go. Please do not misunderstand what I am about to say, Rudy. I cherish each and every one of you. But you are human, and even Senza, just coming into her powers, is no match for the Syndicate. I am not singing my own praises. I am just sharing with you what I know, and I am sharing with you what I am going to do."

"What is that?" Rudy asked, uncertain he wanted the response.

"I'm going to walk into that place. I'm going to get my husband," she said, through gritted teeth, "And I'm going to burn them all to the ground." Ilia stood and strode to the bedroom door. She laid her hand on the doorknob, but then she turned to look at Rudy. "I appreciate you all very much, but I fear this is far out of your abilities, and at just the beginning of mine. I will sleep and wait for nightfall." She turned back to the door, crossed its threshold, and shut it after her.

Immobilized, Rudy stared at the door for some time before turning to pour himself another brandy then thought better of it and poured a whisky instead.

*

The sun was just setting when the rest of the group found Ilia and Rudy. Rudy left a message for Edmond at the inn where they stayed the first night. The innkeeper was more than happy to provide directions, and soon they were all huddled together in the sitting room of their newest haven.

"How was the fruit picking excursion?" Rudy asked.

"We learned a lot about the area," Edmond responded.

"And it was a lot of fun," Senza interjected. "I wanted to get some fruit to bring back, but they charge you to keep the fruit. Can you believe it?" she said, shaking her head in disbelief. "We had to pay to take the tour and pick fruit, but we weren't allowed to keep any of it!"

Anna laughed. "They use the fruit to sell in the community and for medicinal supplies. I think it is pretty clever. Give people tours of ancient trees that are nearly extinct and make the people touring pick fruit and give it back to the community to use and sell."

Edmond chuckled as well. "Quite a system they have going here."

"Did you manage to find any useful information to help our cause?" Ilia asked lightly.

Rudy glanced at her, as the other four sobered. "Yes," Anna responded. "There is a building of interest on the far side of the grove. We wandered into that area to pick fruit and were, rather hurriedly, guided back toward the other side of the grove."

"Yes, and our guide was nervy while trying to do it," Edmond added.

"Nicola and I pretended that we were married, and that I was in a delicate way, so we could go sit near the edge of the property," Senza said, beaming at the group. "Then he was able to disappear for a while to see what he could find out."

Nicola nodded. "I got into the building and looked around a bit. I wasn't able to find Tristan, but I think he must be there. I didn't want to leave Senza too long. People might have started asking where I was, so I couldn't find out as much as I wanted to."

Ilia looked at him. 'I just need to know the layout, Nicola. That's all I need."

Everyone looked at her. After a pregnant pause, all eyes on Ilia, Edmond finally said, "What are you saying, Ilia?"

Ilia stood from her chair and moved around to the sideboard, where she poured a cup of tea then turned to face the group. "I'm saying I'm going in tonight, and I'm going to get my husband."

Everyone began speaking at once, admonishing, protesting, and asking questions. Everyone except Nicola. Ilia waited for them to say what they needed to say, and when they fell silent, she said, "I am going in alone. I am not caught up in some sort of crazed passion that keeps me from seeing reality. Quite the contrary. I know exactly what I am capable of. I am not afraid, but I am certainly determined." She paused for a moment, to gather her thoughts. "I also have the advantage of surprise, as they have no idea what I am."

She took a sip of her tea and continued. "Anna and Senza, I saw Trissa today." Her sisters reacted with surprise and dismay.

"Did she see you?" Anna asked.

Ilia shook her head, "No, thanks to Rudy who scooted me into the inn before she saw me." "Where was she?" Senza asked.

"Just down the street. The two men who were involved in my kidnapping were with her." Ilia glanced at Anna, who had been there and would remember the two men.

There was silence while everyone digested the information. At length, Anna said, "What made you decide to change the plan, Ilia?"

Ilia looked at her sister, smiling. "You know me so well. You know what made me change the plan."

Their eyes locked and held for a moment. Anna said, "Trissa being here has changed things."

Ilia nodded. "I should have finished her that day. I will not make the same mistake this time. I don't want either you or Senza there for that, and," she glanced over at Edmond, "I don't want

Edmond involved in this at all."

Edmond stammered to protest, but Ilia held up a hand. "Edmond you are like a brother to me, and there is no one I trust more than you, but your responsibility is the crew. I do not want to put you in any kind of danger that would impact them and their livelihood. You and Rudy have a job, and that is to go back to the ship and wait for us."

Edmond cleared his throat, then exhaled heavily. "You are right. We will go to the ship."

Ilia turned to Nicola, but before she could say anything he said, quietly, "I will go with you. No. Do not say anything. I know what I promised my wife, and that is to make sure you never go through any of this alone. I know what you can do, moon child. I am not worried." He looked at

Ilia and smiled. "It is dark. Let us go get the Lord Pirate."

Ilia turned to her sisters. "Please go with Edmond and Rudy. Wait for me on the ship."

"What if Tristan can't walk?" Anna asked. "What will you do?"

"I have spoken to him. He knows we are coming, and between Nicola and I, we can get him out of there. We will take a cart to get there. We just need to get him to the cart, and we will be fine.

"I know you all want to be there tonight," Ilia murmured, "but I want you to be safe, and I know the element of surprise we have maintained by my not being visible has helped with that, and them underestimating my abilities will also be very helpful." Ilia paused, biting her lip. "I have one concern and that is the possibility that Trissa has seen Senza and Anna, or even Edmond."

She stared out the window for a moment, seemingly unaware of the rest of the group. Then she shrugged, as though coming to terms with something. "No matter. As long as you are on the ship, it will only be Nicola and I at risk, and though I would not put him in jeopardy," she glanced at Nicola, smiling as he nodded once in response, "I know he has ways of taking care of himself. And that is not even speaking to his abilities to blend in. His martial arts are unequalled." Nicola bowed his head slightly, and Ilia returned the gesture.

"How soon would you like us to leave?" Edmond asked.

"We need to leave as soon as possible," Anna responded before Ilia could say anything. "We need to be careful how we leave, so as to not draw attention."

"I have the perfect excuse," Ilia said. "There is a theatre production happening in the amphitheater. You will go to that and then leave at intermission. Should anyone be looking, they will see you enjoying yourselves. Anyone looking for us will, of course, wonder what has happened to me, but this is the best we can do, and if you are followed, you will be followed to the theater, not the ship."

There was a pondering silence.

"We have nothing to wear!" Senza exclaimed. "We will be a dead giveaway if we are wearing what we have."

Ilia smiled. "Rudy went to the ship and retrieved clothes for you. I figured it would be safer to go there than to alert people of our presence by running all over the island trying to buy apparel. We just don't have any contacts here, so this was the timeliest, and safest option."

Again, the group sat in silent contemplation until it was broken by a woman delivering their meal. She served a meaty stew, with thick slices of buttered bread, wedges of cheese, and tankards of ale. The fare at the inn was simple but hearty. They all ate in silence, each considering what the night's turn of events might produce.

"I feel as though I have been given no options in this charade," Edmond said at length, putting down his spoon, his brow furrowed in frustration. Then he looked at Ilia, his gaze unwavering.

She returned it and said, "You came up with a plan and assumed I would go along with it, and generally I would, as you make good plans." His jaw unclenched with her praise. "However," she went on, "you know very little about magik; certainly, very little about my particular abilities at this point in time. It is I who will have to hinder our enemies, not you.

Humans will be ineffectual in this situation, and I already have the life of my husband to consider. Nicola is a magikal creature and will be able to contend with our foes. The rest of you, sans Senza, who is still developing, will not be able to make meaningful contributions in this situation, and I cannot account for you. Were you to be harmed in this venture, I would never forgive myself." Her gaze swept everyone in the group, landing on Edmond. She shrugged when the scowl remained on his face.

"I love you as a brother, Edmond, but you do not call the shots on every situation just because you are male. I'm sorry. It is my life on the line. Not yours. I will determine how I lay it down." Edmond's eyes widened as her words hung between them.

Ilia addressed the group. "If you want to help Tristan – if you want to help me, you will follow this plan. Senza, I will keep connection with you, so you know what is happening and can keep everyone informed. If we lose connection, do not fret. There can be many reasons for that. Just keep your head about you." She smiled as her sister nodded in acquiescence. "Now if you will excuse me. I am going to sit out back, in the innkeeper's little garden, and refuel a bit." With that she stood, took up her cloak, and left the room.

Edmond spoke first, "I can't believe we are going along with this ridiculous plan!" His anger boiled over. "She will get herself killed. And Tristan and Nicola."

No one spoke for a moment then Anna said, her voice calm and steady, "Have you so little faith,

Edmond? Do you somehow think you can do better?"

He pulled back, surprised at her questions and the anger that shone in her eyes. "No. I thought we would be doing it together. I thought we had a plan."

"No. *You* had a plan. A plan to use a weapon because that is what my sister is. A weapon you know little about. Where does your knowledge come from that you could be so confident in your plan? I have known her for over 100 years, and still, I do not fully perceive her capabilities."

Edmond exhaled a deep breath, running a hand through his hair as he fell back into his chair. "I know. But what about Nicola? She could get him killed. I noticed she didn't mention feeling responsible for him."

"You were not listening, Captain," Nicola said. "She doesn't need to worry about me, because I am wily. You forget that day when the Commander rescued me, I was taken from behind by several ruffians. No one could have gotten out of that. But I fear you, along with most of the crew, believe I am some fragile creature unable to defend myself." He paused, holding up a hand, as Edmond drew in a breath to respond.

"The Commander knows this. When I find my way onto ships, I kill many people on my way to the treasure. You never know this, because I'm so silent and stealthy, my victims never know they are about to die. I am more than capable of going with Ilia and helping her. The two of us together require no one else." He stood. "And now if you will excuse me, I must change clothes and prepare.

Edmond stared after Nicola, letting out a growl of frustration. Then he glanced up to see Rudy staring at him, a grin on his face. "What's so funny about this?" Edmond grumbled.

Anna and Senza stood and excused themselves to go get ready for the theater. As they left the room, Rudy said, "I find you a great deal amusing, Ed."

Edmond stared. "I don't see why."

Rudy sat forward, lit his pipe, then sat back to take a draw on it. "Ed, you are acting like a spoiled little kid. This situation doesn't belong to you. It belongs to Ilia and Tristan. And right now, more specifically to Ilia. Who are you to determine her fate for her? What do you know that somehow better qualifies you to make decisions in this situation? Is it because you are male? I hate to be the one to break it to ye, but women are generally smarter than men in my experience.

It's out of the goodness of their hearts they allow us to make decisions not only for ourselves but them as well. She was a bit nicer about it, but apparently you need it stated bluntly."

Edmond snorted, staring at Rudy. He wanted to rail at his childhood friend, but Rudy knew him too well. He was acting like a little kid, he knew. He sighed and reached for the flask of brandy Rudy handed to him, pouring some into his glass to drink.

At length, he put the glass back on the table with a thunk and said, "You are right."

Rudy grinned at him, tamping his pipe. He scooted back from the table and walked around to put a hand on Edmond's shoulder. "Trust her. We must, for she is really the only one who can accomplish this, and we should not kid ourselves otherwise."

Edmond exhaled his frustration. "I know. I have nothing against Ilia. I just feel useless."

"Well let's get back to the ship and wait for the open seas, the place that is our world. You will be back in your element there." Edmond nodded in agreement, and they both went to prepare for the evening.

*

There was one change made to Ilia's plan. Rudy did not go to the theater. He bribed the driver of the cart they would use so he was able to drive it. No one put up an argument against the change. Senza and Anna were seen in the company of Nicola and Edmond. To have Rudy suddenly join them would draw attention.

"I should have considered that," Ilia conceded. "Of course, it makes sense for Edmond to accompany Senza and Anna. Then Rudy can drive us and be ready to drive us out of there in haste."

They said their goodbyes, reiterated their plans, and reviewed the timeline. Then they were on their way. They did not tell the innkeeper anything but that they were going to the theater. Their items were stowed in the cart under the seat, and their rooms left empty.

Ilia made her way to the cart to join Nicola and Rudy. Nicola was dressed in black and blended into the night as though he didn't exist. He sat in the back of the cart. Ilia sat up on the cart with Rudy, her black cape covering her from head to foot. Rudy didn't say anything but waited for Ilia to get situated then snapped a rein, and the cart lurched forward.

It took about half an hour to get to the far end of the Andolgia orchard and their destination. Rudy pulled into an area where the night shadows covered the cart and horse completely. He held out a hand to steady Ilia as she climbed down from the cart, saying, "Steady as you go, lass. I will be waiting here."

*

As she walked toward the building, Ilia felt Nicola reach out and take her hand. It was the only way she knew where he was, and the warmth of his hand covering hers was reassuring. He pulled her around the building to a side entrance. Ilia was surprised it was unlocked but didn't say anything.

They moved down a dimply lit hall, and Ilia noticed Nicola was no longer black from head to toe. His body had adjusted to allow for the nuances of light coming from the dimly lit hall. Ilia marveled at his amazing ability to change, to absorb every environment they crossed. Had he not been holding her hand, she would have had no idea he was even there.

They continued down the long hall, checking each room until they reached a room on the right side at the end of the corridor. Nicola quietly shifted the handle of the roughly hewn door and pushed it open ever so carefully. Ilia saw two tables in the dim light, and on the far table closest to the wall a large furry creature lay completely immobile. Off to the right of the table was a huge cage, the door standing open.

Ilia wanted to exclaim and run to Tristan, but Nicola grabbed her and pulled her against him as he stood near the wall, behind the open door. "No," he whispered. "Keep your head, or we are all three doomed." He held Ilia against him, her back to his chest, one arm around her shoulders above her breasts and one hand around her waist until he felt her relax. Then he released her and appeared to melt into the wall.

Ilia stood staring at the scene before her, reaching out to touch Tristan with her mind. He responded weakly to her mental touch. "Be ready, my love," she said. "We are here, and we are taking you out of this place." The figure on the table shifted slightly, then whimpered in pain.

Ilia's blood boiled, her magik ready to rage out of her, but she tamped it down. "*Not yet,*" she told it.

She reached out to Senza, "Are you there? We are in." She felt the reassuring pressure from Senza. "Get to the ship."

Ilia advanced slowly, until she was on the left side of the far table near Tristan's head. This was too easy. She knew they were probably walking into a trap. Where was Trissa? Ilia knew Trissa had to be involved. It was no coincidence that she was on the island where Tristan was being held.

As though Ilia had conjured her, three figures entered the room. Trissa was in front of the two men.

Trissa said nothing, but motioned to Adam, as she pointed a gun right at Ilia. Adam's lip curled, as James lunged between the two tables and pulled a knife, holding it to Tristan's throat. "Give your sister back her voice or James here will cut his throat."

Ilia looked at her sister for a long moment. She used both hands to craft the orb and sent it across the room to hover over her sister. Ilia closed her eyes for a moment, and the orb broke over Trissa.

Trissa sputtered and coughed, then smiled. "Hello sister." Her voice came out in raspy bursts, as she massaged her throat. "You remember James and Adam. They are happy to see you, as am I. They are hoping to pick up where they left off last time we were all together, and you have something that belongs to them, I believe. They think you will make men of them." Trissa's words came out jerky and forced, ending in a scraping laugh at her own joke.

Ilia shook her head. "I will never give back what I took from them, and," she continued quickly, as James reached for Tristan again, "If you touch him again, I will castrate both of you."

James's hand stilled. Trissa laughed again and walked toward Ilia. She pointed the gun at Ilia and said, "Get her tied up, Adam. She can't do anything unless she can use both hands together."

Ilia stood, as Adam secured her hands. The bindings had a pole in between them, and her hands were bound on either side of the pole in front of her. "Are you sure you understand how this works?" she asked Trissa.

Trissa stood back with a smug smile. "I know just how this works. You are going to get on that table, and your husband will watch as I peel off your scalp. Then I will have your magik."

Ilia was amazed at her sister's stupidity. "Trissa, it doesn't work that way."

"It does," Trissa screamed. "I have researched it, and I will cut you up in pieces to get to the magik if I have to!" She moved over and grabbed Ilia by the arms, jerking her toward the table.

Ilia pulled back and broke out of Trissa's grasp. She stood with her hands in the cuffs, splayed out, palms down, and she called upon her magik. It surged through her like water through an opened dam. Her fingers glowed. She looked at Trissa, her eyes becoming glowing orbs in her head, the irises disappearing as she said in a tranquil voice, "Since you have done so much research, I'm guessing you have plan B for when plan A doesn't work?"

Trissa stood rooted to the spot, as did Adam and James. This was beginning to feel an awful lot like the last experience they'd had with this woman. Ilia could see a twinge of fear swimming its way to the surface of Trissa's clearly unhinged mind, but she shook her head. "I have backup to help with any unanticipated contingencies this time."

Ilia felt Senza nudge her, she heard Senza's voice say, "Nicola has confirmed there is no one else in the building."

Ilia stood for a moment, puzzled. Then realization dawned, and she said, "You have gone rogue,

Trissa. There is no one here but you and your two sidekicks. You linked up with the Syndicate to use their resources to find us and take Tristan.

Somehow you have managed to shake them, and you are here trying to get my power. You do understand, the Syndicate does not want to work with magikal creatures. It wants to take our magik and destroy us. They will slave us out if we do not supply anything they want, or, as I said, they will simply kill us. You somehow found out they were tracking Tristan. They have been tracking him for some time, but not, I think, because he is a shapeshifter. They want to find out why he is so very good at what he does."

Trissa's face suffused with anger, and she shook her head, "No! You are wrong! When I have your power, I will be in a position of power. That's all I want. I want power. I will create my own organization, and I will be able to do what I want!" She held up the gun and pointed it at Ilia once again. "Now get on that table," she commanded.

Power surged through Ilia, and she flicked her fingers, now glowing with heated magik, at her bindings, and they melted from around her wrists, falling with a clunk on the floor. As she lifted her hands, Trissa lifted the gun. Ilia said in a calm voice, "Shooting me will ensure you do not get my magik, Trissa."

Trissa stopped herself from pulling on the trigger. What she wanted to do in her anger waged with a shred of rationale. She stamped her foot, screaming, "I hate you! I hate you! I want you dead!" She turned and headed over to the table where Tristan lay. "You will give me what I want, or I will kill your mate!" She grabbed the knife James held loosely in his hand. He backed away from her and the table to join Adam on the other side of the room near the door.

Ilia was not worried about them, as she knew Nicola was nearby, completely hidden. She looked at Trissa, and something in her face must have registered as resistance, for Trissa's eyes narrowed, and she turned, raising the knife over her head.

Just as she began plunging the knife toward the wolf's heart, a funny thing happened. She found she was flying, no, hurtling through the air. Her body hit what she assumed was a wall, with such force, she felt bones shatter. She tried to sit up but realized she was still suspended off the ground. She raised her head and looked across the room at her sister, but what she saw was a white, glowing creature, with orbs the color of amber shining from what should have been eye sockets. The creature was holding out a hand, and from it came a white light so strong Trissa felt it was burning a hole through her own eye sockets. She struggled to move and realized she couldn't. Her body was completely broken.

Ilia stepped toward Trissa. "You are finished. Your hubris and greed have overtaken you, and you are no good on this earth. I have ended your time here. You will disintegrate and be absorbed back into moon rays. You have been a disgrace to our kind, and you have now paid the price." With that, Ilia turned away from Trissa, the magik that held her above the ground releasing her to fall heavily to the floor.

Adam and James stood frozen to the spot. Ilia turned to look at them, magik still rolling off her in waves. "You will disappear. If I see you again. I will end you on the spot." Both men turned and fled the room.

Ilia raced to the table where Tristan lay. "Tristan, my love. I am here, and I am taking you home." She leaned down to place a kiss on his muzzle then closed her eyes, running her hands over his body, her magik coating him. "This will keep you from feeling so much pain. We have to move you and I know it will hurt, but this will help."

Ilia glanced up to see Nicola in his black apparel coming into the room, pulling a wagon. He brought the wagon around to the side of the table, and between the two of them, they pushed and pulled Tristan into the wagon. The magik coating did help, as he only whimpered when they transitioned him into the wagon.

"What about her," Nicola asked, nodding his head in Trissa's direction.

Ilia glanced over at Trissa. "She will be gone in a few moments. She is bleeding internally and most of her bones are broken."

She looked at Nicola and their eyes held for a moment. Nicola nodded at her. "You gave her an opportunity to make a different decision. She sealed her own fate." He gave her a small smile of reassurance then said, "Come. We are alone at present, but we may not be for long."

Nicola pushed the wagon through the open door, following Ilia. They made their way down the corridor, and out into the night to the cart where Rudy awaited them. Once Tristan was loaded, Ilia instructed them to drive down the road away from the building. She turned back toward the building and reached her arms up toward the sky, pulling on the power from the waxing gibbous moon. She gathered the power in her arms and pushed it toward the building. There was a mighty shaking, and then the building collapsed, debris flying from it as it crumbled with a loud boom.

Ilia ran toward the carriage, climbing in back with Tristan, her body covering his as they raced away from the fallen building and flying debris. When they reached the main road, she looked up, staring into Tristan's face. He had shifted back to his human form. His eyes searched hers, as she said, "I said I would raze it to the ground, and anyone bent on hurting you with it. I keep my promises."

Twenty

Ilia sat next to the bed where Connor was examining Tristan. Tristan seemed only partially aware of what was happening. Connor gave Ilia a reassuring glance, saying, "He has been in his animal form a long time. What you are seeing is the war within the shapeshifter, not anything due to injuries. He will make the decision soon and will regain full consciousness."

Ilia exhaled in relief. "How bad are his injuries?"

Connor finished putting a poultice on a puncture wound and sat back, looking down at Tristan.

"Broken ribs and possibly a fracture or two in his hands. The knife wound must have been treated because it has healed cleanly. He's malnourished. That is something highly detrimental to a shapeshifter, especially in animal form. I would guess he got aggressive as they pushed him toward starvation. In a lot of ways, it would have been better for him to shift back to his human form. I'm not sure why he didn't." Connor paused for a moment, considering. "He has several puncture wounds. I expect that was being stabbed through the cage."

Ilia felt the anger rising within her, but she shoved it back down. She wanted to be a calming influence on Tristan. She looked at Connor, tears in her eyes. "If I had just gotten to him sooner,

Connor, it wouldn't be so bad."

"Honestly, he is in much better shape than I thought he would be," Connor replied. He stood, gathering his tools, then looked at Ilia. "Give him liquids to get him rehydrated. And spend time touching him and talking to him. That is the best medicine now." He patted her on the shoulder as he moved around the bed and out the door.

Ilia looked at her husband, bruised, battered, and emaciated. She reached over and began to rub his elbow. He loved it when she rubbed his elbows. She talked of what had happened in his absence, and she prayed he would soon become aware of where he was.

*

The sun was setting when Ilia felt pressure on her hand. She jerked awake and realized she had fallen asleep, her head and arms on the bed, her hand clasping Tristan's. Ilia raised her head and looked into a pair of verdant eyes. Tristan was looking at her as though he wasn't yet sure where he was.

"Are you real?" he asked, his voice deep and raspy from lack of use.

"I'm real," Ilia replied. "I must have fallen asleep, but I was waiting for you to come back to me."

Tristan smiled. "You must be real. In my dreams our conversations never made it this long.

Except when you came to me; when you brought the snake."

Ilia smiled. "Yes, I spoke to you. Often."

Tristan released a sigh. "Aye lass."

Ilia's eyes filled with tears, and she began to weep.

"You are going to have to crawl over here if you want me to hold you, lass. I find I can hardly lift my arms."

Ilia scrambled onto the bed and carefully moved into his arms. She cried until she was spent, and Tristan did not stop her.

At length he said, "I wondered many times if I would ever hold you again. But I knew you would find a way. You are a canny lass."

Ilia laughed lightly through her tears. "I was at a loss until I figured out you were in your other form. Once I figured that out, it explained why I couldn't reach you. Our link has always been weaker when you are in your wolf form."

Tristan said, "Aye, and I think I was unconscious for some time and then drugged for some of the time. And then I became too weak, because they never fed me and only gave me enough water to stay alive. I never had much of a chance. It was clever of them. Did you find out who all was involved? What it was about?"

Ilia sat up, wiping her face with a handkerchief she had tucked up her sleeve. "I don't have definitive proof, but I think Trissa joined the Syndicate with Adam and James. She wanted me, but she figured you would be good bait.

The Syndicate has been following you, not because of your abilities as a shapeshifter, but because of your success as a pirate. They wanted to find out how you do it so smoothly with little altercation. I believe that is why you have had that canine sense that someone has been following you."

Tristan nodded. His lips cracked open as he began to speak, and he winced. Ilia rose to get him something to drink and some salve for his lips. She regarded him as she came back to the bed.

His face was gray, making his dark tan look painted on. His beard was thick and long, but Ilia could see his cheeks were sunken from lack of food.

She walked over, put some salve on his lips then gave him a drink. He would have reached up to take the cup from her, but she pulled back. "Connor says to go careful on how much you drink, as it can make you throw up."

Tristan lay back against the pillow and nodded. "Aye, I doubt I would have the energy. Is he going to keep starving me or will I get some food at some point?" he asked, scowling.

Ilia grinned at him. "I can go get some broth. He said I was to get him when you woke." She turned to slide off the bed, but he grabbed her arm, then winced, letting go.

"Stay with me lass. I want to hear the rest of your explanation. And I'm not ready for you to leave me."

Ilia smiled and scooted back onto the bed. "I think the Syndicate met up with Trissa, and she said she could get you if they could tell her your location. She did not tell them about me."

Tristan gave her a sharp look. "They didn't know about you?"

Ilia shook her head. "No, and I think they still don't know about me."

Tristan looked out the window across the room from them. The sun was just sliding over the horizon, its last rays illuminating the ocean waves rocking the boat. "So, this was about me and learning how to pillage ships like me. I never thought of that. I always assumed they used me as bait."

"They did. Well, Trissa did. I think Trissa stabbed you from behind. She was going to torture information out of you, but you shifted after she stabbed you, and you never went back to your human form, so she had to haul this gigantic wolf around and get you to a place where she could keep you.

I think she had Adam and James haul you to that building, and I believe that was the place she was supposed to take you. She was to notify the Syndicate when she had you, but she didn't notify them, because she knew I would come looking for you."

Tristan nodded. "Of course."

"When I finally made contact with you, you gave me a bunch of sensory images you'd encountered as a wolf. They were mostly scents and a few images. Senza has come into her abilities, and she was able to help me sift through the images." She paused at his questioning look.

"Senza has amazing telepathic skills. I think as she continues to work on them, she will become extraordinary with them. Anna helped us pinpoint the Andolgia trees. She is the only one who has ever been around them, having lived 500 years. She was able to help us identify them, and she explained they are endangered. They can only be found in three conservation parks. From her information, we narrowed down the location. Then we went and got you."

"And what of Trissa and her two thugs?" he asked.

"Trissa did not survive. Adam and James only wanted me to reverse the curse I put on them, and when they discovered I wouldn't, they ran. Trissa was dead before I destroyed the building, but if there was any question, she might still be alive, there is none now."

Ilia sat with her hands in her lap looking at her fingers for a moment, remembering the power that moved through them to perform such a feat.

"I missed quite a show, then, did I?" Tristan asked, smiling through his cracked lips. Then, "Who helped you, lass?"

"Nicola went with me. Rudy stayed with the cart we drove to make sure we had a way to escape. I sent Edmond, Anna, and Senza back to the ship."

"I bet Edmond was happy about that!" Tristan said, chuckling.

Ilia laughed, "Yes, we had quite a row before he finally agreed. I think he was laboring under the assumption he could do it better. But I assured him, he could not." She said, with a smug grin.

*

It was a few days before Tristan could get out of bed and slowly amble around the upper deck. The crew were waiting for him and yelled their welcomes to him from below deck. Edmond visited him several times, and Rudy stopped in to check on him, as well. Senza and Anna were waiting to greet him when he made an appearance.

The group often met together on the upper deck to visit and discuss their future endeavors. Tristan welcomed the views from everyone, though it was understood he would make the final decision. Rudy did not join in. He was content to be back in his position supervising the crew on the lower deck.

"Where are we going?" Anna asked one day, as they sat over afternoon tea.

Tristan, who was making daily strides on regaining his health, said, "We are headed for the Isle, though I don't know how long we will stay." He glanced at Ilia before saying, "Since we know the Syndicate is actually looking for me rather than Ilia at this point, I don't want to take any new jobs."

His eyes widened as he remembered something. He looked at Edmond in alarm, "The egg,

Edmond. Where it is?"

"Rest easy, Commander. We delivered the egg. There were no problems. The buyer is aware of the unrest all around. He was not surprised we were delayed, though I did not give him particulars as to why we were delayed."

Tristan heaved a sigh of relief. "I am so glad you remembered to get that done." He caught

Edmond exchanging looks with Ilia, and said, "What?"

Edmond gave a sheepish grin, "It was actually Ilia who remembered about the egg. I was indisposed for a time, and I simply forgot about it. My apologies, sir. Thankfully, Ilia remembered, and we took care of that before we went to get Senza."

"What could possibly make you forget about such a task?" Edmond inquired, his brow furrowing in consternation.

"My love, many things happened when you disappeared, not the least of which your death. We all thought you were dead at one point. Edmond suffered at the knowledge."

Tristan stared at Ilia for a moment taking in what she said then turned his gaze to Edmond. "I'm sorry, my friend. I did not realize," he said, reaching over to squeeze Edmond's arm.

Edmond chuckled. "I now know how I handle your death, so don't die again!" Everyone laughed, happy to be able to make light of such a traumatic incident.

Ilia shifted the conversation. "So, we need to go to the island. How long, and why?"

Tristan laughed, leaning over to kiss Ilia. "I have missed you so much, my love. I can always count on you to cut to the chase."

Ilia smiled. "No more than I have missed you."

Tristan put an arm around her. "I would like to go to the Isle and let Nicola see his wife and child," he said. "We could all use a rest. There are enough places in the village to house us for a time, and the weather is good. The crew can camp on the beach."

He looked at Ilia. "Did you find anything in the books at the house?"

Ilia shook her head. "Not really. There wasn't time."

"So, what is everyone thinking? I have been out of the loop for a bit, so I would like input from each of you. Ilia and I will go to the Isle. I can regain my strength, and she can do research, but I would like to know where you all would like to go. Eventually, whether we search out

Ilia's family or hunt the Syndicate, the place to go will be Portsmith, but I have not contemplated further than that."

"I would like to get to Portsmith," Senza said. "Ella invited me to stay with her and learn more culinary skills."

Ilia smiled. "That is a very good idea."

"Can we ensure her safety?" Tristan asked.

"I put protection spells on Ella's home before we left to get you. We planned on gathering moon children and bring them to her home, but that was when we thought the Syndicate knew about me and would be focused on collecting moon children," Ilia said.

Tristan nodded. "I think it is still a good idea. It is only a matter of time before word gets out about you. Just taking a look at that building your destroyed will make them start looking about."

Ilia bit her lip. She hadn't considered what such a display of power would say to the Syndicate. She had been reckless, and now, her act may have shortened the amount of time they could all go unnoticed.

Tristan sensed her thoughts had shifted. He pulled her a bit closer to him as he said, "What about you, Anna?"

"I think I would like to stay on the Isle. I could help Ilia while you are both there, and when you leave, I could stay and continue researching the materials we have, and I would like to speak with the villagers. I would also like to do some compilation of my own historical research. It has been a long time since I have had a chance to do so. I could stay with Molly until you leave and then move into your cottage while you are gone, if that would be amenable to you both?"

Ilia was not surprised. Anna had taken to the Isle. Ilia looked to Tristan for confirmation, and when he nodded, she said, "Anna, that will work perfectly. So, we have Senza with Ella, Anna on the Isle, and Edmond where do you want to go?"

Edmond looked a little surprised to be asked. "Well, I thought I would stay with the ship. I will go to the Isle, and then I will go to Portsmith. I don't have any pressing plans, and I would like to do some research on the Syndicate. If they knew where Tristan was before, they can find him again. I would like to delve further into what is going on with these rumors of war. I wonder if we should cast anchor somewhere for a time and keep the Anemone out of sight. We seem to be getting popular."

Tristan nodded. "I was thinking the same. I think if we stay on the Isle for a bit then head to Portsmith and anchor there, we will be okay. Rudy can stay with the ship, as I know he prefers, and the rest of us can dust off whatever ambitions we have for the area."

He glanced at Ilia, saying, "I think if we are going to be there for some time, Ilia and I will find a house to rent. We can have a base of operations there. I'm just really uncomfortable with having our base at Ella's. I want to draw as little attention to her place as possible. It's enough having Senza and possibly Edmond stay there. We can find our own place." He smiled at Ilia. She was beaming. Having a home of their own in Portsmith appealed to her.

"Everyone has been paid, Commander," Edmond said. "We were able to fence the diamonds, and I have a buyer for the emerald if we would like to get it moved."

Tristan contemplated a moment. "I know our pockets are padded nicely, all around. But I can't help but think if we go to war, it may be more difficult to get to our fences. Maybe the right move is to sell off the emerald."

Edmond agreed. "If we are going to war, it will definitely become more difficult to move merchandise. I have already run into reluctance from our fences. They are nervous about parting with currency when times ahead are so uncertain."

"Would it be possible to do some exchange with them in product?" Ilia asked.

Tristan and Edmond looked thoughtful. Then Edmond said, "What do we need? Remember that is a huge emerald. What do we need in that vast quantity?"

Ilia shrugged, "Maybe it wouldn't work. I was just thinking that if they don't want to part with their currency, and we are flush at the moment, maybe we could hang on to our currency and barter for food and supplies. We will need to provide for the crew while they are in our employment. Ella will be taking on both Senza and you, Edmond. Tristan and I will need to set up house in Portsmith, and Anna will need provisions on the Isle. No doubt we can provide Molly with product as well. We have an obligation to provide for the village, as we can."

Tristan sat rubbing a clean-shaven jaw. "I like where you are headed with this. Edmond and I will discuss how this might come about if it is even feasible. Maybe we can come up with a plan."

*

Ilia sat at Tristan's desk, brushing out her hair. Her silver curls extended past her chin, giving her the look of a young girl. She smiled at Tristan in the mirror. He was in bed, covered at the hips by a sheet. His hair fell in dark waves past his shoulders, and his green eyes glowed in a predatory manner as he watched her.

Ilia's heart gave a flip. Over the past month, Tristan healed remarkably quickly, his wounds all but gone, his ribs nearly mended. He was still gaunt, and while he worked on the ship, he tired easily, a continued source of frustration for him. He needed fresh fruit and vegetables.

He also retained more of his canine characteristics than he had in the past. He was more watchful, and quieter than before. He seemed more easily frustrated with the inconsequential, which littered everyday life. In this moment, he watched Ilia with the look of an animal ready to pounce, primal desire rolling from him.

Their intimate life had been put on hold, since Tristan needed time to heal, but as Ilia sat looking at him in the mirror, she knew that time was past, and she breathed a sigh of relief. At the same time her heart somersaulted as she met her husband's gaze in the mirror.

Ilia turned, walked over to the bed, removed her chemise, and climbed in. She barely had a chance to get in bed before Tristan's lips found hers and his hands their place on her bare skin. She let her head fall back, as she reveled in the sensations, then wrapped herself around Tristan as he took her beyond her imaginings.

It was sometime later, as they lay wrapped in each other's arms, Ilia had the sensation of complete satisfaction. She reached out to tug on the connection they shared; that link she found for them to communicate so long ago. He was there, and he shared his deep satisfaction with her. As they lay connected in so many ways, Ilia felt Tristan's foundational recovery was complete.

As she drifted off to sleep, she heard Tristan say, "Aye, wife. It is."

*

The day they made port at Marauder's Isle was sunny and calm. The waters were clear as an azure sky, and Ilia felt a quickening in her gut, as she did every time she encountered great magik. This time, however, the magik she was encountering belonged not just to the sorceress but to herself as well. It was strange to encounter her own magik again after disconnecting from it for a time. It was almost like reconnecting with a long-lost child.

Ilia smiled as she watched the shoreline come into view, the dock where Tristan left her that night, which seemed ages ago. It took several trips, even with two row boats, but once they were all together, their accoutrements the last to be deposited on the dock, they all traveled down the pier to meet up with Reed. The ship would be anchored where it was, and everyone would be able to go ashore and take a break from sea life.

Tristan led the first group through the maze, admonishing everyone to hold hands as they moved through. Such a large group could pose problems with members becoming lost. Anna and Senza were carried on the back of bonded members so they would be able to get through.

The fog closed over them, almost solid in its form. They stepped slowly and carefully, but everyone made it through, and Tristan went back to help with the other two groups going through the maze.

Once everyone was through, and all their luggage dappled the sandy beach, Tristan waited for Reed to gather sleds from the village to pull the luggage. Wheels were not effective on sand and the many dunes on the island. Sleds, however, were very effective. The crew loaded the sleds with all the paraphernalia from the ship, and the entire group set off toward the village.

As they entered the village, Edmond veered off with the crew. Three of the four sleds went with most of the crew, while a few members and the final sled remained with the original group to help unload. The next stop was for Nicola, then Anna and Senza stopped off with Molly. Molly was overjoyed to have company and someone to cook for.

Edmond would eventually end up staying with his parents, so his belongings were dropped off with them, and the final stop was Ilia and Tristan's cottage. The crew dropped the luggage off outside the fence, as the magik enshrouding the house did not recognize them, but as soon as Ilia stepped through the gate, the grayness that hung over the property and the vines that smothered it sprang back, and the place once again looked inhabited. The weeds and overrun appearance disappeared, and lush grasses and colorful flowers lined the walkway and the flower boxes Ilia added before she left the house.

Ilia smiled and turned to share her joy with Tristan. She could see he was feeling it as well. The place seemed to enfold them in welcome, and though the sun was setting, there was an unexplainable glow about the place. As they entered, Ilia could tell Molly had been there, ensuring the house did not fall into a depression with dust from the dunes covering everything.

There was a colorful, blue-checked tablecloth on the table with bright yellow flowers. The fire was lit, and even though it was a lovely summer's day, the dry heat felt good. On the counter in the kitchen was a basket with Molly's homemade bread, cheese, her special crab paste, and a jar of honey.

"I'm home!" she exclaimed, turning in circles. Tristan laughed and gathered her in his arms. "Yes. We are finally home for a bit." He lifted her mid-twirl and kissed her long and deep. When their lips parted, he smiled a truly wolfish smile. "Food before or after?"

Ilia laughed, "After. Everything else can wait, but not this." Tristan scooped her into his arms and headed for the bedroom, Ilia's laughter trailing after them.

*

The time on the island was one of regeneration for everyone. Tristan, especially, flourished, and soon his too-thin frame gained its correct proportions. His appetite was restored, and Ilia often wondered if the island would run out of provisions. The crew did plenty of lazing about, but they also had a rigorous exercise program they all participated in every day. Edmond and Tristan were always part of that, which helped Tristan regain the muscle he lost during weeks of starvation.

Molly, Senza, Anna, and Ilia often met up in the mornings to sit on the beach and watch the men go through their calisthenics. Molly sighed. "Gives you a reason for living, watching all these male bodies running around half clothed." They all laughed.

They spent the remainder of their days digging clams and other critters for big pots of seafood gumbo. In the evenings, everyone ate gumbo and freshly baked bread with wine and ale to wash it down. It was a time of great interaction and rejuvenation for everyone.

*

Ilia was standing at the water's edge, watching the full moon rise from its slumber on the horizon. Anna joined her, and soon Senza was there.

Senza was enjoying her time on the Isle, getting to know everyone, and flirting with the young men from the village. She had blossomed during the past several months, losing some of her chubbiness to soft womanly curves, and she had no shortage of attention.

As moths to flame, the three gravitated away from the crowd gathered for the nightly feed and off toward the rising moon. They swayed to the music, pulling strands from the gigantic globe.

At one point Anna said quietly, "How long have you known?"

Ilia stopped pulling strands, surprise registering on her face. "How did you know?" she asked.

"Know what?" Senza asked skipping up to them, her hands full of moonspun.

"Look at the threads as they attach to her," Anna said, pointing to the moonspun. Instead of the shining silver that always surrounded Ilia, the strands became a rich indigo.

Senza stood, staring at Ilia, a puzzled look on her face, then realization dawned, as her eyes opened wide and her mouth formed an "O." "You're going to have a baby!" she exclaimed.

Anna and Ilia both responded, "Shhhhhh!"

Senza covered her mouth, giggling. "But how is that possible, Ilia? I thought moon children cannot have children?" Senza asked, still holding the strands of moonspun in her hand as she pondered this new revelation.

"I don't know. For the longest time I did not even allow myself to consider it, because I knew it to be impossible, but I have been tired, and though I have not struggled with sickness in the mornings, I have not had much appetite, and I tend to feel queasy before bed. But it didn't feel real until I saw the color of my moonspun change when I touched it."

Anna smiled. "This is truly miraculous. As a historian, I can hardly contain my excitement, but as a future aunt, I'm about to jump up and down for joy!" She reached out and drew Ilia to her.

Senza, not one to be left out, reached around to hug them both.

"When will you tell Tristan?" Anna asked.

"I don't know," Ilia said, biting her lip. "I want to tell him, but I am afraid he will leave me behind on the island, and I will not be parted from him again so soon."

Anna nodded. "I understand what you are saying. But do not deceive him, Ilia. There are uncharted waters here, more pronounced than the usual in pregnancy. You will need him to help you maneuver through this."

"Maybe I should stay here. I mean, you and Molly will be here. I couldn't be in safer hands for such things," Ilia said.

"Yes, but on the ship, you will have Connor. There is no one more skilled than he."

Ilia nodded agreement. "I hadn't thought about Connor. You are right."

"I will be with you on the ship, as well," Senza said. "I know I am not very knowledgeable, but I can be a support for you."

Ilia reached over and hugged her, "Of course you will. This baby is going to have two extraordinary aunts." She sighed, then said, "Now let's dance!"

*

It was nearly sunrise when Ilia made her way to the cottage and quietly removed her clothes, climbing into bed as softly as she could to cuddle up next to her husband, who had been in bed for hours.

"I'm awake lass," he said, turning his body to spoon around hers. His hands found their way to her belly and moved down to rest on the spot where she held her secret. "I'm just curious when you were going to tell *me*?" he asked softly.

Ilia froze, then relaxed as he pulled her closer against him. She tried to turn to look at him, but he held her hips pressed against him so she couldn't move. "How did you know?" she asked, repeating the same question she'd put to Anna.

His head lay on hers and emitted a slow growl just over her ear. "I'm an animal, lass. I sensed the change in your body chemistry before you did. But I just wondered when you were going to tell me. You seem to have told your sisters," Ilia flinched at the hurt in his voice.

"I didn't tell them, Tristan. I didn't tell anyone. Anna could see the change in color in my moonspun after I pulled it. That's how she knew. Senza overheard us."

"How long have you known?" he asked.

"Tristan, I am not going to say anything more until you release me," Ilia said, anger sparking in her voice, her body flushing with the magik that had been curled up like a cat on the new life she was carrying.

Tristan felt the heat and released her. He rolled onto his back, one arm tucked behind his head, his hair a long mass of dark mane. Ilia sat up, sitting at the bottom of his body near his feet, the sheet tucked up under her arms. She sat staring at him, willing herself to calm down.

"I knew on the ship, right before we made anchor. I hadn't been feeling the best."

"And you have been off your feed," he supplied.

"Yes." She acknowledged. "I was going to tell you, but then I thought you might try to make me stay here, and I am not going to do that, Tristan. I will not have you go off on another adventure and leave me to not have you come back." Ilia's eyes filled with tears, and she struggled to hold them back, even as they crested and fell down her cheeks, leaving silvery trails.

Tristan reached for her, pulling her into his arms. "I'm not going to leave you anywhere, lass.

I'm going to keep you with me always. If for no other reason than for you to protect me!" he exclaimed, and they both laughed.

"I am wondering where you want to have this wee babe?" he asked. "Your answer will shape our plans."

Ilia didn't respond for a moment then replied, "I would really like to have the baby here with

Connor in attendance, but I know we may still be in Portsmith, so as long as Connor is with us, I'm okay with our home here or our home in Portsmith. I will be sad to not have Anna with us, but she needs to get back to what she does, and we need her researching abilities."

"That makes sense. Now turn around here and look at me."

Ilia turned in his arms, placing her fingers along his jaw, stroking the stubble on his face, "I need to tell you how happy I am that you are giving me a child. I would have spent our lifetime together and been perfectly happy, but this? This is something I could never have imagined."

Ilia smiled, tears still flowing again but for a different reason. He kissed her gently, softly. She pulled him closer, lengthening her body to press against his. He emitted a soft growl as he pulled her even closer. "I love you, lass."

"I love you, husband," she said, sighing, as he began to show her.

Twenty-one

"We still have not planned for finding out how the Syndicate plays into the talks of war. We have Anna looking at the research available here on the island regarding my origins. That is only because the sorceress lived so long and would, at the very least, have heard about Nala. But we don't know enough about the Syndicate and how they work to really ascertain how they play into the war efforts. We have great theories, but no tangible proof." Ilia was sitting with their core group at Molly and Will Reed's house.

"Edmond will be looking for people more closely associated with the Syndicate in Portsmith," Tristan said. "If his searches take him further, we will work that out when it happens. Portsmith is an excellent place to gain intel on the war rumors, so both he and Rudy will be looking into that. Nicola will stay here for now. I want him to have time with his child while time is available." Tristan beamed at Nicola bouncing the baby on his knees.

"What about me? Do I fit in anywhere in this picture?" Senza asked, looking slightly offended.

Tristan smiled at his sister-in-law. "Senza, you will be in a prime location to listen to what people who stay with Ella have to say. We also want you to have some time to enjoy your life a bit. Learn from Ella, practice your abilities to see how far they extend, but I have no doubt we will be in need of your special abilities before all is said and done."

Ilia gave her a stern look, "And I must warn you not to take serious risks. By neutralizing Trissa, we have somehow managed to avoid being a prime focus of the Syndicate, but I made a mistake destroying that building, and it may be one costly enough to cause them to come looking. It will not take much to have them focus on us, and a woman with your abilities would be highly desired in the Syndicate. Never forget, they will not want you to use your power. They will want to extract it from you by any means possible. So, you must be extremely careful."

Senza nodded. "I promise I will be careful."

"Any ideas where the babe might be born?" Molly inquired.

Ilia smiled, her pale cheeks gaining a pink glow. She was sitting on Tristan's lap, and she leaned back against him as he pulled her closer. "We hope to be back here, but it may be Portsmith. It just depends on how things go, but we will have Connor with us no matter what." She glanced over at Connor, who was sitting across the table from them.

"I see," Molly said. "Well, we will just have to be ready for anything. Not much different than any other day." She looked around the room, and they all laughed.

"Does anyone have any questions or concerns we have not addressed?" Tristan asked. "We are going to be spreading to the four winds in a couple of days, and I just want to make sure everyone is okay with our plan." He looked around the room at each face but saw none that held question or unanswered worry.

"Very well then. We are all set."

*

Ilia and Tristan spent the last night in their home in front of the fireplace. A storm blew in off the ocean, and it was necessary to close the shutters up tightly until it abated. When it finally did, they were happy to spend their last night with the windows open, the cool breeze providing the need for a fire. They ate in front of the fire, talked, made love, and eventually slept, as the moonlight streamed in.

As the early hours of the morning were once again upon them, Ilia wrapped in a shawl to cover her nakedness and tip-toed silently out the front door, through the gate, and onto the beach. She dropped her shawl on the ground and walked into the water. The moon was setting on the horizon and thin threads of sunlight began to highlight the ocean. She waded into the water and had a refreshing swim before sitting for a few moments, as the cool air dried the water on her skin leaving goose bumps.

She put her hands on her abdomen where the life she carried was thriving. "This is your home, little one, and this is your moon. No matter where we go. No matter what happens. You are loved, this is your home, and this is where the moon will always find you." She stood for a few moments then turned to find Tristan, naked and holding her shawl.

Ilia sighed. He was so magnificent. His shoulder-length dark hair floated about him in the cooling breeze. His broad shoulders and slim hips were silhouetted against the ensuing light. His green eyes shone out of his handsome face, mostly covered in beard.

Ilia thought she could see so much more of the wolf in him these days. Maybe it was his torture lingering, or maybe it was because he was going to be a father and his primal instincts were on high alert. Regardless, he was a specimen. She walked toward him marveling, as always, at how such a big man was so gentle with her.

"You are freezing, lass," he said, pulling her into his warm embrace, his lips finding hers.

The sun nudged over the horizon, bathing everything in orange and pink. Ilia turned in Tristan's arms and sighed. "One last look, my love. We will have to carry this view with us for some time before we see it again."

"Aye lass," he said, giving the view one last look before turning her back to him. "This view will do," and his lips claimed hers once more.

~The End~